SHANTALLOW

CARA MARTIN

DCB

The publisher gratefully acknowledges the support of the Canada Council for the Arts and
the Ontario Arts Council for its publishing program. We acknowledge the financial support
of the Government of Canada through the Canada Book Fund (CBF) for our publishing
activities, and the Government of Ontario through Ontario Creates, an agency of the
Ontario Ministry of Culture, and the Ontario Book Publishing Tax Credit Program.

LIBRARY AND ARCHIVES CANADA CATALOGUING IN PUBLICATION

Martin, Cara (Pseudonym), author
Shantallow / by Cara Martin.

Issued in print and electronic formats.
ISBN 978-1-77086-552-5 (softcover). — ISBN 978-1-77086-553-2 (HTML)

1. Title.

PS8626.A76928S53 2019   JC813'.6   C2018-906282-7
                                              C2018-906283-5

United States Library of Congress Control Number: 2018967100

Cover design: Emma Dolan
Interior text design: Tannice Goddard, tannicegdesigns.ca
Interior images released under the Creative Commons Zero licence

Printed and bound in Canada.
Manufactured by Houghton Boston Printers in Saskatoon, Saskatchewan,
Canada in May, 2019.

Body printed on 100% recycled paper.

DCB
An imprint of Cormorant Books Inc.
260 SPADINA AVENUE, SUITE 502, TORONTO, ON M5T 2E4
www.dcbyoungreaders.com
www.cormorantbooks.com

For Casey

If morning never comes,
and I wander desolate through the dark,
if hollow footsteps creep close behind,
and even the wind turns against me,
dread feasting sharp-toothed on my soul,
remember me fondly,
speak my name in the gaps between shadows,
softly,
like a secret between friends,
so that the sound of light may guide me home.

— Obscure Celtic Pagan Chant

Shantallow
from Irish *sean talamh*, meaning "the old ground"

Part 1

Part I

1

I don't do this anymore. I don't cut left onto Bridge Road and follow it past Holy Trinity High School, where the trees are shuddering together in the wind, a sign proclaiming "WELCOME BACK STAFF AND STUDENTS" squatting malevolently in front of them. I don't swing a right into Newtown Creek, one of the more exclusive areas of Tealing, tapping my fingers impatiently against the wheel as I cruise by grass as green as a golf course but as stern and precise as a Marine's crewcut. My heart isn't thumping erratically, like a kid making sure his feet don't hang over the bed so the thing that lives underneath won't grab them, while houses with porches only slightly smaller than the apartment I lived in four years ago flash by my windows.

It's not happening. I told myself I was finished with this last time. The last thing I need is to look like a stalker. I'm more like a ghost haunting the last site of my happiness. Although maybe that's being a stalker too.

Meanwhile, the sky overhead is a ceiling of unbroken black, moonless and starless, the same as if there were nothing up there. But I know better. I know that when the cloud cover breaks, the stars will twinkle with ostentatious brightness, appearing three times as plentiful as they do on my street in Balsam, where the street lamps follow the townhouses' example of crowding near to each other. Memories of the glittering Newtown Creek sky — and other useless things — close in on me while I approach the Mahajan house, the sick feeling in my stomach creeping up my throat in slow motion as I take my foot off the gas.

My neck swivels to the right, my gaze darting beyond the cobblestone post with the address "288 Margate Avenue" etched neatly into it to focus on the Mahajans' wide, shapely driveway. A single car is parked on the far left, under a maple tree — a muddy white Kia Rio that I spotted occupying the same space about five weeks ago. Mr. Mahajan drives a silver Nissan Infiniti, and only last November Mrs. Mahajan bought an electric blue Impala to replace her five-year-old Passat. Tanvi doesn't care what kind of car she drives, but her parents gave her a Subaru Legacy because it had a driver death rate of zero on a highway safety study.

Obviously the Kia doesn't belong to any of them. It's not necessarily relevant either.

But then again, maybe it is.

I don't stop. I step on the gas again, zooming by the house as though I have another destination in mind.

The tall trees of Newtown Creek are swaying anxiously around me, shrubbery and the occupants of flower beds shaking with such force that they look like they'd appreciate a coat or a blanket. Ultimately either would only blow away because the wind's picking up steam as I leave the Mahajan house in my wake.

I was never here tonight. No one knows any different.

When things go bad you're supposed to walk away from them and stay away. It's survival instinct.

You don't poke around in the mess, dragging your hands through it like a four-year-old with fingerpaint. You don't stomp through it, getting it on your shoes and trailing it around after you, leaving permanent stains.

It really shouldn't matter who the white Kia belongs to. I'm gone.

My shoulders loosen as the Mahajan house shrinks in my rear-view mirror and then disappears altogether when I hang a left and start working my way back to the main road. The detour has cost me less than ten minutes. I'm good.

Suddenly a lightning bolt zigzags through the sky off to the east, so quick that I can't be sure whether it really happened or I imagined it. My windshield is dry, but now I'm anticipating raindrops, looking at the trees' sinister dance while my mind reaches for a familiar shadowy feeling that's suspiciously like the sensation of falling. A slippery unease as chilly as an ice cube tickles the small of my back, my body jolting into high alert mode. My spine and neck tingle like I'm out of place, backwards in time without remembering the specifics, only that I've been exactly here and now before.

They say that young people have déjà vu more than older ones, that the experiences steadily decrease after age twenty-five. But in this case the sensation could also have something to do with barometric pressure — blood vessels in my head expanding or contracting to compensate for changing oxygen levels.

It's going to storm. It's only a question of when.

Another possible, and more likely, explanation is that anything to do with Tanvi knocks me sideways so that I'm scrambling to regain my balance, waves of regret lining even the best memories. The secrets that I'll never tell anyone because they're ours alone. The times we were the quietest because there was no need to speak. The sweet candy smell of her skin. Tanvi's fingers threading softly through my hair, over and over just the way I liked. The fucked-up arguments. Her fuzzy green Christmas socks with the matching reindeer on them. Tanvi's voice on the phone the first few times she said my name, like I was somebody else. Somebody better.

The things I did. The shitty, shitty, unforgivable things.

Everything runs together like mud, slick and dirty.

I choke out a cough, clearing my throat when what I really need to clear is my head. Empty Tanvi out and start over.

But what do I do instead? As usual, the wrong thing. I swerve into a stranger's driveway — the basketball net in front of the garage jerking around like a kite about to take flight — and begin doubling back to Margate Avenue. Thunder booms in the distance, and my heart drums faster in response: tick-tick-tick-TICK-tick-TICK-tick-TICK-TICK-TICK. There's a race on that it means to win, and my esophagus tightens, wanting no part of it.

There's nothing wrong about a storm; it's just doing what it does naturally. The sky blazes a second time, and this one I witness full on — a spider vein of electricity that doesn't care what it topples or who it destroys.

None of this has happened before. My body and mind both understand that now. This is fresh paint, unwritten and urgent.

The hairs on the back of my hands prickle, and the stars, they keep right on hiding. *That piece-of-shit-looking white Kia.* Whose is it? Parked confidently in the Mahajans' stately driveway at eleven-twenty on a Thursday night like it has every right to be there.

My mind gallops through the car makes and colors belonging to each of Tanvi's circle and comes up blank, same as it did the first time I saw the Kia. It was earlier in the day then; it could've belonged to anyone. A pizza delivery person or a contractor.

I clamp my mouth shut and breathe in through my nose, the itch under my skin screaming at me, urging me on the rabid way some parents cheer for their kids at soccer and hockey games — the mothers and fathers who don't know when to sit down and shut up because they're not helping.

And I do know, but I don't stop either, so I'm not any better than they are. But it doesn't matter anyway; I've got the car crawling toward the Mahajan house and I'm taking in the scene. A long white utility van has joined the Kia in the driveway. If the driver had positioned it any closer to the front door the van would actually be *inside* the house's sheltered entranceway, and a laugh spurts from between my lips, forcing my mouth open.

It was contractors after all. Not somebody else Tanvi was going to wear her killer minidress for. Not someone she'd lie on the Mahajans' sectional couch with, her hand swimming through his hair.

I'm not directly in front of the Mahajan house yet — I'm two doors down, moving at a snail's gait — when someone dressed in black steps into the unlit gap between the entranceway and the back of the utility van. The Mahajans don't have a porch like many of their neighbors do, only that covered square of doorstep — three gentle steps leading up to it — which means you could hang around outside their door in the pouring rain for hours and remain bone-dry.

I kill my engine and lights the second I spot the guy. He's opening the van's rear double doors, a second figure in black joining him. They must be preparing to haul something from the house into the van, trying to make their job as easy as possible. From my position on the road I can't see much — there's a fair bit of lawn between the house and the street, and the gap between house and van is small — but then there's a flash of something decisive, a moment that catches in my lungs.

A black ski mask. One of them is wearing the kind of ski mask you see on closed-circuit security footage of bank and store robberies, the eyes and mouth cut out from the fabric. My stomach plummets, my mind rushing maze-like through the images in front of me, trying to make sense of them. The hanging lantern that should illuminate the entryway is dark. Why would you have the light off if you were planning to carry something out to the van?

You wouldn't. A gaggle of arms and legs of assorted skin tones — people being hustled out of the house — zooms into the gap along with more men in ski masks. One of the group is only a kid, her body twisting and arms and legs flailing, slapping and kicking at black-clad body parts. A cry slices the air, and I don't know how long I've been sitting and watching from my car, but I've seen enough. My left hand closes around the door handle, forcing it down and throwing the door open.

Usually I'm better at long-distance running than sprinting, but not tonight. One second my running shoes are hitting pavement and the next I'm hurling myself into the nearest figure in black, my fist jabbing into the stranger's neck. A drop from the clouds spits on my chin. The van doors are gaping open behind me — rear windows ominously whited-out — and a male voice shouts something that I don't have time to decipher.

A second guy lurches forward and punches me square in the nose. Cartilage crunches, my knees starting to buckle as my eyes swim. "*Fuck*," someone's muttering. "Who the fuck is this asshole?"

I spin to stare into the back of the van — at Tanvi sitting on the floor between two other people not in black who I can hardly make out because my pupils are drowning. My head down low, I charge into the nearest inky target, grabbing him around the middle and toppling him to the ground.

I go with him, my fall broken by his body.

Someone yanks up my feet and somebody else grabs roughly at my shoulders, wrangling me into the air. *No. No. Get the fuck off me.* Desperation blends with fury in my limbs. My fingers drive into fabric, then skin. I fling my arms around the waist of the figure underneath me, chafing the back of my hands against the cement and kicking behind me with all my strength. The sky crackles, sudden light blinding me while rain pummels my skin and my bloody nose weeps like a bathroom tap. People are shouting and screeching chaos, my head spinning and my bones howling. Something hard jabs against my head.

The blood from my nose drips into my eyes, my body slanted with my feet up and head down. I can't see anything but stinging, soupy red. I don't know what's happening. Only that Tanvi's in the back of the van and she shouldn't be there. The guy on the ground is struggling out from underneath me, but I'm still holding on, cold dread spreading inside me — the moment freezing.

The moment just before they do whatever they were going to do in the first place, and I can't stop it. She's gone.

"I think he saw my face," someone barks.

Then Tanvi's voice sails above the anarchy, thawing the action. "Don't shoot him. You can ..." The sound dies in my ears as my right cheek bursts, head slammed violently to the side by nothing I see coming, a twin punch bulldozing simultaneously into my abdomen, dragging me feet first into total darkness.

Part 2

2

Last August was too hot for words, like the month before it. With three and a half weeks of summer vacation left I was fed up to the teeth of my daytime summer smell of sunscreen and multiple layers of deodorant. My company T-shirt weighed me down as though it was an alpaca sweater, and my arms and legs were so brown I wouldn't have identified them as mine if I'd seen them in a photo. I'd gotten so lean that I almost didn't like it, lean like I'd only been pre-puberty.

Between my seasonal landscaping gig and part-time supermarket job I didn't have much chance to run that summer. If I had, I would've been a dead ringer for the hanging skeleton people put up outside their houses at Halloween, except that I'd have been the one in the "Golding Green Thumb" shirt. According to the company dress code, no matter what the weather app said, the company T-shirt had to remain on.

Despite the blistering temperatures, there were no water restrictions in Tealing. The town was far from running dry. Freakishly, the rainstorms weren't infrequent that summer — it was just that up to that point they'd occurred mainly in the dead of night.

Most mornings the air was already thick with humidity by the time the Golding Green Thumb truck idled at the end of my driveway, and by ten o'clock the sun was ready to fry bacon and eggs on the sidewalks and fatally punish pets whose owners had been stupid enough to leave them locked inside cars. It was no different that very first day I saw Tanvi; my safety glasses were sticky-glued to my face with perspiration and my hearing-protection earmuffs were fixed snugly in place, sending a constant stream of sweat down my neck as I tamed the grass edging the Ghims' front walkway with a string trimmer.

Heather was down near the end of the driveway, pruning bushes, and Santiago was in the backyard, taking care of the lawn. There wasn't a cloud in the sky — it was a warm, vibrant blue that would seem like the product of an artist's imagination come winter. It was also roughly the same blue that had hung over my head the day my dad came home, and occasionally my eyes would still snag on a patch of summer sky and trip backwards in time before I could catch myself.

Showing off on a two-wheeled bike, my legs pumping hard and my stomach full of welcome home cake and grilled hot dog, my dad watching with a squint, a celebratory cigarette tucked between his lips. "Look at that," he said, tapping ash like he was adding an exclamation point. "Not a baby anymore, huh. Next thing you know I'll be teaching you to drive stick." My father smiled toothily, winking as though the two of us were in on a private joke. The men of the family, me five and a half years old and him nearly twenty-six, the best yet to come.

Or not.

I hit the off switch and inhaled the smell of fresh-cut grass, landing back in the Ghims' front yard with sweat dripping off my chin, my early-morning shower staler by the minute. I'd just bent to set down the trimmer, my mind switching to thoughts of the water bottles in the truck's cooler, when someone padded out from the neighbor's front door.

The shock hit me in the center of the chest first. Then my lungs forgot to breathe and the rest of me forgot to shift my line of vision and pretend I wasn't staring. I stood frozen on the Ghims' property, gaping at this strange girl on the neighbor's grass — a girl I'd never in my life laid eyes on before, but knew just the same.

The girl from my dreams. Not someone who looked vaguely like the teenage girl on the phone only a stone's throw away from me, the *exact* girl. I'd have known her anywhere. In the dreams there'd been only fear. The two of us standing in a wooded clearing, breathing raggedly in tandem, clothes disheveled. In the dream it was always night. So dark that I was surprised human eyes could pick up enough to light work, but mine did.

Every time it was the same thing. Terror pinching at the girl's face, carving into her cheekbones and glowing in her eyes. I was scared too, my eyelids pulsing with it. The clock was running down for us, and we had to run. We'd been running before we'd reached the clearing and we had to run *again*, faster than we ever had and with no fixed end in sight. Something was coming for us. It was behind us in the woods, and it was quicker than we were and never got tired.

We were losing hope, overwhelmed like in the dreams where your legs won't obey you and instead feel like lead. This girl and I, we were doomed and we knew it. That was how the dream went. Chased by something I never saw, only sensed.

Each time I woke up as we started moving again, hurling ourselves in between the gnarled trees ahead. A dream with no end and no beginning. No purpose that I could make out.

Standing with one foot on the Ghims' walkway and the other on the grass, I drew my hand across my brow and then my chin, clearing the sweat from my face as I took in the real-life girl. South Asian. Approximately my age and height, long black hair framing high cheekbones and arresting brown eyes that might have made me stare even if I hadn't seen her before. A cellphone was kissing one of her ears, and she was in bare feet, layered tank tops — one purple and the other white — and butt-hugging drawstring fleece shorts. I watched her toes claw at the grass, disappearing between the long blades while she frowned heavily at whoever was on the other end of the phone.

It was then that she glanced up and caught me looking. She held the phone away from her ear, bitterness flaring in her eyes as she called out, "Why don't you go hump someone else with your eyes. I'm trying to have a private conversation."

My jaw dropped to the ground with a cartoon thud. I turned into the mute caveman I'd been acting like, body and gaze shifting instantly away from her. Keeping my eyes straight ahead, I marched stiffly down the driveway to retrieve a bottle of water from the truck, cursing myself for being so obvious. By the time I'd worked up the courage to face her again, the girl was gone.

But I couldn't stop thinking about her. I stole glances at the neighbor's house on and off all day, waiting for her to reappear as I continually recalled her image from my dream and measured it against the real thing. What did it mean to dream of someone you'd never met and then stumble across her in waking life? Had I seen the girl somewhere in Tealing before without realizing it and swept her into my subconscious? She didn't go to Abbey Hill High School. If I'd spotted her there I would've remembered it.

It's not like I could've cross-examined her about where I might have known her from after what had gone down between us. Not like I could've confessed I'd seen her in my dreams, either. Confronting her seemed like a bad idea, destined to provoke more hostility. And yet, near the end of the workday, while we were all clearing up and returning tools to the truck, I hopped over the invisible division between the Ghims' yard and their neighbor's property.

I trekked up the circular paving stones leading to the neighbor's front door, my head down and my cheekbones sucked in like I was ready to eat humble pie. My middle finger gently tapped the doorbell, my weight shifting anxiously from my right foot to my left.

A black woman in her forties opened the door, a toddler clasping a hunk of circular cheese standing behind her leg, peeking out at me. "Yes?" the woman said semi-patiently.

"I … uh." The girl had definitely been South Asian. How did the woman at the door and her kid fit into the picture? "Are you a resident of this household?"

The woman's head tilted irritably. "Yes, I am. But I'm not interested in buying anything." She scanned the lettering on my shirt. "We don't need someone to do our landscaping, thanks."

"Right. Okay. Sorry for bothering you." Confused, I turned to go. Needling curiosity swung me around at the last second, the door nearly shut. "*Wait*. Is there a girl here?" My hand chopped sideways through the air next to my head. "My height. Long dark hair. Wearing shorts and tank tops."

The door ajar by a mere foot, I watched the corners of the woman's eyes crinkle, one side of her mouth jerking up before she forced it back down. *Really?* her expression seemed to say. *You're using your landscaping job to creep on girls?*

"I owe her an apology," I added quickly. "I think she wanted quiet while she was on the phone … and privacy."

"Mmm." The woman's lips drew together. "Well, she's not here now. She's not *a resident of this household.*" The woman cracked a smile as she echoed my ridiculous terminology, the door clicking firmly shut before I had the opportunity to say anything else.

The disappointment tasted like sharp thirst and amputated grass. Santiago had explained the science behind the scent of newly cut lawn on my first day at work. It's not the nice summer smell that you think it is; it's a plant's SOS signal. A release of airborne chemical compounds that mean it's in trouble and could use some help.

I could've used some help on the neighbor's doorstep too. The girl's name or some other clue. But like the lawn, I wasn't getting any; I had no choice but to walk away empty-handed. Whoever the girl was, I must've been hard at work while she'd made her exit. When I climbed into the Golding Green Thumb truck that evening I wondered if I'd ever get that close to her again. I'd lived in Tealing for three years, and as far as I could recall I'd never seen her outside of the pictures in my head before. If she didn't live next door to the Ghims I had no idea where to find her.

The last thing I expected was that I'd spot her again any time soon. Tealing wasn't a bustling metropolis, but with a population of 137,000 the majority of people who lived there were strangers to me and always would be. However, only fifty-three hours after leaving the Ghims' place, the girl sped by me in a red sedan while I was out for one of last summer's infrequent runs. She was curled up in the passenger seat of the car and I was jogging across Nelson Street, away from the lake. Rationally, I couldn't be positive it was her; it was only a glance into a moving car at night.

A couple of days later I was strolling Tealing's Midnight Madness with Jeffrey Cope and Arjun Grewal, walking back and forth across Main Street while munching grilled corn on a stick and gravitating between stages featuring old-school cover bands and distinctly wholesome entertainment — little kids doing martial arts demonstrations or girls with ringlets in their hair performing Scottish dance routines. Despite the family atmosphere of Midnight Madness, most of Tealing's teenage population stopped by for at least a couple of hours. It was a place to be out at night that no one's parents could be suspicious of — most of them didn't realize some kids liked to veer away from the crowded downtown Tealing streets and head down to the lake, only a few blocks away, where the minimal lighting offered a chance to hook up with someone or indulge in underage drinking between foot patrols by the police.

An alternate version of me had already left Arjun and Jeffrey behind to swagger down to the lake and dive into trouble. Actually, that alternate version of me wouldn't have been friends with Arjun and Jeffrey to start with. The friends I would've had in their place wouldn't be on the honor roll; they'd be lucky if they ever graduated high school. They'd jeer at the cops who periodically herded teenagers away from the lake on Midnight Madness night and easily find somewhere else to party, somewhere the cops didn't care about because it wasn't frequented by the middle and upper classes. Those guys — my alternate version friends — would think of guys like me, Arjun, Jeffrey, and Justin Chen (who wasn't with us that night because his grandparents were visiting from China) as pussies.

My eyes rushed through the crowd, my pulse racing. *Her*. Off to the left near a bakery stall, tossing her long black hair over one shoulder. That day in the Ghims' yard, I'd seen a mirror image from my dream when I'd first clapped eyes on her. On Main Street, it was the real girl my gaze tripped over — the real flesh and blood girl who made my ribs ache and my mouth burn. I couldn't keep my eyes pinned to her for more than a few seconds; the crowd was swelling forward and backward, people jostling their way through the fluctuating gaps in the thirty or so feet between us, stealing her away from me.

I tripled my pace and started weaving my way toward her, Arjun and Jeffrey falling back. If I'd known her name, I would've shouted for her at the top of my lungs too. It felt like a final chance.

Fast as I was, the Midnight Madness mob was swifter. They swallowed the girl whole and left me standing uselessly in front of the bakery stall alongside half a dozen strangers waiting to buy cupcakes and pastries. My hands wound around the back of my neck as I spun on my heels, scoping for her in all directions and not finding her.

You can't lose something you've never had. You can *find* something you've never had, but you can't lose it. Only that's exactly how it felt when the girl vanished from view, and when Arjun and Jeffrey joined me by the stall a minute later I couldn't jettison the feeling and go back to being the person I'd been before. The girl was written all over me.

I told my friends the parts of the story that made sense: the girl on the lawn who thought I was an asshole; the girl I couldn't stop thinking about and who'd popped up at Midnight Madness only to fade from view. Arjun and Jeffrey must've sensed there was no use in talking me out of her; we spent the rest of the night hunting her down, my friends pointing out every teenage South Asian girl they saw. We scoured the crowds gathered at each of the stages, examined the lines for every food stall, and carefully combed through the relentless stream of families making their way back and forth across Main Street. We even trooped down to the lake, where the cops must've recently patrolled because, aside from a young couple making out by the playground swings and rival gangs of bloodthirsty mosquitoes swooping around our necks, it was deserted.

I stayed out on Main Street after Arjun and Jeffrey left. I stayed so late that I saw the cleanup crew begin to disassemble the various stages and wheel away garbage carts, and the vendors pack up their temporary stalls.

She wasn't in my dreams when I fell asleep later, either. The following day was Saturday, and my shift at Central Foodmart didn't start until two, but I was awake by nine that morning, lying in bed with the A/C unit in my window going full blast and restlessness jogging through my veins. It wasn't a good feeling; it was too insistent for that. Like trying to sleep through the noise of a leaky faucet — the angry ping of the water pelting the sink.

I didn't fall back asleep. My head was starting to pound and my throat was scratchy, like second-hand vinyl. Getting up didn't help. I couldn't click into gear and took so long in the shower that the water ran cold. Then I parked myself in front of English Premier League soccer with a plate of waffles I couldn't finish and fell into a daze that lasted hours.

Last summer my ten-year-old Camry had still belonged to someone else, a friend my mother had made on her bus route, and my transportation choices were limited: the bus, my bike, or my mom, when she was around. But my mother had left for her own shift hours earlier, and I hadn't heaved myself off the couch in time to catch the bus. Out of options, I pulled my bike out of the garage and pedaled to the supermarket, the adrenalin surge from the ride carrying me through my first couple of hours behind the cash register. The third hour I guzzled fluids and stopped smiling at the customers, and the fourth I grumbled to Desiree — who was manning the checkout lane next to mine — that I'd picked up Lyme disease.

It was after eight when the assistant manager on duty cashed me out, nearly two hours before the scheduled end of my shift. I walked out of the place bleary-eyed and fuzzy-headed, joints aching and my flesh unnaturally heavy on my frame. The nearest bike rack was across from the Foodmart's parking lot, directly outside the larger of Tealing's two movie theater complexes, and my mind was a black hole as I stumbled toward it.

The combination lock clicked open in my hand, my gaze roaming idly toward the wide set of stairs that led customers to the theater box office. The girl was sitting near the bottom of the stairway in navy overalls that fell just below her knee, a striped T-shirt under them and slip-on canvas shoes on her feet. Her head was in her hands and her expression was downcast, not unlike when I'd seen her on the lawn. My mind stalled, my hand taking over for it by clicking the lock closed again.

I lumbered in the girl's direction, too sick to be nervous, the excitement that would've had me reeling on any other day dialed down to medium-low. "Are you okay?" I asked from the bottom of the stairs.

Her gaze shot up to mine, tender flecks of red criss-crossing the whites of her eyes. She was pretty in a way that stuck in the middle of your throat, with eyes deep enough to drown in. Those things would've been obvious in my dreams, too, if I'd been able to feel anything but fear. "What are you going to do about it?" she retorted.

Nightmare memories sprang back with a start as I stood in front of the theater staring down at the hurt in her eyes. Us in the dark clearing in the woods, her lip swollen on the left side and her eyes frantic, her forehead scratched and bleeding. *"No," she protested firmly, digging her fingernails into my arm. "That doesn't make any sense — you know you're faster. You have to be the one."*

That was what she'd said to me, at least once in my dreams. We'd argued in the clearing, her using a voice no different from the one she'd answered me with on the stairs.

"Forget it," the real-life girl told me, snapping me out of memory and back to the present. She laughed bitterly, her elbow pointed into her knee and her hand resting along the curve of her face. "It's all right. Just walk away."

I sank my fingers into my pockets, ballooning the fabric out as I shrugged. "Where do you want me to go?" I joked, as though there was still some small hope I could cheer her up. "Are you sure you're okay?"

"I never said I was. You look like shit, by the way." She rubbed her eyes.

"I feel like shit," I confirmed. My brief remission was passing. "The flu, I guess. I couldn't finish out my shift — I'm just about to head home. Listen." I hesitated, looking away from her. "I'm sorry about the other day while you were on the phone."

"That was you?" She studied my face, blinking slowly as her mouth hid behind her palm.

I smiled without meaning to. *She hadn't even known it was me.* I'd been obsessing about her for days, and she'd haunted my dreams for weeks before that, but my existence had barely registered with her.

"Figures," she added leadenly. "Look, it's been a bad day. And that was a bad day too."

I thought she was trying to say that she wanted to be left alone and that I'd have to walk away from her again without knowing her name, without knowing the slightest thing about her. My throat had gone from scratchy to raw, and the crisp pain at my temples was screaming at me that I needed to get home and collapse into bed, but the hunger coiled around my lungs wouldn't loosen its grip. It wouldn't let me leave.

"Sorry," I said, my voice hushed. "Sorry there have been a lot of shitty days lately."

"Yeah." She sniffled and flung her hand away from her face. "Thanks."

At war with myself, I turned and made for the bike rack, the woolly sensation in my head nearly convincing me this was a dream too. I forced myself to take step after step, the losing side of me pummeling at my ribs and shouting that it wasn't too late, that I could still turn back, even as I bent to unlock my bike.

"Hold up," she called from behind me. I swung around and watched her close the distance between us, her long black hair glossy in the dying sunlight. "Do you want a ride?"

For the second time in sixty seconds I clicked my bike lock shut, straightening my spine and grinning wearily in relief. All I'd had to do to meet fate was stop chasing it. In the end, she had come after me.

3

"Where am I going?" she said as we pulled out of the plaza parking lot, the trunk of her Subaru tied down with the string she miraculously had on hand so that we could transport my bike.

"Bridge Road and Norris Avenue," I advised. "Take a left here." The air conditioning was amped up to maximum and goosebumps broke out on my skin even as I felt my forehead flush. The sun was low in the sky, and a can of Fruitopia rattled in the cupholder between us, the sound more unsettling than it should have been.

"What's your name?" I asked, wrenching my eyes away from her to point them at the road.

"Tanvi," she said distractedly, braking lightly well in advance of the upcoming red light. "What's yours?"

"Misha." My throat rasped, the flu or whatever bug I'd picked up reminding me that the two of us weren't alone in the car. It was chaperoning us.

"Misha what?" Tanvi's brown eyes flashed in my direction. The bottom dropped out of my stomach and kept falling, the world spinning faster on its axis.

The fever, I told myself. But no, it was entirely her. I'd climbed into the car with Tanvi only minutes earlier and I was already changing. The flu wasn't a fraction as contagious as she was. She was doing something to me that I didn't have words for; I could barely catch my breath whenever I looked at her.

"Antall." I forced out the syllables. Normally they were simple to say. "Thanks for the ride. I don't think I would've made it on my bike."

"It's okay," Tanvi replied without looking at me.

Modulating my voice, I meted out directions one step at a time, unsure whether she actually required them or not. "You barely look old enough for a driver's license," I said, fishing for information as we arrived at the set of lights nearest my house.

"Technically, I'm not." She adjusted her overalls strap, her eyes on the horizon when I wanted them back on me. "That's why I'm being so cautious — I don't want to get stopped. I have my learner's permit, but I'm not insured to be driving unsupervised. If anything happened my parents would kill me."

"So, you're ... what, sixteen?" I asked after a long moment.

She nodded almost imperceptibly. Then she raked one hand through her hair with sudden aggression, her cheek twitching and her gold bracelet shifting position on her wrist. "Remember what I said about it being a bad day." Tanvi's lips slapped shut, the temperature in the car abruptly dropping another couple of degrees.

"Translation — quit the chatter," I murmured. "I hear you." I motioned to my street, reciting the house number and then pointing it out for her as we approached. If Tanvi had been someone else I might have been able to figure out how to stop her from disappearing now that it was almost time for me to get out of the car. With her, I had no idea.

Frustration coated my tongue as we swerved into my driveway. Had I known then what the Mahajan house looked like I could have felt defensive about the modest three-bedroom townhouse my mom had worked so hard to land a mortgage on. The narrow, three-storey house's bare-bones style — plain brick and vinyl siding — and deck of cards-sized front lawn might have made me uncomfortable in my seat.

But in the moment all I could think of was her. She wasn't a dream. We weren't standing in the clearing in the woods, the sky as black as dirty oil and gloom pressing in on us from every angle. She was a regular teenage girl next to me, one of her overalls straps threatening to slip off her shoulder.

Tanvi shifted into park and furrowed her eyebrows. "You like what you see?" she asked pointedly, right hand firmly clutching the gearshift. Brown eyes stared at me appraisingly, a current of antagonism headed directly for my forehead while I refused to duck.

"Excuse me?" I said.

"You've been staring at me practically the entire ride. I figured you must like what you see."

If she'd seen me in her nightmares she would've stared too. On the lawn and again in her car. No matter how she tried to stop herself.

"I do," I admitted. *I like it a lot.* The hairs at the back of my neck stood on end. My calf muscles clenched and my jaw along with them, the falling sensation expanding inside me like a mushroom cloud, annihilating everything else.

A sour smile skimmed across Tanvi's lips, only to be replaced with a frown. "What if I followed you inside?" she asked. "What would you do?"

That wasn't a fair question, and I frowned back. Outside a dog was barking wearily, as if purely by habit. Arctic air from the car vents brushed my arms like invisible fingertips.

"You don't want me to?" Tanvi asked, leaning back against the headrest.

Then her cellphone chirped, demanding her attention and giving me extra time to work out her desired reaction. Was she messing with my head? Baiting me so that she could relish shooting me down?

What could I do or say that wouldn't be the wrong thing? Who the hell was this girl? Why was she stalking my nightmares?

Tanvi fished her phone out of her overalls pocket, biting the side of her lip as she glanced at the screen. "My friends back at the movie theater," she volunteered with a glance. "They realized I was gone."

"Why did you leave?"

Tanvi shrugged, her dusty pink lips drooping at the corners. "I didn't want to be there."

"Because of your bad day?"

"Uh-huh." Any anger coming off her had dissolved, sadness gusting in to take its place. My defensiveness began to fall away as the change registered.

"I don't think you really want to be here either," I observed, heart punching against my rib cage. "Why'd you drive me home?"

"I don't know." She laid a finger against the amethyst centerpiece of her bracelet. "Don't you ever do something without really knowing why?"

"All the time," I replied. Not the whole truth, but it made Tanvi smile.

"Actually, I do know," she admitted with an incline of her head. "I didn't want to think. I wanted" — her lips lingered, blooming in slow motion — "a break. But I don't want to talk about what from. That defeats the purpose."

"Okay," I said quietly, the ground beneath us shifting and whatever was going to happen between us tonight beginning to come into focus. "Then … come in if you like." I unbuckled my seatbelt, the joint pain and headache worse now that I was opening the car door and stepping onto the asphalt. Nervous energy collided with the flu symptoms, struggling to overtake them. Leaning down, I peered into the car. "I do want you to," I said.

The dog yelped brokenly from down the street. My mind flickered, tall trees dwarfing me and darkness descending, dream memories flooding my senses.

Tanvi blinked once and stopped her engine, the trees receding in the bright light of day. Sunshine glinted off the car as I straightened, making me squint. I watched her unfold her body and stand solidly in the here and now on my driveway, so cute in her overalls that she made my eyes hurt along with my limbs.

I headed for the trunk, wrestling my bike out of the car and locking it away in the garage while Tanvi waited. Then I loped to the front door and slid my key into the lock, Tanvi right behind me. Stepping into the entranceway, I skirted to the right, leaving her room to slip inside. Two staircases lay ahead. One up and one down. Our basement was partially finished but mostly we used it for storage; I never took anyone there.

Before I could kick off my shoes and lead her upstairs, Tanvi's hand curved around my waist. Slowly, she stepped up close to me, the toes of her canvas shoes jamming against the toes of my black oxfords. Her waist was higher than mine, her legs longer, but I'd been right that day I first saw her — our heights matched.

She leaned her face toward mine, her head tilting one way and mine the other, automatic adjustments we didn't have to think about. The space where our mouths met caught fire. I tasted popcorn on her lips and in her mouth, her tongue salty sweet. Restless too, warm and hungry. One of my hands skimmed over her long hair and then her back, two of my fingers gently fish-hooking the overalls strap she'd had to fiddle with in the car.

Tanvi's fingers skated around the back of my neck, her body sinking into mine, the kiss deeper with each second. Her breasts crushed against my chest, my hand swimming up and down the strap, ready to slide it down and set her free.

Then Tanvi eased her face away, mischief sparking in her eyes as she turned to dart upstairs. My feet were heavy on the steps as I trailed after her. She laughed when she heard the stomp. I laughed too, my lungs short on oxygen.

She was halfway into the living room, her presence among the familiar furniture making the place feel like somewhere new, when I stopped, a wave of nausea bending my head and fastening my lips shut. Tanvi's strap slid down her arm of its own accord when she spun to look at me. "What is it?" she asked. "Do you have a girlfriend?"

"No." I leaned one shoulder against the wall, steadying myself. "Why? Do you have a boyfriend?"

"No," she said quickly. "Not — no."

Three negative answers to a single question in the space of three seconds. That didn't sound like an unqualified no to me. Unfortunately, I didn't have the energy to follow up.

"I need to lie down for a second," I murmured, lurching over to the couch behind her. Who catches the flu in summer? And at what felt like the worst conceivable moment. Fate was playing with me, making me the butt of a joke. I would've been furious, but I didn't have the energy for that either.

"Don't run off on me yet," I pleaded. "I just need a minute." Or a full body transplant.

I collapsed onto the couch, Tanvi staring pensively down at me as she perched on the arm. "I'll get you some water," she offered, drifting off in the direction of the kitchen.

My hair was sticky wet, like when I'd been running, and I knew if I kept my eyelids open I'd soon be vomiting partially digested waffles onto the carpet. The room was whirling.

But if shutting my eyes allowed Tanvi to disappear again, I'd never forgive myself. "Thanks," I rasped after her, my eyes closing like blackout curtains, forcing the decision.

Behind my eyelids, the trees gradually closed in. There was nothing I could do to stop them. Their bony, twisted branches reached for my arms and shoulders, tearing into already bloody skin. My calves ached from running. My lungs howled silently, ready to give up the fight. The wind blew through my bones, threatening to crush me into rubble. It whispered cold into my ear. Things I couldn't and didn't want to hear. Tanvi was with me, struggling to keep up the way she always did and saying what she always said when we reached the clearing.

I shook my head, my heart beating out of its rhythm. "I won't do it," I protested hoarsely. "That's not going to happen, so you can forget about it right now."

"You might have to." Tanvi's shining eyes pleaded with me. "It could be our only chance."

"I don't care." I tugged her forward, staring into the murky tree line ahead, ready to drag her along with me until she'd give in and start running again too.

When I pried my eyelids open again — who knows how long later — the living room was in near darkness and a noise scratched steadily overhead. I blinked up at the ceiling, searching for the cause and not finding one. But it was still happening, persistent and eerie like something that didn't belong here. Something lost and hungry.

I shivered as I sat up. Low voices drifted in from the kitchen, chasing the scratching sound away. My eyes had been open when I'd heard the scratching. I was sure of it. Yet I must've still been dreaming.

A pint glass filled with water stood on the coffee table, within arm's reach. I grabbed for it, the mingling voices separating themselves into two separate entities. Mom and Tanvi. Cautiously sipping, I listened to snatches of words that didn't add up to anything I could understand.

As I staggered into the kitchen, fever flooded me with worse shivers than the dream sound had provoked. I saw Mom with one hip parked idly against the counter as she stood listening to Tanvi utter more words than I'd heard from her so far. Mom was still in her work uniform. Navy pants and a pale blue button-down shirt with a Tealing Transit logo embroidered on the arm. Her glasses, which she needed only for distance, hung around her neck on a chain. At the sight of me, Mom's eyes popped, her hand instinctively reaching for my fore-head. "You're burning up."

"I know," I replied, but it was Tanvi I was looking at. She was still here. Still one hundred percent real, unharmed and unafraid.

Tanvi's eyes were mainly on my mom's. "I better go," she said lightly, her overalls strap neatly back in place, like it had never been otherwise. "Hope you're feeling better soon, Misha." She steered a neutral glance in my direction. A dark-haired mystery in a pair of overalls and a striped T-shirt.

"Thanks," I said, as though that was the end of it. Short and sweet. It could've been.

Only when she made for the stairs, I went with her. I followed her down and stood in the open doorway of my house, trying not to shake as I molded a hand to her shoulder. "Who are you?" I said. "Tanvi *who*? Am I going to see you again?"

In your dreams, a voice whispered inside me.

"Tanvi Mahajan," she replied, not answering my other question. "You should go back in. You look like hell."

"It's an improvement on earlier, then," I noted, my fingers slipping from her shoulder. "Outside the theater you said I looked like shit."

Tanvi grabbed herself around the middle, the two of us close enough to have touched each other whenever we wanted. "I'm trying to be nicer now that I know you a little better." A slight grin swelled her cheeks. "Your mom seems pretty okay."

"She's been through a lot." I didn't know what had made me say that. It must've been the flu warping my judgment.

"Really?" she asked.

"Yeah. Bad days …" Bad years would be more accurate. But I didn't want to get into defining "bad" any more than Tanvi did.

She nodded, winding a strand of hair around her finger and pulling it across her cheek at a slant. Tanvi peered down at her shoes, slowly releasing the lock of her hair to slip both hands into her pockets. Her gold bracelet peeked out from one of them, the amethyst centerpiece catching on the fabric. "My aunt died last week," she confessed, her chin close to her chest. "She was more like a cousin. Only eight years older than me. She lived with us for a couple of years."

Tanvi held up one hand, palm out, to stop me from telling her I was sorry. "It was partly my mom's fault," she said. "That's the worst thing about it. She wouldn't let Alice come back home." I watched Tanvi's chest fill with air, weighed down by the revelation. "Don't say anything. I'm just going to go now."

My shoulders sagged with second-hand grief. Tanvi didn't care if whatever grimy virus had gotten a hold of me took her down too, and this was why. She'd lost someone close.

I shrugged helplessly with my elbows, a mixture of pride and sudden awareness of my comparative insignificance stopping me from begging her for some kind of second chance.

"I know where to find you," Tanvi said, kicking her right leg out to casually tap my shoe with hers. Then she swept toward her car without a backward glance, the dog down the street howling at the rising moon and my fever carrying me back me into the house to dream more murky dreams of places I'd never been and a girl who was still more a stranger to me than she was anything else.

4

The flu kept me out of my Golding Green Thumb shirt for days. I sprawled around the house like a dying dog, too restless to stay in one spot but too weak to accomplish anything except Netflix binging and looking up Tanvi Mahajan on the Internet. The first thing I found was a group photo of Holy Trinity's sophomore girls' volleyball team. A pack of pretty, long-haired girls in red T-shirts and black shorts crowded into the frame, the front row of girls kneeling so that it was easy to locate Tanvi amid the row of grinning teammates standing behind them. With Tanvi's legs fresh in my memory, I wasn't surprised she played volleyball, only sorry I couldn't see her legs in the picture.

The school website had an entire page dedicated to their various volleyball teams' achievements. This past season the sophomore team had killed it, winning a regional championship. I skimmed through the articles and then scouted out Tanvi's various social networking pages. Because we weren't friends I couldn't see a lot. Mostly food porn and photos of trendy clothes, lipstick, and animals doing crazy things. The usual.

Every day I almost sent her a message and then held off.

When school was back I'd have no trouble finding her in person. But I shouldn't look for her at Holy Trinity either. If she didn't want to see me again, I needed to let it go.

It was obvious ... in theory.

Then, five days after Tanvi had driven me home, while I was crashed out in my bedroom after dinner, listening to tunes and relishing the comparative coolness after a long day in the sun, my cellphone vibrated.

"It's Tanvi. How long did you have your flu?" the text demanded.

I phoned her right away. "How did you get my number?"

"I ran into a friend of yours online. Arjun Grewal. He passed it on." She paused while I absorbed the idea that she must have been looking me up the same as I'd done with her. "He said something like, *you're* the one we were looking for at Midnight Madness." Voice gathering strength, she continued. "You were looking for me?"

No point in denying it. She had confirmation. I sat up, flinging my legs over the side of the bed and pinching my phone tightly, as though someone was trying to wrestle it away from me. "I saw you there," I admitted. "But you have a habit of vanishing."

A gravelly bitterness peppered Tanvi's laugh. "Really? Because I feel pretty stuck for someone who has the power to vanish into thin air. I'm a disaster zone. I haven't been able to leave the house in forty-eight hours. If I have to spend another night in here with them I'm going to lose it. I need a recovery estimate from you. Hopefully one that's going to make me feel better instead of worse."

"The first two days were hell," I said truthfully. "The third day was medium-hell, and then I was out of the woods." Guilt at having infected Tanvi melded with warped pride at hearing that part of me had stayed with her. "Trust me, you'll feel better soon."

The phone line's eerie silence droned in my ears, Tanvi's dream voice echoing in the blank space: *you have to be the one*. She'd wanted me to leave her behind in the clearing. I wouldn't do it in the dream, and awake, I felt a shadow of that same responsibility toward her. It was a potentially hazardous feeling. Hearing from her again wasn't necessarily a good thing.

An adult male voice muttered something in the background. "I'm on the phone," she told him. "I don't need anything right now."

"Your dad?" I asked.

"They won't leave me alone. It's so phony."

"What do you mean?"

"Nothing," Tanvi said dismissively. "My head is killing me. You must've been ragingly contagious the other day. It was only one kiss."

"It was your idea," I reminded her. "And it was a good one, except for the timing." Tanvi in her overalls and canvas shoes. Tanvi in the clingy fleece shorts that showed off her muscular volleyball legs and sexy ass. Tanvi's hair in my hands, our mouths burning. Tanvi lying underneath my weight, wanting me with her eyes, slipping nimbly out of her clothes and then helping me with mine.

I wasn't delusional. I knew the night would never have ended that way, except in my head. But it didn't mean that ending wasn't out there somewhere, waiting for the right time to fall into place.

"Listen," I said, "I know you can't go anywhere, but if you want, I can come over."

Tanvi hesitated a beat. "I wasn't kidding about being a disaster zone. I can't keep anything down. I'm in sweatpants and my grossest hoodie with my parents popping their heads in here every five minutes. Nothing would happen between us."

"I didn't mean it like that. I meant, you're sick — I'll be your visitor." Take her mind off Alice and her parents. Be whoever she wanted me to be. Give the future an opportunity to fall into place.

"My parents would probably say no," Tanvi pointed out.

"Don't ask them. Like when you took your car."

"*Misha.*" The undiluted delight attached to my name made me smile. "I like the way you think. But don't be surprised if my parents hurl questions at you. If they ask, say you're buddies with Taye, my friend Imogen's brother. But only if they ask."

"Don't tell them we were complete strangers when you offered me a ride home?" I teased.

"Try it and see where that gets you," she challenged, firing off her address before disconnecting.

288 Margate Avenue.

I knew the street, all right. Golding Green Thumb had multiple clients on Margate. Nice people mainly, with more money than they knew what to do with. But why couldn't Tanvi have given a more neutral address? One that didn't make me feel like I was about to drive off a cliff with my foot on the accelerator?

I rolled on a fresh layer of deodorant, dug my bike out of the garage, and pedaled to Newtown Creek. Twenty-three minutes in an evening sun that would've turned me into a puddle in thirty. The well-manicured lawn was in shade, its healthy green glow sneering mutely at me as I sauntered up the driveway and leaned on the doorbell.

A forty-something-year-old white woman in a gauzy floral top and black leggings promptly opened the door. Her shoulder-length brown hair draped over one shoulder as she tilted her head.

"I came to see Tanvi," I said politely. With adults, politeness was my default. After years of practice, it was second nature. "I heard she was sick. Thought I'd drop by and try to cheer her up."

"Come in, Misha," Tanvi called from down the hallway.

One of my feet made to cross the threshold.

"Wait a second," the woman urged, her right hand reaching out to hold me in place. She swiveled, glancing at Tanvi as she shuffled into view. "Aren't you going to introduce us? I don't think we've met before."

"This is Misha," Tanvi said, a step behind the woman and at least three inches taller. Tanvi's voice dragged, and she was wearing a ratty yellow hoodie, but the rest of her was as stunning as the first time I'd seen her in the flesh, her mouth a polished mahogany and her long black hair back in a ponytail that showed off her cheekbones. "And Misha, my bodyguard is named Helena."

The woman — Helena — laughed reluctantly. "You can call me Mrs. Mahajan, Misha." Slowly, she stepped aside, allowing me to enter. "Where do you know Tanvi from?" Eagle eyes immobilized me before I could reach Tanvi. I stopped dead on the hardwood floor.

"Oh, I'm a friend of Taye's, so we've been running into each other for a while." I glanced at Tanvi for confirmation.

"I think Misha might be a sexual trafficker from Eastern Europe," Tanvi chirped. "You should probably call the cops."

"You're making him nervous," Mrs. Mahajan chided, smiling wearily at me as if to say, *You see what I have to deal with here?*

I grinned uneasily back, my T-shirt sticking to my spine. Then Tanvi grabbed my arm, talon-like. She pulled me along with her, steering me through a hallway that dwarfed the two of us, an ornate beaded chandelier dangling overhead like a cluster of melting icicles. We swung into a large room with open double doors. I loitered just inside the doorway while she curled up on a charcoal-colored sectional couch positioned opposite a mammoth wall-mounted television.

A trio of photographs in identical square white frames decorated the wall directly behind the couch. Dramatic black and white prints, each image placed no more than three inches from the next. The first, frothy sea. The second, mist embracing mountains. The third, sunshine breaking out between storm clouds.

A leather armchair rested on the far side of the couch, beyond it a thin birch-veneer desk littered with an assortment of more casual photos, a sprig of fresh flowers, and a bell-shaped table lamp. Bay windows cast the room in golden evening light, the butterfly palm next to the desk casting a hazy shadow on the hardwood floor.

"I told you nothing was going to happen between us," Tanvi murmured, more into one of the plush couch pillows than to me. "You're wasting your time."

"If I was a sexual trafficker from Eastern Europe, I wouldn't take no for an answer." My legs cut across the distance between us in long strides, a grin breaking my face in two. I swooped down to scoop her feet off the couch and hold them against my thighs. Her legs were hidden by shapeless white sweatpants with a logo that ran down one leg, but I could feel the shape of her feet under my hands. Narrow, long like the rest of her.

Tanvi didn't struggle. She laughed, the reflex action distorting into a cough.

I set her feet gently down on the couch, dropping my body into the section across from her. "So, was that your dad's second wife at the door?" I asked. Tanvi looked full East Indian. Or Bangladeshi or Pakistani, maybe. I couldn't see anything of Helena in her.

Tanvi dove into a hoodie pocket to extract a lozenge. "My aunt." The lozenge clinked between her teeth. "One of my legal guardians. She and my uncle raised me. They adopted me after my parents died." Tanvi wiggled her toes restlessly in her sock feet and hauled herself into a seated position. "You don't have to put on a sad face. It was a long time ago. When I was a baby."

I obliged her, rearranging my face and resisting the urge to ask for details about what had happened to her parents. "So, when you said your mom wouldn't let your Aunt Alice come back …"

"I meant *Helena* wouldn't let her come back." Tanvi wrestled with the nearest couch pillow, holding it in front of her like a shield. "Alice was her half-sister. You would think being blood relations would mean something."

In an ideal world, maybe.

"Why didn't Helena let her come back and stay with you then?"

Tanvi's squat fingernails scratched at the pillow. "Alice had issues. I hadn't seen her in two years. When she first left she texted sometimes. Then that stopped too. My parents didn't want her bringing her problems here. That's what they kept saying. I'm sure she knew they didn't really want her being in touch with me, either. But if you can't depend on your family, who else is going to help you?"

A middle-aged South Asian man in a button-down shirt and chinos ambled past me, holding a glass of something fizzy. "You must be feeling better if you're ready for visitors," he noted. Crossing into the center of the room, he set the glass down on a wooden end table. "More ginger ale. Want to try some crackers or toast?"

Tanvi shook her head decisively, her face graying at the thought of solid food. "Maybe tomorrow."

The man, sporting a classic Ivy League haircut — side-parted top and slicked-down sides — paused to cast his eyes on me.

"I'm Misha," I said anxiously. "Nice to meet you, sir."

"Good of you to come and brave infection to cheer Tanvi up," Mr. Mahajan replied. "You don't go to Holy Trinity?"

"Abbey Hill High."

Mr. Mahajan's eyes remained unimpressed, the rest of his face holding on indifference.

"I'm on the cross-country and track teams," I added. And the honor roll. I was no one to be worried about. "Going into eleventh grade this year."

Tanvi smirked at me from the other end of the sectional. *Too much information. Shut up, Misha.*

Mr. Mahajan arched an eyebrow, hand diving into his upper-crust hair. "It's an important year," he declared.

Tanvi sipped soundlessly at her ginger ale, her eyes avoiding mine.

I'm no mind reader. But there were times when I thought I could read Tanvi's, and that was one of them. I stayed silent on the couch, allowing the uneasy quiet to settle on the furniture and weigh down my shoulders.

"Don't stay too long, Misha," Mr. Mahajan added as he began to withdraw. "Tanvi needs her rest."

Kapow. Tanvi glared at her uncle's back, crossing her eyes. I stifled a chuckle and stared at her sock feet and smooth, lush lips. The tiniest details about her seemed startlingly incredible. The mild smell of grapefruit that infused her skin, despite being sick. The shallow cleft in her chin. The sharp smarts behind her mysteriously infinite eyes. You couldn't miss that Tanvi was something special. But she wasn't exactly making things easy for me. Did she want me to screw up and for her "parents" to toss me out to the curb?

"Obviously he was really impressed by me," I kidded once Mr. Mahajan had vacated the area. It wasn't until he was clear of the room that I remembered he was her uncle and not her real father; he could've fooled me.

Tanvi smiled tiredly. "He didn't dislike you. That's just what he's like when I have someone over the first few times. His mind game trick is to say as little as possible so that the other person feels compelled to keep talking and reveal themselves."

"He sounds like a psychiatrist."

"Close. He's in financial services." The ginger ale hadn't left Tanvi's hand. Thirst welled up inside me as I looked at it. And at her.

This wasn't about the dreams anymore. If I let it, this was something that would shadow me during the day and keep me up late into the night. The thoughts of when I'd see Tanvi next and where we were heading.

"Is he your mom's brother or your dad's?" I asked, conjuring Mr. Mahajan's image and searching for a resemblance to Tanvi.

"My mother's. They were fraternal twins." Tanvi's dark irises began to melt. A single tear punched out of the corner of one eye and cascaded down the side of her nose. "He and Helena both make me sick after what they let happen to Alice. It's so easy to say you care about someone, but the proof is what you do." Yellow hoodie sleeves flew to her face, Tanvi batting at her eyes. "You suck too, by the way. You told Helena you were going to cheer me up."

"The night's not finished yet," I said. "Give me a chance." Tanvi's sadness got under my skin in a way that it shouldn't have. We barely knew each other.

I smiled crookedly, ignoring my instincts and leaping up from the couch. Storming to the unoccupied center of the room I crouched, my arms swinging backwards, then swooping under my legs and upward as I jumped into the air. Reaching maximum height, I tucked my legs and arms in, rolling through space. Landing on my feet, I let out a yelp of victory.

Natalya had taught me the back flip during a visit to my grandparents' house when I was seven. It was the nearest I'd come to flying, and I'd never let myself forget how to execute the move.

The secret was to trust yourself. And not to be afraid. If everyone let themselves be ruled by their fear of falling, none of us would ever learn to walk.

But I hadn't planned to do the flip for Tanvi. The second I was safely on the ground my face began to burn. A dog could do tricks. A five-year-old kid with a store-bought magic kit.

"Not bad," Tanvi said. She tugged her socks off and trooped toward me, motioning for me to step aside.

I returned to the couch and watched her throw her arms back, as though she was about to repeat my performance.

Crouching just as I had, Tanvi stopped abruptly. "Ugh, I don't think I can right now," she said, her fingers stretching across her abdomen as she straightened. "Not without losing whatever's left in there."

"Lie down already," I told her. "If your parents" — was I supposed to call them that? — "come in and think you've been doing back flips for me they're going to tell me to go home."

Tanvi sank into the sectional again, her socks abandoned on the floor. "I took gymnastics as a kid. And bhangra, ballet, taekwondo …"

Sure. Her guardians would've had a bursting-at-the-seams college fund for her, too. Naturally they signed her up for every activity going.

"I took squash," I offered. "And rock climbing." No one had to teach me to defend myself. Learning the opposite is just as tricky.

"Not gymnastics?" Tanvi said with a wink in her voice.

"No. My sister taught me how to do a back flip. Handstand, back walkover, and round-off too. She was the one in gymnastics." Natalya's gymnastic ribbons were hanging on the wall of her room when we left my dad behind.

"How old is your sister?" Tanvi's bare toes peeked up at me, completely at ease with their continuing nakedness.

"Nineteen. She moved in with her boyfriend this past winter, but they have an apartment in Tealing."

"Your mom's okay with that?"

I shrugged. Keion was nine years older than Natalya, and as far as I knew he'd never made my sister cry. The single time I'd heard them argue his voice had remained level while hers was the one that briefly machine-gunned the air. The nights she got home late from her job at Jean Machine, Keion had chili, pasta, or lemon-pepper salmon waiting in the oven for her. When they were apart he sang Natalya songs over the phone because he knew it made her smile. On their anniversary he'd brought her a kitten from the local shelter, although he preferred dogs. Natalya was a cat person.

"My mom likes him," I replied, while Tanvi's feet pretended it didn't make any difference whether she was wearing socks or not because they were only toes, ankles, arches, and the bits in between.

Only feet.

"They're good together," I explained. "He drives a cab right now, but he's studying part-time to become a nurse." Anybody who ever met him would tell you he'd make a good one. Keion found something to like about ninety-eight percent of the people he encountered. If he had bad feelings about a person, not only was that person not worth your time, he or she was probably lethally dangerous. "Back in April he talked a guy with a switchblade out of robbing him. Then he let the guy go without reporting it. He said the guy didn't want to hurt anyone, that he was just in a bad place."

No lie. Keion was like a good Samaritan you see on a news report but have trouble believing exists in real life.

What I didn't say: Natalya knew a good thing when she saw it. She didn't need to take her time to decide about Keion. She'd seen enough of his antithesis to be clear on what she didn't want.

People say "grow up" as though it's such basic advice that they can't believe someone is making them utter it out loud.

For better or for worse, Natalya grew up fast.

"Not too many people would do that," Tanvi said approvingly. She told me she didn't have any brothers or sisters. Not from her biological parents and not from her aunt and uncle, who couldn't have children. According to Tanvi, before her parents' accident her aunt and uncle were planning to adopt from India. They'd wanted a girl. By a twist of fate, their niece had turned out to be the one.

The topic bounced effortlessly around. We talked about the teachers who made students jump through hoops for their own amusement and the teachers you knew cared because they always went the extra mile, even for the students they didn't like. How when you're a kid the days seem so long. A week was forever. How you think you'll understand things better when you're older, that you'll know what to do in any situation.

"And you think the things adults tell you are the truth," Tanvi said. "My nanaji used to tell me incredible stories about the animals in his zoo. Like fairy tales about their lives, but always with happy endings."

"Wait, *who* has a zoo?"

Tanvi's laugh tickled the air. "My nanaji, my grandfather on my real mom's side. He doesn't really *own* a zoo, but he's the curator of the zoo in Peterborough. He oversees everything."

Whatever we talked about, I never stopped noticing her feet, or the way her hands moved when she was excited. Had she tossed them around like that when we'd argued in the clearing in my sleep? Had she said my name then? What was coming for us in the woods? Why didn't the dream ever move beyond that fixed point?

And how long had I been sitting in the Mahajans' den? Outside their bay windows, the sun had set and a yellow moon had taken its place. The days were growing shorter. Hot as it was, summer had begun to die.

"I should go," I said. Before Mr. Mahajan returned to tell me it was time to disappear. It was better if I offered first. I wasn't Catholic like the Mahajans, and I wasn't Indian. I needed to do something to make up for the deficit. I wasn't even as polite as I could've been with her uncle because Tanvi hadn't wanted me to be.

As I stood to go, Tanvi frowned and hid her hands inside her pockets. I almost stayed instead.

Launching myself off the couch and vaulting toward her, I bent to kiss one of her bare feet. Like nothing more than a peck on the cheek. Lips grazing soft skin.

Until it happened, I didn't know I was going to do it.

"You're crazy," Tanvi declared, the same magic in her voice as when she'd said my name over the phone. She stared up at me with eyes that didn't know what to expect. As though suddenly anything might happen.

"Maybe," I admitted, my chest exploding. My eyes ached in their sockets and my throat opened and closed like the gills of a fish. I pried my lips apart, controlled my breathing. "We should get together again — when you're feeling better."

Tanvi nodded with her mouth shut. I was standing next to her part of the sectional couch, beside her outstretched legs. She hauled herself up, reaching for the center of my T-shirt. Fabric bunched in her hand, she yanked me down toward her. The tang of ginger ale fizzed on my lips as our mouths collided.

Anything anything anything, her body said.

And from that moment, it felt like we were each other's destiny.

5

Ten days after I went to visit Tanvi, my body reclined on a floating
lounge chair in the center of the Mahajans' oval, Caribbean blue
swimming pool. Her flu was long gone. Tanvi's chair bobbed nearby,
a water bottle crammed into the chair's cupholder and her eyes open or
shut behind her sunglasses. I couldn't say which.

Four days of summer break stood between us and the start of the
school year. Under my skin new fissures were forming — slender spaces
where Tanvi had seeped in and begun to crack me open.

It was my choice. But it didn't feel that way.

Choosing to breathe was a choice. There are ways to stop, if that's
what you wanted. Most of us didn't. We hung on until some part of
us broke and couldn't be fixed anymore. Usually it was the heart.

In the previous week and a half I'd learned new things about Tanvi.
She had a summer job as a hostess at the local Molto Troppo. Tanvi's
grandparents — Helena's mom and dad — owned the chain of popular mid-range Italian eateries. Tanvi knew the menu by heart. She
said she couldn't help cringing whenever people ordered a cappuccino
with their dinner. In Italy, coffee was meant to be drunk at the end of

the meal and a cappuccino was something you had at breakfast. Her nonno had instilled that knowledge in her the same as if she'd been a blood granddaughter. To him, there was no difference.

I learned that her closest friends called her T.V. because her middle name was Vanessa. Imogen was on the volleyball team with her every year, and Riya, who was South Asian too, had been friends with Tanvi ever since they were in the same third grade class. Like me and my friends, they were all on the honor roll. As a kid, Tanvi had been afraid of dogs because a German shepherd had knocked her off her feet and stood over her with its teeth bared, snarling. She still felt nervous around big dogs until she got to know them.

The night Tanvi told me the truth about Alice, the fissures under my skin had yawned into chasms. Tanvi's aunt overdosed in a seedy Toronto motel. She was a drug addict and a prostitute and no one noticed she'd left the living world. It was days before the maid found Alice slumped in the suite bathroom in a bra and yoga pants. Tanvi cried on my shoulder — then clenched her hands into fists — when she spelled out the details.

Tanvi's aunt had been clean for the majority of the two years she'd lived with the Mahajans. Although they still owned the restaurant chain together, Helena's parents had broken up decades earlier. Her father had remarried, and the union had produced Alice. When Alice ran into trouble with drugs, neither of her parents wanted to know her. Helena stepped in to help, getting Alice into a rehab program and then offering her a place to stay.

Tanvi had worshipped her like-a-cousin young aunt. They'd danced in her bedroom together. Alice showed her how to create the perfect smoky eye and confided in her about the ex-boyfriend she missed. When the weather was fine they played badminton and soccer in the yard, and when it was bad they holed up in the den losing themselves in video game marathons. Slowly at first — then not so slowly — Alice fell into her old ways. All the way down.

I'd kissed her hair when Tanvi had told me these things. The smell of grapefruit tunneled through my nostrils.

We'd talked in whispers. We'd held hands.

She told me about Ashish too. The twenty-year-old son of family friends she'd had a crush on for years, until they'd crossed the line together a couple of times and Ashish got spooked. They didn't talk anymore. It was over — she was definite about that.

The things Tanvi knew about me made a shorter list.

She'd already met my mom, and knew she drove a bus. And she knew I had a sister who worked at Jean Machine and an almost brother-in-law.

I told her my dad was a loser who'd done time more than once. My mom stayed with him longer than she should've. Then even her patience had hit a wall. We moved in with my grandparents. Thin facts that only scratched the surface.

But the past didn't count from the Mahajans' oval pool. It was long finished. Something that had happened to the person I used to be. Surrounded by so much blue and sunshine that felt like a luxury now that I wasn't sweating over the condition of someone's lawn, the most amazing girl I'd ever met not twelve feet away in a two-piece yellow swimsuit, I couldn't sit still for another second.

I lowered myself into the pool and breaststroked urgently toward Tanvi, the water cool against my skin from having baked on the float-ing chair for lazy minutes. Meanwhile, Mrs. Mahajan had just left for work. We were entirely unobserved.

My wet arm draped across Tanvi's legs on the pool chair. She yelped, jolting in her seat.

"Were you sleeping?" I asked.

Grinning dazedly, she yawned and sliced her arm into the water. A tidal wave of pool water smacked me in the face and shoulders.

Sputtering and laughing, I heaved myself over Tanvi's chair, my hands reaching under her armpits to lift her, the chair tipping with my added weight. Tanvi laughed along with me. Higher and harder. We splashed into the water together, my hand snaking around her waist, hers fanning across my chest.

Our lips fused, bodies treading water in the middle of the pool, then swimming for the nearest end where we could grab hold of the pool's edge.

Tanvi pulled herself out first. One fluid motion, like it was effortless.

I went after her. Just like the day on the stairs. Tanvi first, me second.

We stumbled into the shed together. My jeans and shirt hung from a hook in the corner — waiting for me to change back into them — and a pile of immaculately pressed white bath towels gathered on a small white nightstand. Water puddled under our feet on the terracotta tiles. Behind us the bar fridge hummed with life, its only occupants half a dozen cans of Fruitopia. Strawberry. Tanvi's favorite flavor.

Not one garden tool lingered inside the shed. The eight foot by eight foot pine structure resembled a rustic northern cottage from the outside but served only as a guest change room.

Inside the shed's walls, there was zero possibility of anyone charging in to interrupt us. We were the only people around for miles. That's how it felt. Tanvi and me with our mouths welded together. Our hands gliding over wet, warm skin. My fingers slipping into her swimsuit bottoms, sliding them down to tile. My knees on the terracotta floor so my mouth could reach her where I wanted.

Where she wanted too.

Where she tasted first like chlorine, and then like her.

And afterwards she reached into my shorts. Her hands on me, and her mouth saying, "No one ever did that before."

I hadn't either. Other things, but not what I'd done for her.

We changed into our street clothes and flopped onto the den's sectional couch together, the two of us occupying the same space. Tanvi combed her fingers through my hair, her touch so gentle that it hardly seemed possible. "I had a dream about you last night," she said.

I shifted my head, staring at Tanvi incredulously. Held my breath and waited for her to tell me what I already knew. The forest clearing. Black doom. The two of us together, running for our lives. Days could pass in between my nightmares, but they never left me alone for long.

"It was winter," she continued. "So cold. Perfectly formed snowflakes the size of my fist were falling around us. The sky was an amazing purple as though it was getting dark. You had a dog that looked more like a coyote. It was wild looking, but beautiful. The three of us were walking through the snow; we were going to see Alice together. In my dream, she wasn't gone. She'd never died. It never got dark, either. No matter how long we walked, the sky stayed purple."

My fingers skimmed Tanvi's arm, lungs slowly emptying only to fill themselves afresh.

We hadn't shared the same vision. Hers had been the opposite. A good dream instead of a nightmare. Hopeful. Tinted with wonder.

"It sounds beautiful," I told her.

"It was. I wish it was true."

I could picture it. Just as she'd described. Giant, elaborately flawless crystalline snowflakes filling the air. Drifting idly to the ground in no hurry to land. Tanvi in sheepskin mittens, Sorel boots, and a parka. Infinite purple sky. A journey without end.

"In the dream, you weren't afraid of the coyote?" I asked. Big dogs, even in the distance, made Tanvi flinch. I knew that. She had to make a conscious effort to fight her fear of strange dogs, unless they were small enough for an old woman to carry comfortably in her arms.

"No," she replied. "I knew it was yours. You loved this dog — or whatever it was — so much in the dream that I liked it too."

The fissures under my skin — the cracks Tanvi had rendered and stretched day by day — ached and throbbed. Inside me, tectonic plates shifted. Heat escaping from underneath.

"Remember what I told you about my dad? The robberies. The arguments with my mom." My voice burned, my outer crust crumbling.

"Yeah." In Tanvi's hands my hair was silk. Her fingers swam through it with mermaid grace.

"There was more. He dislocated my shoulder once. I was about eight and a half. I was standing in front of my mom. He used to … he used to hurt her, all the time it felt like. Mostly when he was drunk. But this time it was me, because I wouldn't move and let him do it. He pulled me away from her. I fell. He dragged me through the kitchen and the hallway. Then he opened the front door, yanked me outside, and locked the door behind me."

Tanvi was silent, her fingers never stilling. The purple sky of her dreams blossomed behind my eyes. Maybe it *was* real, in a sense. I could almost feel the snowflakes brush my arms and land on my lips.

"Is that why your mom left him?" Tanvi asked, her voice unwavering.

"We left that night. He ended up in jail again a few months later. He was always in and out. Couldn't hold down a job. Even his mother — my grandmother — doesn't know where he is now."

"Since after the last robbery?" Tanvi prompted. I'd told her that much.

"Right." The jewelry store. Him and his partner got their hands on nearly half a million dollars' worth of gold, platinum, and precious gemstones, and then vanished.

"I hate him," Tanvi said. Fury stole into her mouth and her limbs. I felt its warmth through her fingertips. "No one should ever hurt anyone else in that way, but especially their own family. I hate that he did that to you and your mom. And I hate that he didn't get caught when he doesn't deserve that money, he doesn't deserve anything good."

"People don't always get what they deserve," I said.

"No, they don't," Tanvi agreed wistfully.

A clap of noise broke us apart. The sound of someone smacking wood.

"You're looking much too comfortable," a male voice said sternly from the open double doors. "Tanvi, sit up."

I retracted my arms with a speed that would've rivaled any action movie hero, untangling myself from Tanvi on the couch. Mr. Mahajan stood in the doorway, his shoulders squared and his mouth an indignant slash. His Ivy League hair — not a strand out of place — appeared more severe than I'd remembered it, not allowing for the smallest margin of error.

Next to me, Tanvi quickly resettled herself in a seated position. Not even our legs touched. The only noise in the room came from the air conditioner. It whirred steadily in complaint.

"*Dad*," Tanvi said finally, not chiding him exactly. Not exactly apologetic, either.

My cheeks smarted. I forced my restless legs — and restless everything else — to transform into stone.

"*Tanvi*," Mr. Mahajan said, echoing her tone with a precision that would've had me laughing in some other circumstance.

Then he spun on his heel and strode away, leaving us alone in the den.

"Sorry," Tanvi said under her breath. "That was embarrassing."

We could've closed the den doors. We'd known he was on his way. Then again, it could've been worse. We could've been up in Tanvi's bedroom doing what we'd been doing out in the shed.

"It's okay," I told her. "But maybe I should take off. He looked pissed."

"No," Tanvi said decisively. "We weren't doing anything. He's just trying to make a point." Her brow furrowed, her lower lip jutting out. "But it's meaningless. His eyes are closed. My mom's too. They only see what they want to see. Meanwhile Ash, someone they would never expect to …"

"What?" I asked.

"Ashish and I" — Tanvi bit down on her thumbnail — "we slept together."

My calf twitched, threatening to turn into a charley horse. The facts Tanvi had shared about Ashish hastily reorganized beneath my skull, neural pathways rewiring themselves and a red-hot poker forming under my ribs. Ashish Kohli. Current Harvard student. Summer intern at the Tealing mayor's office. The son of one of Mr. Mahajan's university friends, Ashish and Tanvi had practically grown up together.

But it wasn't just a childhood crush. Not just a couple of kisses or a series of hurried make-out sessions, either.

"So it was serious?" I said.

"No." The syllable idled on Tanvi's lips, her brown eyes distant — looking back into the past. "If anything, it was puppy love. I'd liked him for so long. But it wasn't real. I'd constructed an image of him in my head, but so much of it was just … like a childish fairy tale almost. And after we were together, he felt so guilty that he said he felt like he'd betrayed my family. But even then, I made it happen again. At the time I wanted him to be mine so much that I couldn't see clearly."

"I was going to tell you about him." Tanvi paused, one of her hands clutching her left kneecap. "More about him, I mean. It just felt soon. And we were a big mistake — awkward to talk about."

It didn't feel soon. Not after what we'd done in the shed earlier.

"But you're over him?" The hot poker stirred the contents of my chest, whisking them into mush. "You said it was done."

If Ashish was in the past, what should it matter what they'd done together?

Yet if I had the power to jump back a few minutes in time, I would've already done it. One short leap. Then I would've let Tanvi feed my hair through her fingers and tell me about her dream, but I would've kept my mouth shut about my dad. She didn't need to know that buried part of me. The fissures had wrenched too wide, and I'd allowed it to happen. I hadn't made the choice to stop.

"It was done before it ever started, believe me," Tanvi told me. "He's in love with a girl he goes to school with. We should never have happened in the first place. Like I said, it was a mistake." Tanvi drew her legs up onto the couch with her, wrapping her arms around her shins like closed butterfly wings.

My brain burned into a fireball as I sat stonily next to Tanvi on the couch. Ashish was twenty and went to Harvard. He'd slept with Tanvi, who'd wanted him to be hers so much that she couldn't see clearly. I was still in high school and still a virgin. My competitive edge was zero. I couldn't make the equation results come out any differently.

"You're so quiet," Tanvi said. "It's making me feel weirder."

"I'm just thinking."

"Thinking what?" Tanvi asked, her head cushioned by her knees.

"I don't want to get any deeper into this and find out you still have a thing for this guy." The words twisted out of my throat like braided hair pulled tight enough to give someone a headache. *Ash*, Tanvi had called him initially. She was still using his nickname. "You said you liked him for so long. It sounds like something that was taking up a lot of emotional space."

"It was," Tanvi admitted. "And now it's not. Honestly, I wouldn't string you along like that." Her left hand unclamped itself from her shins and touched my thigh. "Okay?"

"Okay," I said, the part of me I couldn't control disagreeing with half a dozen instincts pointing me in the opposite direction. The part of me that had given up worrying what I could lose by being with Tanvi. The part of me that had already surrendered.

"Okay," I repeated. And we were.

Better than okay. For months on end afterwards.

The world didn't end. The fissures under my skin didn't stop my heart. Greenland ice sheets didn't split apart like fault lines.

Nothing changed, except Tanvi Mahajan and me falling in love.

6

Leaves turned gold and red and fell from the trees, congregating on lawns instead. The days grew shorter, requiring longer sleeves and then jackets. The outside world smelled of mulch. School assignment due dates came and went. Cross-country practices and meets, too.

I had dinner at the Mahajan house, off and on. Tanvi came over to my house for dinner too. She and my mom chatted like old friends. Natalya and Keion had us over to their apartment, and Keion fed us his sticky pork noodles. When Natalya and I had a second alone in the living room afterwards my sister beamed at me from the corner armchair.

"She's great," Natalya said conspiratorially. "But you already know that. You guys will come by again, right? Don't keep her all to yourself."

"You sound like a kid talking about a Christmas present," I teased.

"Okay, maybe. But I'm allowed to be a little pushy with my little brother once in a while. You know Keion and I like good people."

"I know. Thanks. I'm glad you like her." And we did hang out with her and Keion again. But what Tanvi and I liked best was when there was no else around. We'd curl up on my couch, or Tanvi's on the rarer occasions when the Mahajans were both out. If we were confident we had a place to ourselves for a stretch, it was the bed. Our hands and mouths knew no borders.

Tanvi was three months older than me and eligible to drive unsupervised before I was. By the end of October she could pick me up in her Subaru.

At the end of December we hit a pre-New Year's Eve party thrown by a Holy Trinity friend of Tanvi's. The snow came down heavy that night. A snowball war broke out in the backyard. Girls versus boys. The girls were vicious. One of the guys took an ice-cake to the eye, another suffered a bloody nose. "White flag going up," a guy named Cal hollered when he saw the blood run down his friend's face and into the crevice between his lips. "No one needs to die here today." He convinced everyone to stop, drop, and make angels in the snow instead.

"Typical Cal," Tanvi commented. "Always making peace." She rolled on top of me while my arms were flapping through the snow, her whispered breath hot when everything else was cold. "I'm so excited about tonight. I can't wait to leave this party."

Her dad was the one to pick us up. That was Tanvi's idea, part of the master plan. She told her father Keion was coming for me in his cab. Instead, minutes after we'd arrived back at Margate Avenue, she snuck me under the Mahajans' beaded chandelier, up the curved staircase, and into her bedroom, then reported to her father that I'd gone home while I texted my mom that I was sleeping over at Jeffrey's.

Not drunk and not sober, we were the perfect in-between. We stripped in silence, kissed in silence, stifled the giddy thrill noises of occupying a forbidden space together while in the hallway someone turned off an overhead light and then closed a door behind them. As we burrowed under the blankets, sweating into each other's skin, Tanvi guided me inside her. She'd been on the pill for five weeks by then. It felt so good and right between us that I wanted to stop the clock — stay in her bed until my heart stopped beating. Ghost lovers, unseen and unheard by anyone except us.

For hours we stopped and started, catnapping in between and finally following through again completely in what must have been the early hours of the morning. Sleep seemed like a wasted opportunity. I thought we'd be up all night, too aware of each other's presence to give in to it.

We'd climbed into bed with Tanvi's purple drapes gaping open in the darkness. But when I woke up I was spooning her, my arm sprawled over Tanvi's waist and my face buried in her hair. Dull, gray light leaked through the gap in the curtain, and she was mumbling something so low and indistinct that I wasn't sure whether it was words. I leaned over her, listening closely. She was still out like a light, but her lips were moving.

"That doesn't make any sense," Tanvi whispered. "You have to be the one."

I jerked away from her in shock. The dream had caught up with her. As though it was contagious and I'd carried it back to Tanvi's house with me. Infected her.

My sudden movement woke her. Tanvi rolled over and opened her eyes, smiling sleepily like nothing out of the ordinary had happened, other than the two of us sleeping together for the first time. "Hey," she whispered happily. "Good morning."

It should have been. Now I wasn't sure.

"What were you dreaming?" I asked. "You were talking in your sleep."

"Really? I didn't think I talked in my sleep. What did I say?"

"I don't know," I lied, heart hammering in my chest. If I didn't admit to them, the dreams didn't exist and couldn't touch us. But I couldn't stop shivering under the blankets. And that raw scratching noise overhead, like something being belligerently dragged across Tanvi's ceiling, it was just a settling noise. Nothing to do with my dreams. It couldn't be.

"Huh. Weird." Tanvi said, shifting her head on the pillow as if she was listening too.

She reached for her phone to check the time, and the second Mr. Mahajan had left for work and Mrs. Mahajan was in the shower we sprinted downstairs and approached the door to the garage. "Shit," Tanvi muttered, fishing in her purse. "I don't have my car keys." She pushed me in the direction of the front door. "Wait outside in case my mom comes down — the alarm will be off now, so you can go through. I'll meet you out there in a minute."

I headed for the door while Tanvi retraced her steps upstairs. Outside, yesterday's snowfall glistened in the sun, like a million tiny stolen diamonds had been scattered among the pristine white drifts. The sight immediately lightened my mood. Last night with Tanvi had been one of the best nights of my life, and I needed to get a grip. Dreams were just brain litter. Everybody's house made noises. We could be happy and stay that way.

Trudging along the perimeter of the Mahajans' driveway, my boots repeatedly disappeared under the snow. Overhead, the moon was still visible. It looked as at home surrounded by blue sky as it did by blackness. A gibbous moon, more than half light but less than full. I trekked onto the sidewalk and past the neighbor's house, not wanting to chance Mrs. Mahajan spotting me from one of her windows. It was safer to keep moving, turning back now and then to look for Tanvi, the morning moon keeping me company.

Not five minutes later she emerged from the Mahajan house in earmuffs and her long suede coat. She hurtled in my direction, kicking up a whirl of snow with each step. As she caught up I flung my arms around her and kissed her forehead. She leaned into me, breathing heat onto my neck. "You must be starving," she said, producing a croissant from her pocket.

"Thanks. You think of everything." I tore a piece from the croissant and shoved it between my teeth. "What do you think they would've done if they'd caught us?"

"Who knows?" Tanvi's gloved hands settled into her coat pockets. "Sometimes I wonder if I'd have more room — or less — to screw up if my real parents were alive. I can't help but wonder how things would be different. How I'd be different. In multiple ways, probably, if my parents were here."

"That's true. Everything that's happened to us so far has led us to this exact point." I pointed to the snow at our feet. "Maybe we wouldn't be together. We might never have met."

Tanvi's neck arched, her chin swimming up to the sky, succumbing to the realm of possibilities. "Anything could've happened." She eyed the pale moon pensively.

"And still could," I said. "The path we're on, we could completely change it at any moment. We can just make the choice and do it. Be who we want to be. Do what we want to do. It sounds obvious, but it took me the longest time to realize that."

"Really?" Tanvi prompted, eyes widening in curiosity.

I trudged slowly alongside her, diving into my reply with a casualness that contradicted the actual response. "I used to be different," I began. "When I was younger, the way my dad acted — the things he did — they made me see my family as a certain kind of people." The kind who had problems that regular people didn't. The kind who went to the emergency department for things that weren't accidents. The kind who were late with the electricity bill and would never get ahead.

When my mom got the job in Tealing and I started school here I brought my old problems with me, fighting anybody who tossed me a surly word. One night after a parent-teacher meeting where my mom was warned of future suspensions if I didn't shape up, Natalya cornered me in the hall. "Holding on to anger is like drinking poison and expecting the other person to die," she said. "You ever hear that before?"

"Don't start," I protested. I'd had plenty of lectures from multiple sources. The words didn't touch me. It was almost like they were talking about someone else.

"I don't get you." My sister slumped impatiently against the wall. "You act like you have no choice. But only you get to decide who you really are. And you're brand new here. So why can't you just stop it? Decide you're not going to be that way anymore. Or are you actually *trying* to turn into Dad?" Natalya turned her face to the side so she wouldn't have to look at me. Then she stomped away down the hallway without glancing back.

It's not simple to change. It's not a single conversation with your sister, and not something I could easily explain to Tanvi, either. How I changed everything in eighth grade. My friends. My grades. The way I spoke to people. The way I walked. The don't-fuck-with-me aura I'd projected nearly without being aware of it.

On Margate Avenue, Tanvi's grip on my arm tightened as I wrapped up a highly edited version of my story. She rooted her boots to the ground, stopping us both on the spot as if she sensed there was more in my head than I'd shared. That it wasn't only about doing my math homework, learning not to raise my fists, and avoiding running with the wrong crowd. It was about doing everything right. Every little thing you can imagine. Getting the *best* grades possible. Impressing your teachers with your effort and intelligence. Wearing clothes that said preppy rather than potential future prison inmate. Picking friends who were on track to become doctors, chief executives, and lawyers.

Saying "sorry" and "excuse me" like someone who'd been raised right from day one. Never getting high. Never getting angry — unless the situation unquestionably warranted it, and even then only within controlled limits. Only drinking at events where everyone else was, but never to the point where you couldn't control yourself. Being someone people trusted. Someone they would never think to be afraid of. Someone you would never glance at in the street, or any-where else, with the tag "loser" flashing invisibly across his chest.

I wasn't my DNA. I wasn't my social class. I wasn't anything that was set in stone. Not unless I wanted to be.

Tensing under Tanvi's grasp in a late December wind I could suddenly hardly feel, I wondered how she'd managed to guess about the gaps in my story. How does someone begin to fill in blanks they should never have known existed?

But it wasn't that.

As I searched Tanvi's eyes, freezing on the inside while my skin went numb, she said, "*Look*."

Following her gaze, my eyes collided with a dog. Gray, mostly. Flecked with fox red and murky white. Large enough to worry Tanvi from roughly thirty feet off.

It stared back at us with mild curiosity from the edge of a neigh-bor's front lawn. The quality of the stare was what drilled the truth into me. Not a dog. Something that lived its own life, its own way, free from constraints. An eastern coyote, its genetic makeup part coyote and part wolf.

"It's okay," I said under my voice while I tried to turn away. "Let's go."

Tanvi held fast to me. "You're not supposed to turn your backs on them. We need to face it and back away slowly to show we're not afraid."

The coyote didn't care about us. I wasn't scared. But maybe I should've been, with Tanvi next to me. And as soon as that occurred to me fear ignited in the center of my chest. Primal fear. The kind our ancestors must have felt gathered around a fire, trying to keep away the things lurking in the dark.

The pressure on my arm anchored me to the moment. Morning on Margate Avenue. The Mahajan house a dash away, the coyote standing between us and safety, taking a tentative step closer to us in the snow. It was a beautiful animal, objectively. Familiar like a neighbor's dog is familiar, yet not familiar at all. Wild and unpredictable. A hunter.

We didn't know what it might do.

As solidly as my body stood on Tanvi's street, my mind was half somewhere else. Adrift in a nightmare I'd been having for months, Tanvi bleeding next to me, rivulets of red dripping down her face. Death closing in from the darkness, terror advancing ahead of it, smothering hope.

My brain jumped to a protection chant my grandmother had taught me as a kid, when I used to have nightmares of a different kind.

> Moon and stars, forever shine,
> Moon and stars, friends of mine,
> I close my eyes and trust your light,
> I close my eyes and say goodnight,
> Watch over me while I am gone,
> Watch over me until the dawn.

The words were of no use to anyone while awake. And I didn't believe in dream catchers, chants, or spells anyway. With a gust of wind, my mind rebooted, recognizing its mistake and leapfrogging into the present to join my body.

"Come on," Tanvi said urgently, her fingers vise-like on my arm.

We stepped slowly backwards together, the coyote's stride quickening. More curious now. Emboldened.

I tore my arm free from Tanvi. Hurled both hands into the sky, clapping them above my head and shouting with a ferocity I normally kept strapped down. "Get out of here! Go! Get the fuck away from us before we shoot your scrawny ass!" Years ago, at one of my old schools, a wildlife expert had led an assembly about how to handle an encounter with a coyote. The information began to trickle back to me as the coyote neared, its coat so thick you instinctively wanted to run your hands through it, even as your legs longed to carry you away. Whatever you do, *don't run*. That's what the wildlife expert had said. If you run, the coyote will likely attack. Make yourself look as big, loud, and hostile as you can. Act like an asshole. Become everything you hate.

Beside me Tanvi was roaring, waving her arms rabidly at the moon and stomping her feet, her lips curling away from her teeth. Any kid passing would've looked at us and died laughing. It was a ridiculous scene.

But not to the coyote. It turned and ran from us, hotfooting its way down Margate Avenue like it had better places to be while we hurled verbal abuse at its tail.

"Oh my God!" Tanvi exclaimed once the animal had shrunk into a speck in the distance.

We jogged back to her garage, breathless and on a strange, natural high that comes from facing even the smallest potential danger and pushing through to the other side.

"Remember my dream months ago?" Tanvi asked as we climbed into her front seat, hearts still jumping under our ribs, drumming to the beat of a horror movie thrill. "That was exactly how your dog looked in the dream."

A laugh pogoed in my chest, behind it a sinking feeling, like a limb swallowed by quicksand. Our dreams were stalking closer, converging with reality. However much I wanted to deny it, the words Tanvi had whispered in her sleep were no coincidence. We'd driven the coyote away — under a sky as bright as any day in June — but darkness had crept a step closer and stared us knowingly in the eye.

7

The Camry came to me in February, via an eighty-one-year-old man on my mom's bus route who wasn't allowed to drive anymore because of macular degeneration. His bad luck was my good fortune, and I drove Tanvi everywhere I could to make up for the months she'd chauffeured me around Tealing. The man only wanted four hundred dollars. It was a steal, easily paid for by my shifts at Central Foodmart.

On Valentine's Day we drove to an out-of-town Lebanese restaurant. Tanvi bought me boxers covered in tiny red hearts. I gave her a plush otter that lay on its back like it was floating. We exchanged boxes of chocolates and devoured half of them on the way home, my mind running wild because every time I looked at Tanvi, my eyes tripped and fell down to her legs, where her embroidered black minidress rode up her thighs, making promises.

Sometimes I thought of things I shouldn't, too.

How had it been with Ashish?

Better or worse than with me? Tanvi never said. But several photos of him were tucked into the Mahajan family album, where he sat next to her on a park bench, grinning like a guy about to get what he wanted without even having to ask. Some photos were only a year or two old, others snapped when they were children. Tanvi flat-chested, her legs skinny and awkward but her eyes unchanged.

A second album contained photographs of Tanvi with her mother, Antoinette, and her father, Anand. That album was only half full. In the final image Tanvi, held in her father's arms with his back to the camera, points at whoever is taking the picture. Her eyes are alert, her expression one of amusement. The night her parents drove to a Toronto hospital to visit an old auntie and a torrential rainstorm forced a transport truck into their path she was precisely nine months and twelve days old.

It's that photo of her that rips my heart into pieces.

Somewhere I had a father I was better off without and Tanvi didn't get to keep the parents that she should've had for longer than nine months. The girl in the photo doesn't know she's about to be robbed. Judging from her face — the shining eyes and beginnings of a smile — the universe is everything she needs it to be.

I thought I could be part of that. And she could be that for me.

For months it seemed true.

Then the final days of March rolled in. Initially they were almost indistinguishable from the days and weeks that had preceded them. Snow and ice were melting, the runoff dangerously swelling creeks and exposing bald patches of grass and miniature teepee piles of crumpled beer cans and cigarette butt litter. But Tanvi and I were unchanged. It was rare that a day went by without us touching base. We were close. Happy. We were the kind of people who thought we didn't believe in saying cheesy things only to be repeatedly proven wrong whenever we were within each other's orbit.

It was sickeningly sweet, and we ate it up.

But words are only words. Their meaning is subject to change.

That was something I used to know, but had forgotten. Denial is like blindness — either temporary or permanent — and when I spied a coyote darting across a residential street on my way to the Tealing mall I refused to register it as the powerful animal I'd encountered on Margate Avenue. He was too skinny, his fur and skin attacked by mange. It couldn't have been the same coyote Tanvi and I had scared off in December. It must have been a different animal.

Arjun was looking to pick out a birthday gift for his mother that Saturday. I met him and Justin at the mall, where everything he saw was wrong. Too cheap, too expensive, the wrong size, not her style.

We drifted into the food court for a break. Justin's finger shot out, identifying Tanvi at a table close to the burrito counter. Ashish Kohli sat across from her, wearing a plaid shirt with the top two buttons undone and tenderly holding her hand. A friend might hold your hand that way, if you were dying. As far as I knew neither of them was.

Tanvi and Ashish took no notice of us in the distance. Their eyes were filled with each other.

I jerked to attention, twisting my face away from them. Then my entire body. I stalked away from the food court with Justin and Arjun in tow. "That looked incriminating," Justin noted. "But appearances can be deceiving."

And sometimes things are exactly as they appear.

Ducking into a clothing store, I texted Tanvi to ask what she was up to. Sixty seconds later she replied that she was at the mall with Imogen. "What're you doing?" she wanted to know.

"Catching you in a lie," I messaged. Then I turned off my phone and told my friends I had to go. Be anywhere but where I was.

I climbed into the Camry, my fists shaking on the steering wheel.

I peeled out of the mall parking lot and sped in random directions, my brain detonating over and over. Right. Left. Right. Right. Left. Past the movie theater. Beyond the recreation center and library. Navigating a wide circle around the Newtown Creek Park where two hawks soared overhead, scouting for prey — and where I'd curled up on a blanket with Tanvi, believing her feelings were the equivalent of mine. Trusting her more than I'd trusted anyone outside my family.

Hours later, when I pulled into my Balsam driveway, I couldn't feel anything or remember exactly where I'd gone. The scenery in my mind blurred together like soggy newsprint.

Visually, the human hippocampus resembles a partially formed seahorse. Or one that's curled up and died. That's what mine felt like as I stepped into the house. My hand automatically searched out my phone in my pocket, switched it on so that it sprung to life. Six messages waited for me. Each of them from Tanvi, saying different things. She was sorry. She didn't tell me because she knew how I felt about Ashish. She ran into him while at the mall. It wasn't planned. They were just talking. It didn't mean anything. She was sorry sorry sorry and she needed me to return her call.

"I saw you together," I texted. "You were holding hands." Nobody holds your hand like it's a precious, fragile object without the act meaning something. There had to be more.

My phone wailed between my fingers, like an ambulance siren coming up on your bumper. I ignored it, navigating to Ashish's Instagram account instead. The most recent posting was a photo of Tanvi and Ash. They were standing, facing each other, noses so close that it would've been tough to fit a can of Coke between them. Ashish's gaze was supremely serene, as if the girl in front of him was the answer to everything and he'd never have another moment's doubt in his life.

His caption read: "Never wrong a girl who has your heart. She is precious and rare."

Someone called Sarvesh commented: "And gorgeous. What's she doing with you ;)"

"You two are too cute together," somebody else said.

A third exclaimed: "You better send me a wedding invite!"

My mom had joined me in the hallway. She'd changed out of her uniform and was wearing jeans and the long V-neck sweater that

Natalya had given her for Christmas. "You're home early," she observed. "How are Arjun and Justin?"

I shook my head, stupefied. Tanvi and Ash were together. Everybody knew it. Why was she continuing to lie to me? She easily could have slept with Ashish again already. It was possible that they'd never stopped.

"What's wrong?" my mother asked. "You look like someone just ran over your puppy in the street."

"Nothing … just … I'm going out again in a second."

Patrick from work, Central Foodmart's laziest stock clerk, was having a party I'd never intended to go to. But I was going now. I couldn't stand in the hallway all night with Tanvi's lying texts spitting repeatedly into my phone, insulting my intelligence.

My phone felt hot in my hand. Like an outdoor ATM during a heat wave.

I texted Desiree for Patrick's address. Neither of us liked Patrick. He blamed everyone else for his mistakes and spoke like there was a megaphone superglued to his mouth. Desiree couldn't believe I was going to his party.

I couldn't believe it either.

I couldn't believe my relationship with Tanvi had been gutted like a fish in the time it takes to point a finger.

My mom insisted on driving me over to Patrick's house, a split-level semi with Christmas lights still over the garage and a mob of cars parked up and down the street. Tanvi blinked inside my head when I barged through the front door without knocking, a fog of smoke and hip-hop music enveloping me. In the house people were doing shots and dancing. Or standing around with their spines hugging the walls, watching the others. The music was too loud for talking, and the air smelled like old bingo hall air — dank, smoky, sweat-stained yet spiked with perfume.

It didn't matter. I wasn't there to talk or to breathe.

Most of the people I edged past were strangers. A few years older than me, like Patrick. That didn't necessarily matter either. I kept walking, taking in the living room scene as I went. Girls in heavy mascara and cherry-red lipstick. Naked legs under short skirts. Skin-tight jeans and halter tops. Ultrabrite smiles.

I reached the kitchen next. Several closed-lid Rubbermaid coolers lined the floor, and both sides of the double sinks were crammed to the top with ice. It glistened under the track lighting. Tiny rectangular ice floes, melting imperceptibly. A guy in an orange beanie and a scarf so big that it threatened to swallow his upper body like a boa constrictor was doing a line of coke off the counter while a girl in a denim skirt sat next to him blowing smoke rings.

"Hey, Misha," the girl said languidly.

I zeroed in on her thin eyebrows and freckled nose, realizing it was Margo from work. "Hey, what's up, Margo?" I bent to pluck a can of beer from the nearest cooler.

"Some of the people we know from Central are in the basement playing pool," she offered.

I thanked her and headed downstairs. If Tanvi thought she could play me and get away with it, she was dead wrong. I was striking back. In the basement I located Patrick and other people from work. A crowd of us played pool and knocked back beer, and then shots, Tanvi holding Ashish's hand the entire time, their heads pulling together like magnets. Fingers picking at each other's clothes, making them disappear.

I talked to girls I knew and girls I didn't. Short girls. Tall girls. Girls in bare feet and girls in knee-high boots. It took a little time, but in the end I found one. A girl who was looking for the same thing I was.

Her name was Katrine, and she straddled me on the basement couch, her red hair falling around my face while we chapped each other's lips. I'd forgotten what it was like to kiss anyone but Tanvi. My body slipped into autopilot, but my mind wouldn't let go. It was locked on Tanvi, seething and breaking. Still in shock hours later. Stalled. Stuck in a moment in time. The moment where everything I thought I had didn't mean anything anymore, and she was the reason.

On the couch I pushed my hands gently into Katrine's shoulders, forcing her away from me. "Back in a second," I told her, but I knew I wouldn't return. Tanvi's hold on me was so tight that I didn't really want anyone else, even as revenge.

"I might still be here," she said, trying to be cute. She slithered off me, retreating into the shadows.

Patrick clapped me on the back while I sprinted up the steps to the ground floor. "Having a good time, bro?"

I nodded with my mouth shut, stomping into the kitchen. The coke was long gone. So were Margo and the guy in the orange beanie and boa constrictor scarf. The ice cubes in the sink had transformed into water. I reached in to pull the plug and hung my head over the counter, the pita I'd eaten at lunch making a hasty exit.

Yeah, I was having a good time, bro. The time of my life.

And now I was leaving.

Keion came in his cab when I texted him, like an indie 911. He shook his head at me as I dove into the front seat next to him. "I've never seen you in this sorry ass state," he said. "What's going on?"

"I don't know," I told him.

"Yeah, you do."

"Yeah, I do," I admitted. I'd walked too far out on the ice and realized it could crack under my feet. "But not now, okay? I need to get home."

Keion nodded as we pulled away from the curb. "I can see that, all right."

I leaned my head back against the headrest and shut my eyes; I'd downed too many shots to keep them open. Sleep curved its velvety black wings eagerly around me. I didn't fight it.

In some other place, Tanvi stared at me with eyes like a starless night sky. "*Shantallow*," she said, her cheeks slick with blood and her lips not moving. "*Run.*" My shirt was torn at the elbow. It flapped as I ran, my ribs twitching underneath my skin, clawing me from the inside.

"We should have reached a road by now," Tanvi said. Misery bent her voice, like a branch drooping under the weight of too much snow. "How can there be no road?"

I jolted myself free from sleep. Keion's eyes were on the road ahead. "*Shantallow*," he hissed. "*We shall all be changed.*" Sharp fingernails scraped violently against the passenger side of the car. Keion grinned maniacally, his teeth broken and gray. Only he wasn't Keion anymore. My father was at the wheel. Soil spilled from his mouth. Chunks of his skull were missing, the glare from a passing car illuminating the clumps of raw, uneven flesh left in their place.

"Hey, hey!" a voice called. "Wake up, Misha." A car horn blared. It sliced through my fear, hurling me back to the world. My head knocked back against the headrest, Keion's right hand closed firmly around my arm. "Whoa. You were having a night terror or something. I couldn't wake you up. You damn scared me." He promptly released his hold, his right hand joining his left on the wheel.

"I'm okay," I said unconvincingly. "Must've been all the beer."

We were back in Balsam, a couple of blocks from my house. Keion sighed through his teeth, his concerned eyes worse than any lecture. Thirty seconds later we veered onto my street. About six houses down from mine a guy with his hood up sat on a neighbor's steps, hunched against the wind. He cocked his head in my direction as I exited the car, like we knew each other.

Keion called after me, "Be good, Misha. Call me if you want to talk."

I was as shaky as hell, freezing on the inside. The dream had been so real that I easily might have thrown myself from the car to escape it. One of my hands flew instinctively up in the air to wave off

Keion, my feet pausing until the cab was gone and then padding me over to the neighbor's front yard like they had their own ideas about what was supposed to happen next.

"Thought that was you," the guy said from the stoop. He tugged his hoodie down, revealing a familiar face. Black, maybe nineteen years old, maybe twenty-two. I'd never known exactly in the first place. I couldn't remember his name, either. Craig, Greg, Kevin, Gavin. Something like that. We'd run into each other a couple of times on big jobs last summer. He'd worked with another Golding Green Thumb crew.

"You live out here too?" I asked. My dad's fucked-up face flickered behind my eyes. I grabbed the railing to steady myself.

"Nah. Closer to Bishop. I'm just waiting for a friend to get home. My mom locked me out for missing curfew." I nodded dazedly, feeling as if I'd never be warm again. "You look spooked, man," he added. "You all right?"

"Been better," I confirmed. "I got mixed up with one of those rich Newtown Creek girls — you know, the kind of people whose lawns we slogged over all summer because they're too uptight-rich to bother their asses doing it themselves."

"Oh yeah." He chuckled dryly. "So this girl was slumming with you?"

"And then she figured it out. Screwed me over with her ex." I knew how pathetic I sounded, but once I kicked into gear I couldn't shut up. My lips kept flapping open in the wind, telling him how out of my league Tanvi was with her perfect house, rich parents, even wealthier restaurateur grandparents, and Harvard ex-boyfriend. It was better than ranting about my psycho dreams.

"Her grandparents own Molto Troppo?" he echoed. "I'd rather have a Big Mac than the pseudo-Italian microwave shit they serve in that place. You should've dumped her before she dumped you. Don't sweat it, though. A girl like that isn't worth the trouble. You need someone who will have your back. Someone who's for real."

I nodded, wishing I could take back all my sloppy, self-pitying words. "It's gusty out here, man," I told him. "You want to wait in my house until your friend shows?"

He slipped his phone out of his hoodie pocket to glance at the screen. "No, I'm good. He should be here soon. Thanks, though." He swung his hood back into place while I turned to go.

The night didn't feel over. The last thing I wanted to do was to sleep. But I was worn out through and through. Still soaked in alcohol too, regretting everything but the first two beers. Inside the house I collapsed on the bed in my clothes and fed my earbuds into my ears.

Next thing I knew, Tanvi was glaring down at me from beside my bed. Sunlight passing through the window etched a fuzzy halo around her head. Her dark hair twisted partially around her neck, and the skin under her eyes was puffy and raw. "Congratulations," she said, bitterness clogging the air. "You win."

"What?" I mumbled, lips heavy from sleep. "What are you talking about?"

"I saw the photo from last night," Tanvi said. "On Snapchat. You and whoever that girl was."

I pushed myself up on my elbows, the color draining from my face, leaving me a ghost. I felt it happen and saw the evidence in Tanvi's eyes. I was a dead man.

"You didn't know there was a photo?" she continued.

That prick Patrick. It must've been. Or someone else from work, thinking they were being funny.

"You and Ashish." His name collapsed into rubble on my tongue. "You started it."

"And you thought you'd end it." A punishing smile hollowed out Tanvi's face. "Mission accomplished. I thought we were better than that. I thought all the time we spent together since last summer, all those things we told each other, really meant something."

My arms hung apologetically at my sides. "I don't know what the photo from last night looks like, but we just made out. I've never seen that girl before in my life, and I couldn't take it any further … because of you. You're the only girl I've ever been with for real." I shook my head, my vocal cords slashing themselves into threads. "I would never have done that if I hadn't seen you two together. I saw his Instagram — the things people were saying. You looked like you were about to kiss."

"There was no kiss. People don't know a thing." Tanvi rubbed her eyes, bolts of agonized, jagged red forming inside them. Forked rivers of disappointment. "All we did was talk. I would never have cheated on you, Misha. You didn't even give me a chance to explain. You just believed the worst right away."

"You still care about him," I countered. "You can't tell me that you don't."

"I'm not going to try to tell you anything. We're done. Don't call me. Don't come by. I don't want to see you anymore." Tanvi spun and tore out of my room, her steps urgent and self-assured. The smell of grapefruit wafted behind her, killing me quietly.

Hot on her heels, I shouted, "Wait! Don't act like this is all on me. What happened with that girl didn't mean anything. Less than you holding Ashish's hand." My sock feet hit cold pavement as I followed Tanvi outside. "But it won't happen again, I swear."

Her pace accelerated. I lunged and cried, "Wait, goddamnit it. *Wait.*" My fingers shot out and closed around Tanvi's arm, holding her in place from a step behind. The fabric of her coat bunched underneath my hand. "Can't we even try to fix this? After all these months together you're just going to let go like that?"

"You did," she said, refusing to turn and face me.

I held on a second longer. Then another. Feeling how alive Tanvi was. The strength coursing through her bicep from hours of volley-ball. Beyond that, from the sheer force of her will. A girl who could make her guardians second-guess their own wisdom. A girl who could stop you in your tracks and re-chart your course. Match you thought for thought, word for word, step for step. A girl who could decide to love you, and then stop — like you'd been nothing all along.

But strong as she was, I was stronger. I could keep her there. Make her listen. Swing her around on my driveway and force her to look me in the eye.

Tanvi would struggle.

She wouldn't just give in.

She wasn't afraid of me. She'd never had to be.

Blood rushed through my ears. My heart pumped out cold hate, circulating it throughout my body. It filled my mouth, and it tasted like venom, yesterday's beer, and the things you promise yourself you'll never do. The fingers of my free hand crunched into a fist. The smell of Tanvi's skin turned my stomach. Still I held on, transferring the feeling through the fabric of her coat, wanting her to know it was there.

Without blood, you die. It's essential.

Hate only kills, even when it tricks you into believing otherwise.

That morning in March was the start of our demise. There was no one chasing us, no wounds to show for it. Overhead the sky was a gentle, washed-out blue. The trees on my street were spindly, adolescent and few. Aloof bystanders with no desire to hurt us. But Tanvi and I might as well have been standing, quaking, in the clearing from my dreams.

We were doomed.

8

For days I left Tanvi alone. I hoped the damage we'd done would blow over if we gave each other space. When I couldn't stand to wait anymore and broke the silence, my calls and texts went unanswered. Every time she ignored me felt the same. Anger fed my organs. It circulated at the speed of light, infecting every scrap of tissue in my body. I couldn't stop its path.

Tanvi had inverted her old ability to vanish, using it against me. My rage festered at how easily she'd made me disappear. I wasn't innocent. But neither was she. "You're in love with Ashish," I ranted into her voicemail, following a slew of other groveling messages pleading with her not to give up on us. "You're probably together with him now. If you wanted out, you should've just said so in the first place instead of turning everything around and blaming me."

But every time she ignored me the anger petered out, leaving me empty. Every teenage girl in Tealing could've straddled me, her hair falling around my face, cordoning me off from the rest of the world while she kissed me until my lips were bruised, and it wouldn't have stopped me from wanting Tanvi back. The rage and emptiness chased each other around in a shrinking circle, Tanvi at the epicenter, shutting her eyes and making me fade to black.

While my mom was out on her route one night, Natalya dropped by with a container of sweet potato chili Keion had made. My sister had her sympathy face on from the moment she bumped into me in the kitchen. "I told myself I wasn't going to say anything, but Mom's worried about you." Natalya bit her lip as she closed the fridge door. "She thinks something's up with you and Tanvi. Is she right?"

I shrugged. "We're taking a break. Things were getting complicated."

"Complicated how?"

"It's nothing to worry about, okay?" I held my shoulders straight, lightening my tone. "My love life is my business. Not something my family can fix. But I'll be all right. I'm not pressing any panic buttons. This is what high school's like, remember? Nothing lasts."

"But you two seemed so good together."

I'd thought so too. I needed Tanvi back in my life. I needed her, but she was fine without me.

Once my sister had gone, I jerked open my bedroom closet's sliding door, pulling a fistful of hangers aside. A border of empty space — no man's land — gaped between my blue-checked button-down shirt and a black suit jacket that I'd nearly outgrown. I stepped into the chasm, aiming high. Launching my foot savagely into the wall, the crunch of sheetrock echoed in my lungs. A long shudder of relief.

I stood back, breathing raggedly. The vaguely foot-shaped hole stared accusingly at me from the wall. I hastily repositioned my clothes in front of it, listening for Mom's footsteps on the stairs. When I didn't hear them, I knew I was in the clear.

I could patch it later. She'd never know.

I should have steered clear of Tanvi from the beginning. If it weren't for the dream, I would never have approached her outside the movie theater. She would've remained a stranger. A pretty girl I spotted from the Ghims' lawn once instead of a knot that tightened every time I picked at it, a problem I couldn't solve and only knew how to aggravate.

When I crawled into bed that night — a half-written English class *Frankenstein* essay on my desk — the dream had begun to seep into the edges of my consciousness. Darkness lurked just beyond my eyes, beckoning me forward. This time I went willingly, ready to see Tanvi, ready to tell her all the things I couldn't say to her while awake because she wouldn't listen to me anymore.

But the dream didn't care what I had to say. It unfolded the same way it usually unfolded. Stopping in the middle of things, like it had begun. Dreamless sleep fell in after it. Then things that would vanish from my mind the moment I woke up, my cellphone ringing in the near blackness of my bedroom.

Tanvi's name illuminated the screen. It had been eight days since she'd done anything but try to get rid of me, and I winced and answered, needing to hear from her but afraid of what she might say.

"Hi," I rasped. "What time is it?"

"Early. Two minutes to six." Tanvi's voice rippled in my ear. She'd been crying. Something I'd heard only often enough to recognize the distinct timbre of her pain. "Listen, I know we've been a war zone lately, but I need to talk to you for a minute."

My gratitude fused with guilt, my tone as gentle as a sheet of fabric softener. "It's okay. We can talk. There's no excuse for what I did. I miss you. I'm sorry about every—"

"Not that," she said. "Not now. It's Alice. She called me."

"What do you mean?"

"I know how that sounds, but you can see it on my phone log. Her number is right there."

"Somebody must have been assigned her old number," I theorized. Alice had died eight months earlier. The loss wasn't fresh anymore, but Tanvi carried it with her like a scar, and the mind and the heart played tricks. Especially late at night.

"You don't understand." Tanvi's teeth chattered over the phone line. "She spoke to me. I was having a dream. About you and me. It was horrible. The kind of nightmare you have when you're a kid. The phone woke me up and —"

The ghost of a centipede slithered up and down my spine, running for its life. Under the blankets, goosebumps sprouted from my arms, panic rising. "What kind of dream?" I interrupted, although I already knew the answer. We ran, and never escaped. Each time, we failed.

Tanvi had had the dream at least once before — the night we'd first been together — but then instantly forgotten it. Now it was obvious that my silence about the nightmares hadn't protected her. The dreams wouldn't allow themselves to go unacknowledged any longer.

From the supposed safety of my bedroom I imagined I heard something being dragged across the ceiling. My spine tingled, my fingertips turning a raw, frosty purple.

"It doesn't matter," Tanvi said dismissively, her speech slowing and turning deliberate. "The point is, Alice was on the phone when I answered the call. *I heard her voice.* She told me, 'When the time comes, don't let the darkness inside you.' Then she said, 'I love you, Zia.'"

That had been her Aunt Alice's running joke. Calling Tanvi *Zia* when technically Alice was the aunt in a relationship that functioned more as cousins.

"Are you serious?" I asked.

"It was Alice's voice, Misha." Tanvi had grown eerily calm. "I called the number back. It's out of service."

A beat of silence reverberated in my ears. "I'm coming over."

"Okay," Tanvi said slowly. "I'll be sitting on the steps out front."

I shoved my bare feet into running shoes. Pulled a hoodie on over my T-shirt, cold sweat gathering on my lip like a phantom moustache. Phone cradled in my hand, I sprinted down to the garage in the sweatpants I'd slept in.

With every step I moved further away from understanding. Last summer the nightmares were new. They'd never stopped, and now they were plaguing Tanvi too. Her dead aunt had supposedly called her from a telephone number that was out of service. Alice's message to Tanvi echoed in my brain as I raced toward Newtown Creek. A useless, unspecific warning. Meant to scare Tanvi, maybe. But why?

The sun was rising. By the time I reached Margate Avenue, crimson clouds lit the sky. I got out of the car, feet pounding along the pavement that delivered me to Tanvi's door. She sat on the top step in blue flannel pajama bottoms, her leather jacket buttoned up to her clavicle and both of her hands wound around the back of her neck. "Here," she said, breaking her pose. "See for yourself."

The phone log corroborated everything Tanvi had said. At 5:51 a.m., a call had come in from Alice. I dug my own phone out of my hoodie and punched in her number. "We're sorry," said the same automated female voice who tossed out an apology any time a call couldn't be connected, "the number you have dialed is not in service. Please check the number and dial again. This is a recording."

Tanvi stared knowingly up at me while I pulled the phone away from my ear. "Nobody there," she declared confidently. "The number doesn't belong to anybody anymore."

I handed back her cell. "Someone must have faked it somehow. Hacked the line." It was the only idea that made any logical sense.

"Come on, Misha. I know Alice's voice. You think I'd be fooled that easily? It was her. And what she was saying was intended directly for me." Tanvi's eyes glowed with impatience. She'd expected more from me, even after Katrine. She expected me to accept the truth when I heard it; she had no way of knowing I was trying to shield her from something that neither of us could guess how to deal with.

I glanced at Tanvi's polka dot ankle socks and then the sharp curve of her cheekbones. The countless times I'd rested my hands there tugged at my ribs, tightening my chest.

"If it's genuine, what do you think her message meant?" I asked.

Tanvi shook her head, her dark hair reflecting light from the rising sun. "The darkness … I don't know. Darkness is the opposite of light. It's hopelessness or evil. But Alice said 'when the time comes,' like it's a test for some point in the future. Or maybe something bad is going to happen to someone close to me."

"If it really is a message from Alice, she wouldn't want you to think like that. She wouldn't say something intending to torment you."

Tanvi's fingers streaked across her forehead, the nails she kept trimmed short leaving miniature marks on her skin that dissolved while I watched. "I don't know what I'm supposed to do."

"I need to tell you something." The confession twisted in my throat. It would be hours before the sun burned away the crisp morning chill. I folded my hands into my armpits, fighting the cold. "I've had a dream about us too. A recurring dream. We've been running from something — I never know what. But it's coming through the dark. We're in a clearing, surrounded by tall trees, and we're beaten up and bleeding." I stopped and held my tongue, unable to tell her I'd known her face longer than she'd known mine. It was too late. That confession should've been made months ago, or not at all.

Tanvi's head dropped, her eyes tumbling the furthest, falling into a rabbit hole where impossible things occurred and wouldn't let themselves go unnoticed. "It sounds the same," she agreed. "I hardly ever remember my dreams. I probably wouldn't have remembered tonight either, except the phone call pulled me out of it in the middle. But it sounds the same. It was so dark, and we were alone and terrified." One of her hands crunched into a fist, her mouth tensing. Had it been a month earlier, I would have seen Tanvi's wisp of an exhale in the winter air. "I don't understand. What does it mean?"

"I have no clue." My arms were restless from wanting to hold her. All this time I'd kept quiet about the dream, never imagining it could bring us together.

"How come you didn't tell me about the dream before?" she asked.

"Because it sounds crazy." I peered dazedly up at the sun, wondering what kind of twisted game life was playing and how long we had before Tanvi's parents discovered us outside. Not long enough.

"What happens afterwards?" Tanvi's chin quivered as she met my eyes, her expression neither distant nor intimate.

"There is no afterwards. That's as far as it goes."

Tanvi shook her head, as if rejecting the nightmare and its hopeless scenario. "Do you think the phone call from Alice has something to do with the dream?"

I found myself nodding and shifting my weight between my feet. "It sounds like whatever happens, she doesn't want you to give up."

Tanvi rose rapidly from the step, her arms curved in toward her chest, maintaining her body heat. "I think so too," she said, suddenly reaching out to brush the back of my hand. Her eyes held on to me longer. "Thanks for coming over. You were the first person I thought of after Alice's call. Hearing from her completely threw me. I called you on impulse, and then wasn't sure whether I should've. But you've listened to me talk about Alice so many times."

"I'm glad you called. I've been wanting to see you. We need to talk."

"I don't know what we need," Tanvi said wearily, our earthbound problems elbowing their way back into the picture. "But for now I really have to go. My mom and dad will be getting up soon. If they —"

"Right." I took a half step back, like I could afford to wait for her because we had all the time in the world and however things worked out would inevitably be for the best. Over the past few days, my barrage of angry and heartbroken texts and phone messages had worked against me. If I came on too strong again, the negativity could cement in Tanvi's mind. I had to want her back with less urgency than she wanted me. "Call me later?" I said lightly.

"I will," she promised. A strand of her hair fell forward, partially obscuring one of her eyes, as she bobbed her head.

Mentally, I swept her hair aside, gently sliding it back behind the slope of her ear. Mentally, I leaned into her and kissed her goodbye.

We understood each other. We made each other happy. It was too much to give up on. Hadn't Tanvi proven that by reaching out to me? And hadn't I proven it by rushing over to her house when most people still had their heads buried in their pillows?

I turned, hearing the Mahajans' front door close behind me while I walked back to the car. All day I kept my phone so close to me that it was practically another organ. Lungs, liver, kidney, cellphone. The morning and afternoon were hopeful. Evening less so. At Central Foodmart, I touched my phone in my pocket every ten minutes, feeling phantom vibrations against the top of my leg. I snapped at a customer who criticized my grocery-packing skills. He responded, "Young people these days know nothing about customer service. Just do it the way I'm telling you to without complaining about it."

Gritting my teeth, I replied, "Sorry for the misunderstanding, sir."

When Tanvi finally called later that night to tell me she'd thought long and hard about us, I wouldn't accept her decision. Alice and the dream had complicated things for her, and she still had feelings for me, but when it came down to it, we couldn't trust each other. We needed to be apart. That's what she said.

First, I begged for another chance. Like a dog that will sit, fetch, roll over. Lick your hand in apology and whine for forgiveness.

Second, I called her names. Things I'd never called a girl before.

Third, when Tanvi screamed back at me over the phone and then hung up, I didn't hesitate. I didn't kick another hole through the wall. I didn't slam my fist into anybody or pick a fight. The refrigerator remained unharmed.

There are so many ways to hurt someone. You're practically spoiled for choice.

But I didn't have to think about how with Tanvi. Not even for a second. I flicked through my phone, finding what I needed within moments and shamelessly releasing it to the entire world.

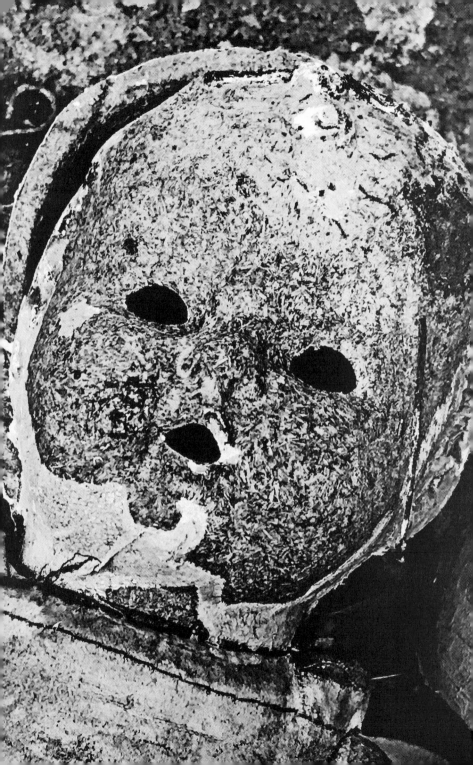

9

We'd promised each other no one else would see the photos. I meant it at the time. Back then, I was someone Tanvi could trust, and we'd only been kidding around, striking funny poses and acting up for our phones. That January afternoon in her bedroom I'd snapped at least twenty images, Tanvi naked except for her favorite bracelet in each one. She took almost as many nude photos of me. Afterwards Tanvi made me delete all of the images on my phone but one, so I asked the same of her. We deliberated over which photo each of us would be allowed to hold on to.

Tanvi wouldn't let me keep any of the sexiest images of her. The digital photo I was left with was from her belly button up. Her hands cup her bare breasts like a pushup bra, her nipples exposed as if they're being offered to whoever might want one. The pose and uncovered skin made it a sexy photo too. But only from the neck down. Tanvi's tilting her head, sticking her tongue out of the side of her mouth and pulling a goofy cartoon character expression with her eyes.

I logged in to Tanvi's Snapchat and Instagram accounts and immediately loaded the image, tagging a dozen male names from among her followers. She only had two passwords that she used for all her social networking sites — the process couldn't have been simpler. For a caption, I added, "The 34Cs are getting heavy. Anyone want to hold on to them for me for a while?"

Tanvi would take the photo down the instant she saw it. One of her friends would tell her about it, or someone would flag the image. Then it would vanish. But not before a handful of people gawked at Tanvi naked from the waist up, analyzing the quality of her breasts.

The thought was more satisfying than kicking any wall.

At first.

For a few minutes I sat back and watched the likes and comments roll in, disbelief that I'd followed through and posted the photo battling with a burning seed of regret.

"Is this for real or Photoshopped?" someone asked.

"Sweet rack, TV! Happy to handle it for you any time."

"Yo, you got a full-body nude pic for us?"

"I can think of some other things I can do for you while we're at it!"

My phone rang furiously in my hand. The landline sprang to life seconds behind it. Text message notifications crowded frenetically onto my screen. Reverberations of guilt throbbed inside my skull as I felt gloomier by the second. The pressure spread out along my forehead like mutant beating wings.

Delete. Delete. Too late, I realized I couldn't do this to her. With a couple of clicks, I made the photos disappear from all of Tanvi's accounts. But deleting something after six minutes wasn't the same thing as never posting it to begin with.

With my mom out on an evening shift I had the house to myself. I switched off the landline, powered off my cell, and went dark. For the next hour and twenty minutes, my life was as quiet as an abandoned graveyard.

You can't lose something you've never had. Tanvi Mahajan had never really been mine. We were like an optical illusion. Something that deceives by appearing to be other than it is. In our case, a trick of the heart rather than a trick of the eye.

Even if that were true, she didn't deserve her breasts plastered across the Internet. Betraying Tanvi's trust for a few minutes of warped satisfaction was one of the worst things I'd ever done, and now I'd done it twice in short order. Turned our entire history to steaming shit.

The femur can still fracture, but it can support up to a ton of weight before it snaps. Anything can be broken if you try hard enough. And some things shatter without any effort at all. Some things are built to self-destruct.

After long minutes of silence, somebody was leaning on my front doorbell. Slamming the wood with their fist too, as angry as I'd been earlier. Dread rising in my throat, I shuffled down to the door.

An apology would ring hollow — useless and meaningless. I said nothing as I opened the door for Tanvi. Her right arm sailed through the rift between us, her hair disheveled and her mouth set in a battle-field grimace.

I let her do it. Stopping her would ring hollow too.

The crack of her open palm against my cheek didn't last long enough. The sting was mild. The same pain that gathered on your face when you stayed outdoors too long on a winter day. Tanvi rushed past me, into the house, while I stared at the spot she'd deserted.

"What are you doing?" I called after her.

Overhead, tectonic plates shifted by force. Thumping, thudding, smashing into pieces. I spun and ran, taking the steps two at a time. Standing in the open doorway to my bedroom, I surveyed the damage. Tanvi had dashed my mirror to the floor. Glittering shards converted the hardwood into a minefield. Bent over the top drawer of my dresser, Tanvi clawed at the pair of boxer shorts she'd given me for Valentine's Day, ripping them to shreds and flinging the ragged remains over her shoulder.

"Stop," I said half-heartedly.

I deserved it. Anything she could think of. But my mom didn't. She'd be home any minute now, and I would have to explain the unexplainable.

"You shit!" Tanvi shouted while I reached down under the bed for my running shoes.

She reeled to the far side of the room, stopping in front of the bookshelf while my feet pushed their way into my Nikes. Random books morphed into airborne projectiles. My Darth Vader pencil holder scratched my chin as it rocketed toward the wall behind me and fell dead to the floor. An old set of headphones followed it, last year's bronze medal for the 1500-meter run three seconds behind.

"All the time you talked about your dad like someone you'd make sure you'd never turn into," Tanvi yelled, her lips going blue. "And look at you, the minute things get complicated you act like *trash*." She snatched a Sharpie from the shelf, twisting to scrawl on my wall. "You were right," she said, facing away from me.

Two long strides across the room and I could read what she'd printed, in capital letters an inch high: TANVI LOVES ASH.

Glass crushed under my shoes. The abrasive sound scraped at my eardrums. Years hurtled by me, howling inside my head, draining me into bone. My shoulder roared in its socket. A jagged memory — one of many — squeezed at my windpipe, pausing my breath. Eight and a half years old. Lying crumpled on our doorstep, like a dead bird that had flown headlong into a window. Inside our house, my dad turned on my mom. I heard him raging from the other side of the door. Taking the place apart, and her with it. With me out of the way, there was no one to stop him.

I never could stop him anyway. The only thing that ever stopped him was leaving him behind.

"You were nothing," Tanvi said. She adjusted her arm and pressed the Sharpie into the wall again, taking back everything she'd ever given me with her words, stripping me down to pain and shame. "Nothing."

Charging toward her, I clutched her wrist. Wrestled her arm away from the wall. If I was nothing, how could I accomplish that? If I was nothing, why did it feel so good to squeeze her wrists together to force the Sharpie from her hand?

Behind her on the wall, Tanvi had added an "L" twice the size of any of the other letters. "*Loser*," she sang to my face.

She twisted as she yanked backwards, sliding one of her hands free from my grasp. Wildly, she swung, her hand catching me under the eye while I weaved, missing the worst of it. She came at me again. Propelling herself forward like a slam dancer. I flung out my arms to stop her from knocking me off balance. She struggled against me, skirting left. Glass shards shifted under her heel like a current, sending her down.

Tanvi gaped up at me from the floor in shock, her eyes searching for something familiar and comprehensible to hold on to, and not finding it. Her upper body had fallen safely away from the scattered glass. The shards lay grittily under her jeans and her shoes, where thick fabrics would have offered protection.

I stood over her, understanding streaming through me with a fullness that burrowed into my core. It twinged along my back and filled up the spaces between my ribs, making me whole. This is what it felt like to have power over someone. To know if they hurt you, there was always a way you could hurt them more. They could never really win.

The warmth oozing inside me died as swiftly as it had materialized. A chill sped in after it. Disgust. Self-loathing deeper than any fracking well and equally toxic. I hated myself more than I'd ever hated Tanvi. Hated with a cold, sinewy vengeance that although I hadn't shoved her to the floor — and had never hit her — for the briefest second or two, it had felt good to watch her fall.

Sick.

I was sick. Destructive. Weak. Pathetic. I was ten times worse than the people I'd shunned for the past few years, telling myself I was superior, that I had changed.

Tanvi was right. I was a loser. I was the kind of trash that couldn't recognize itself and believed she was the problem.

But it was me. Under the surface, I was broken. Under the surface, I was shards.

Frowning, I lowered my hand to help Tanvi up. Silently, and with surprising grace, she took it, rising nimbly to her feet. Then she swept the pieces of glass gingerly from the back of her jeans and exited my bedroom without another word.

Weeks later I heard through the grapevine that she wasn't with Ashish. That had only been her rage talking.

I was never alone with Tanvi again. Never any closer to her than a July day she edged by me in a Baskin Robbins parking lot, her eyes bulldozing me into rubble with the potency of an atom bomb.

Not until we were taken.

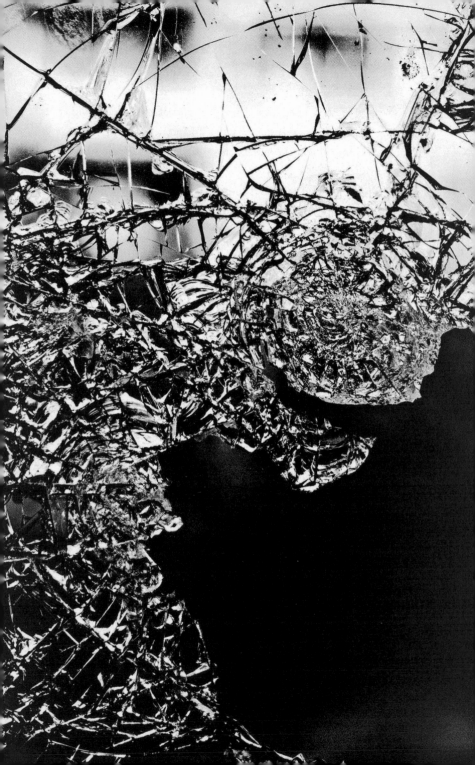

Part 3

10

When I come to, I'm lying face down on hard plastic, my eyes blinking back gritty tears and blood and stomach pain twisting me into a fetal position. My hands want to fly to my abdomen, to protect it from something that's already happened, but they can't. They're frozen behind my back. I thrash around like a fish out of water, my mouth gone like a horror movie creature — solid flesh where the opening should be.

"Easy," a male voice tells me. "You're not going anywhere."

"Maybe he can't breathe with his nose fucked up like that," a second guy suggests.

My head flips frenziedly back and forth, my nostrils inhaling clots where oxygen should be and the world sliding away from me while I plummet toward something else.

"Hold still," one of them growls, yanking the fleshy covering from my mouth. I splutter and cough, then gulp down air. I've barely filled my lungs when something smacks my lips. Wriggling and heaving I sit myself up like an old man, breathing raggedly against whatever they've used to reseal my mouth — layers of duct tape, probably. I can almost see its silver gleam, and I keep fluttering my eyelashes, fighting off the onslaught of wet, but it's like driving through a monsoon without windshield wipers. Nearly impossible.

They've left a small hole in the center of the tape this time; a fine stream of air seeps in where my lips part. I'm not going to drown in my own blood in the back of a stranger's van.

Shifting my weight, I accidentally knock against the figure next to me, who nearly topples me with a shove to the shoulder. I regain my balance before I hit the floor, knees forming a tent in front of me and my hands scraping against plastic behind them. My brain's skipping double dutch, overclocking as my vision finally begins to clear.

White Kia. Utility van with whited-out rear windows. Men in ski masks.

They kidnapped Tanvi and whoever else was at the Mahajan house, including me. They thought I saw one of their faces. In truth I didn't see anything, but being in the van is the better case scenario. Better than being left behind. But where are they taking us? The ski mask floating close to me is the first thing to come partially into focus. White skin around the eye and mouth holes. The guy's gripping something in one of his hands, his posture tense. Tanvi's furthest away from me, but she's the one I see next. Sitting cross-legged, hazy brown legs disappearing into volleyball shoes. Hair hanging in her face, partially obscuring the slash of duct tape over her mouth, and her body swaying slightly from the movement of the van.

I count all the figures inside the vehicle. Two guys in the front seat, one of them at the wheel and the other in the passenger seat, both of them in baseball hats and all-black clothing. Another two are crouching among us in the back of the van, one with white skin under his mask and the other black, each of them cradling a gun. Four abductees total: a young white girl who can't be much older than ten, Tanvi, me, and a black guy about our age with a grown-out buzz cut whose chin and neck are smeared with red. He must have tried to fight off the kidnappers too. His face is vaguely familiar, and when he stares point-edly back at me his eyes are beaming a message.

I can't know what it is; I can only guess. *Be cool. We'll have a chance to clean up this situation later. Wait for it.*

My eyes hold on his, making sure he knows I hear him. *Cal*, I think suddenly. He goes to Holy Trinity with Tanvi; they shared a class last year. Tanvi and I were at a pre-New Year's Eve party with him. He was the one who de-escalated the snowball war, but back then I didn't think she really knew him outside of school.

Clearly, it's different now, and that ceiling of unbroken black is closer than the sky; it's crammed into the van with us, smothering me with the facts. Cal was hanging out at Tanvi's house until a few minutes ago. They've gotten close enough to sit next to each other on the Mahajans' sectional couch, her long legs stretched out so that her feet can rest on top of the coffee table as they joke around, or worse, lower their voices, building secrets together.

But that would be the good news, comparatively. They could be so much closer than that. Lips on lips and skin on skin. Her tongue between his teeth. One of his hands gripping her naked waist. The two of them sliding into an easy groove together in the dark.

It's too easy for me to imagine. Way too easy, and none of my business. I did this to myself, months ago. All in like a born loser who'd rather go down with the ship than try to swim for safety.

My eyes leap to Tanvi again. Her arms have been secured behind her back, same as Cal's and the white girl's. The girl's wide eyes wing around the van, taking everything in as she leans into Tanvi and Tanvi leans back in response. The girl's long blond hair spills onto Tanvi's shirt as though it belongs there as much as Tanvi's does, and I automatically think of Natalya.

Things were good when my dad came home. But the bad showed up soon after him and lasted longer. Years longer. I'd hear my father's voice splinter, and my sister would run to my room before he could split open like a force of nature and rain down havoc. The first few times my dad lost it Natalya pulled me under the bed with her. "Do this," she'd say, pressing her hands over her ears and humming. "Don't stop until I tell you."

You could still hear him. My mother's voice too. The pleading when he splintered and the screaming when he broke and let his hands do whatever they wanted. Even with my palms clamped to my ears and the muffling effect of my own hum, I could hear them. But it was like being trapped inside a corner of your own skull, with everything else happening miles away where it couldn't touch you.

After the first few times Natalya didn't have to tug me under the bed; I dove in there with the dust and waited for her to shove in beside me, both of us humming like an old refrigerator or a hive full of bees.

"Everybody sit tight," the guy in the passenger seat barks. "We don't want to hurt anyone. Don't give us any reason to. If you follow instructions, we'll all get along fine from here on out."

Tanvi glances at me from behind her hair, less easy to read than Cal. The white girl coughs next to her, folding her chin in close to her chest, trying to vanish. Tanvi's gaze falls away from mine, resettling on the girl as the air expelled from her young lungs jams against the duct tape, forcing her to chug it down again.

Outside, thunder groans. The low, bassy rumble reverberates inside me like a fist barreling into my gut afresh. My legs tremor, my cheekbones hollowing out with the effort of sucking back a whimper. My head tips on my shoulders, the top of my blood-drenched T-shirt jeering up at me.

"That's what happens when you try to be a hero," the guy in black closest to me says, his syllables tart with indifference.

The van picks up speed, veering right. We could be getting on the highway, putting distance between us and the Mahajan house.

How long until someone notices we're missing and starts looking for us? We could be miles away by then.

There must be other cars on the road. Not many because of the weather, but some. They'll be white-knuckling their way home in the storm; a nondescript utility van is the last thing they'll remember.

My head bobs repeatedly, like a ball on a string. I force my eyes open wide, fighting the ache spiraling out from my center like a Catherine wheel. Nothing good can come from passing out a second time, and you can never believe someone who says they don't want to hurt you. Whatever necessitates the words makes them a lie.

Woozy, I see my dad's fists float in front of my face like mist, the skin on the back of his hands smoother than you'd expect. Paler too, without a single freckle and only the faintest vertical scar marring an area just above the wrist of his left hand. The stink of his stale cigarette smoke wedges into my nostrils — nostrils unable to suck up air but that plummet back into history. I blink violently, resisting the vision and squirming in my restraints.

"Calm down," a muffled voice snaps from far away.

Closer, my father's wiry voice worms into my ears. *Don't let the world kick you in the teeth the way it's done to me, Misha. You still have a chance. I fought, but not hard enough. It wore me down, and I let it beat me. Don't let yourself get so tired that you let the world win.*

My dad didn't always explode when he was drunk. Sometimes he threw himself a pity party and invited me along. The two of us against the world. A team you'd never want to belong to.

"Calm the fuck down," the voice repeats, a hand whacking into my chest, pushing me backwards. I go over like an upended turtle, organs rearranging themselves inside me like puzzle pieces made of barbed wire.

One of the guys in the back of the van with us erupts into laugher.

"Shut up," a voice from the front seat admonishes.

The laughter stops dead, its ghost hovering in the air.

It would hurt less to stay down, curl up like a slug, and give the puzzle pieces a chance to settle into their rightful places, but I force myself up again with a grimace.

Can't let myself be pulled under. Have to stay lucid. The weaker they think we are, the worse things could be for us.

The wind whines shrilly against the windows, and I fasten my gaze to Tanvi while I sip in air through a slit that must not be any wider than a fingernail.

If anything can keep me grounded here, it's her.

Tanvi stares back at me, a long, unbroken moment — the dark eyes and high cheekbones I'd recognize in any crowd breaking me in two and putting me back together in the same instant.

We'll get through this. It's going to be all right. That's what I try to say with an unfaltering gaze. But with my face bathed in red and rear-ranged like a Picasso portrait, the message must not look anything like I intend. My lips sting under the scrap of punctured duct tape, chafing with the unspoken words. Tanvi reflects them back to me like a carnival mirror, a hail of thunder punctuating her expression. *It's going to be tonight. This will cut through us.*

Lightning throttles through the van's front windows, hurling stark shadows into its recesses. For a split second I imagine I see him again. Dad and his smooth hands, skulking by the rear doors. His mouth gapes inanimately, and his back arches in a way I've never seen before. Unnatural. A puppet with its string pulled cruelly.

You still have a chance.

Then the light fades and he goes with it, leaving the eight of us in the van to our fates.

Shit. If I had a CT scan it would show a concussion. I'd put money on it. I'm zoning in and out of consciousness like a drunk cascading across highway lanes.

When my eyes drift back to Tanvi they're revealing something new, whether she can decipher it or not. The truth. It contracts at the corners of my eyelids and lengthens my chin.

There aren't any sirens in our wake. No one is coming for us.

We're disappearing.

11

The van skids sharply, losing traction on the wet road. Every one of us in the back goes tumbling, the young blond girl flung the furthest. She lands in a heap with one of the kidnappers, the gun springing loose between them on the van floor. Cogs spin swiftly in her mind, her face a flash of possibilities. I know what she's thinking. Grab the gun. Shoot the bastard.

Too late.

He's reaching for the pistol, closing his fingers around the handle and waving it in her face. "Be good, little girl," he warns.

Tanvi's voice strains against her duct tape, the words mumbled but her alarm as clear as an air raid siren. The blond girl stumbles, landing hard on her kneecaps before scooching back to her former spot next to Tanvi. "That's what you'd like to be anyway, isn't it?" The guy with the gun chuckles snidely from behind his mask. "A good little girl."

Cal struggles to his feet, a hum of protest exploding from his lungs. "Fugg yoo asshull."

The black guy pushes Cal's shoulders, forcing him down again, his gun pointed squarely at Cal's chest. The white guy aims his gun away from the blond girl to train it on Cal, and then me. "We should've left them tied up back at the house," he complains, shooting me a dirty look. "Both of them. They're already more trouble than they're worth, and for all we know they're worth fuck all."

"No one asked you," the guy in the passenger seat bellows. He must've witnessed the whole episode, but he's already turned to face the road. He doesn't want us to be able to identify him; none of them do. It's a good sign, and my heart beats faster in relief. They believe we'll walk away from this. "Don't be a prick," he continues. "There's no room for that while we're on the job. We couldn't take the chance that the last kid saw one of our faces. So we've got four now, and we'll get paid for each of them."

The white guy's eyes harden. "Those two won't net a fraction of what we'll get for the girls."

"The icing on the cake," the black guy intones, cradling his gun.

But the white guy's precisely right when it comes to me. Any kind of ransom is out of the question. Every cent Mom has is tied up in the house and monthly bills. No one can float her the cash, either. Both my grandfathers are dead. Dad's mom hasn't seen us in years. We abandoned her baby boy; that's how she sees it. Any damage he did to us isn't his fault. Only her son's pain counts for something.

Meanwhile, my maternal grandmother would sell her organs if it meant getting Mom, Natalya, or me out of a jam. Trouble is, they're the only things she owns that are really worth anything.

My eyes vault to the blond girl huddled in close to Tanvi. Her jaw's pointed defiantly into the air. The pose reminds me of someone, but I can't put my finger on who. Like Tanvi, the girl must be worth her weight in gold. The two of them were targeted. Cal and I were just last-minute add-ons. If Cal's family turns out to be as hard up as mine, the guy in the passenger seat might start losing his patience.

That could be bad news for all of us.

Uneven ground churns under our wheels, pebbles pummeling the van's undercarriage and exterior. We've hit dirt road.

Outside, the storm is still raging, explosions of light and sound erupting around us like carnival fireworks. Impossible to say how long we've been driving. Filling my lungs takes most of my concentration. The stomach pain isn't going anywhere, either.

Inside the van, tension crackles like static electricity. This is what it used to feel like when my dad came home late, banging the front door open as if it didn't matter that he woke us. Sometimes falling noisily on the stairs, grumbling loudly to himself, and sometimes blasting TV infomercials or crime shows from a horizontal position on the couch, his shoes still on. If Mom complained, stared at him in the wrong way, or even sometimes when she was careful not to react, he'd spew like a volcano, not quitting until he was empty. No one could fall back to sleep on those nights. Anything could happen.

One morning I found him passed out cold on the stairs. Mom, Natalya, and I each navigated our way carefully around him, tiptoeing down to the kitchen to eat our breakfast in silence rather than risk waking him up. Not so grim, comparatively. We counted ourselves lucky while holding our breath.

If he were still around, he wouldn't pay my ransom either. He'd find other things to do with the money he made on his last big job. Women. Booze. Drugs. Special projects that would attract other sleazebag criminals and eventually get him arrested.

It's a wonder he's been able to stay under the radar this long. At nearly half a million dollars' worth of merchandise, the score was probably more than he expected. Definitely enough to keep him going these past three years, especially if he's in Mexico or somewhere in Central America, which is the popular theory in my family.

The cops drop by periodically to ask whether we've seen or heard from him. He must be miles away, I always tell them. If he were still around, he would've fucked up again by now.

Hands down, the best thing about my dad is his disappearance.

I never thought he had enough sense to stay gone.

It's the only thing I have to thank him for, and I don't think about him much these days, except as an example of who not to be. The only reason he's squirmed his way into my skull now is that stowed in the back of a mobile crime scene, air ringing with silent panic, my hands tied behind my back and my nostrils leaking blood clots, a familiar feeling — waiting for the shit to hit the fan — has razored under my skin, approaching bone.

He's banging through the front door, half looking for a fight, the other half wanting to be left alone. That's what it feels like.

Which side of him wins depends on the flip of an invisible coin or a hair trigger that no one can see. The difference is, all those years ago I was afraid of what he'd do to me. Afraid of what he'd do to Mom and Natalya, too. Afraid for all of us.

And now I'm not scared of these guys. Not for me. But nothing can happen to Tanvi.

Nothing worse than we've seen so far. Not if I can help it.

The van stops dead, the black guy opening the rear doors and hopping down onto trampled, overgrown grass. "Watch your step, folks," he says, motioning us forward with his gun. The white guy has his weapon drawn too. He grabs Tanvi's arm, yanking her up.

"After you, miss," he declares, his tone malice crowned with sullen deference. His hand on Tanvi's back pushes her forward, the blond girl leaping up to move alongside her. Cal goes next, glaring at the white guy despite his pistol. I heave myself into a standing position, battling the pain. The barbed wire puzzle pieces clatter noiselessly in my chest, my steps stiff with the effort of appearing unbreakable.

I force myself to jump down from the van, the same as everyone.

Stupid idea.

Landing whacks the air from my lungs, barbed wire fragments kicking my ribs from the inside like steel-toed boots. My feet sink into the wet grass, my head hanging limply as I absorb the hurt. When I look up, the dickhead white guy from the back seat has dropped out of the van and planted himself in front of me. He grins at my discomfort. With his eyes, at least. The ski mask's mouth hole is a small circle, not enough to give his lips' reaction away.

My gaze careens past him, to the lean dirt road reclaimed by nature. Our way in and out. With no moon or stars to illuminate the area it's like trying to see with hands clapped over your eyes, peering through the gaps between your fingers. Somewhere in the distance the road winds into dense woods, any sign of civilization obscured. Overhead, the soot-black sky threatens more rain.

The crew of kidnappers gathers tightly around us, the two from the front seat of the van with their ski masks firmly back in place the same as the others now that they don't have to worry about being sighted by cops on the road. They have gym bags looped over their shoulders and handguns of their own at the ready.

"Let's go," one of them commands. "Turn around and start walking."

We turn in ragtag unison, the squelch of the grass underneath our feet the only noise I can hear and a flashlight glare guiding us. An abandoned old house looms ahead, surrounded by trees maintaining an uneasy proximity, the forest ready to overtake the entire property the way it took the road. The second-storey windows stare spitefully down at us like mismatched eyes, the pale blue shutters of each of them open wide, but one of the window blinds pulled shut while the other window gapes darkly. The house's grizzled white paint has cracked and worn away in streaks, like stained sheets that no amount of bleach could revive. A triangular peak divides the roof in two, patches of tiles missing from both sides. From the porch roof also, which slopes gently to the left, an accident waiting to happen.

A simple, double-doored outbuilding in a similar state of disrepair huddles next to the main house, an ugly afterthought. Its fastened-shut doors sag inward, beginning to give in to time and the elements.

The main house's lower windows have been boarded up, and the porch steps teeter underfoot as we climb them in single file. This place has been forgotten for a long, long while, and resentment oozes out of what remains of its neglected façade.

One of the kidnappers suddenly charges past us, forcing the front door open. It creaks on its hinges. "Wait," he orders, entering first. Soon dull light leaks out from the open doorway.

"We should get them cleaned up before we make the call," he hollers from inside as the other kidnappers herd us through the door, past a decaying staircase, and into a shell of a room. "Especially the last kid. We don't want to give them any reason to be difficult."

My eyes rake over our surroundings, looking for anything we can use.

The kidnappers have been here before. They've made preparations. Folding chairs have been strategically placed in every corner of the room, bare wooden floorboards swept while the ceiling grows moss and the room's grungy paint sloughs off in strips. If I could still smell anything, the place would reek of mold, dust, and old death. Something's eaten through the bottom cushions of an ancient rust-green sofa against the far wall, next to an antique wheelchair coated in layers of dust. The fireplace is bricked up, a large wooden cross balanced on the mantelpiece, leaning against the wall behind it. A stack of paper cups, still wrapped, stands beside a collection of water cooler bottles and small pile of recently purchased food — sliced bread, canned fruit, tinned tuna, and a giant box of Special K.

Four battery-operated LED lanterns light the decrepit space. The kidnapper who beckoned us inside holds a fifth in one hand and a gun in the other. "Everybody sit down on the floor," he commands. "It's not the Ritz-Carlton, but we have the basics." The lantern swings under his grasp as he motions to his accomplices. "Un-gag them." His gaze swerves ninety degrees, colliding with mine. "Any trouble and we press mute again. That's how this works."

The black kidnapper veers toward the blond girl, sliding off her tape with unexpected gentleness. She winces anyway. Then sucks in oxygen like someone who narrowly escaped drowning. Hacks like a textbook example of bronchitis. The cough doesn't give way to normal breathing. She sputters and chokes, bending at the waist, waiting for a lung to squeeze out of her newly un-gagged lips. A third guy hustles to the supply wall, ripping open the paper cups.

No one else moves. Not until the dickhead tears off my duct tape, his arm extending to point me in the direction of the middle of the room. "You heard the man," he growls. "Down."

Seconds later I'm sitting on the floor and the blond girl's gulping water from a paper cup. They've freed her hands. Next to me, Cal's ass hits the hardwood floor. "Shit," he groans.

"Shut up." Dickhead waves his pistol at us. "You want the tape back on?"

Cal silently shakes his head. The kidnapper who's been issuing directions to the others plants his lantern on the floor. "Lauren," he calls, opening a compact plastic box, "take these. Wipe their faces for me." He holds out something small and white. A swatch of fabric.

I watch the blond girl freeze with the cup pressed to her lips. The blond girl who must be Lauren but whose connection to Tanvi is a mystery.

"I'll do it," Tanvi offers as the duct tape is ripped from her mouth, leaving her lips raw and abraded. The distorted sound of her voice — counterfeit confidence, fear, and a hard shell of protectiveness congealing into a pulpy clump in her throat — makes me shiver and wish I'd done everything differently. Stayed the person she'd made me feel like I was in the beginning.

"No, you sit down," the kidnapper says decisively. He must be the leader. None of the others are challenging him or interrupting. "She can do it. Either she does it or one of us will."

The blond girl — Lauren — reluctantly takes the offered material. Crouching in front of Cal, she runs the fabric delicately over his chin and neck, blood lightening in places and then disappearing. But his busted lip needs stitches. No amount of dabbing with a wet wipe will disguise where his lower lip opened up and oozed flesh.

"Sorry, Misha," Lauren says as she veers away from him and toward me. She winces as she looks over my face, trying to decide where to begin.

"It's okay," I tell her. "Go for it." *But how does she know my name?* Did Tanvi say it while I was unconscious, before they gagged her?

Lauren sucks in her breath when the wipe gingerly meets my chin. As it skates down my neck, she gains confidence, the towelette accelerating. The kidnappers shuffle noisily around us, one or more of them disgruntled. My ears reach for their words, but fall short. Lauren's wet wipe has scarcely made contact with the bridge of my nose and I'm flinching under the impact, recoiling with such force that I accidentally stretch my rib cage — like someone hooked a pair of pliers around the bones and tugged.

"Mark, go upstairs," a somber voice demands. "Try there." The aggression and distress behind the directive tightens my thighs, my leg muscles jerking me back toward Lauren. What's going on? Something's not unfolding according to plan.

"Here," the same voice says with more restraint. An arm lowers a paper cup to Lauren. "Give him this, too." The kidnapper's lightly freckled hand drops two plain white tablets into her palm.

"No," I protest. Asleep, anything could happen. And any brain-bending substance could make me nearly as useless awake.

"It's just a painkiller. You look like you need it."

"I'm fine," I say shakily.

The lead kidnapper — every aspect of his face except his mouth and the skin directly around his eyes still covered by the mask — lowers himself in front of me, sitting on his haunches. His hand grasps for my stomach, fingers stretching carefully across my abdomen. On a normal day, the action would hurt less than scratching an itch.

Tonight, tears kick their way into the corners of my eyes. A gasp seeps from between my lips.

"Sure." Lukewarm sarcasm flattens the leader's words. "You're perfect — you could bench-press two hundred pounds."

"It won't look good if you're crying on the video," one of the other men says from behind me.

"He's right," the leader confirms. "It's better that you don't look like somebody who belongs in an E.R. waiting room. This is just tramadol, I promise. It'll fix you up."

"And if I won't take it?"

The kidnapper tilts his head, the mask doubly sinister askew. "Two options. One of us can force them down your throat, or we can all sit here waiting for you swallow them yourself, delaying the release of the four of you. Is that what you want?"

No choice then. We need to get out of here as fast as possible. The situation's unpredictable and could nosedive quickly. Anyone willing to commit one felony might just as easily commit another. "Okay, but let her do it." I cock my head at Lauren. She nods in agreement. Slips a tablet between my lips, then raises the cup to my mouth, chasing the first pill down with water. Half of it slides down my chin. The second try is marginally neater. With both pills sluicing into my stomach, I peer at Tanvi seated roughly four feet away.

She's absorbing the details of her surroundings, her eyes continually skirting back to Lauren and to the position of the two kidnappers on their feet, guns at the ready. "One more thing," the leader declares, reaching into the plastic box — a first aid kit — and pinching at two small squares of gauze. "He needs these. Put them in his nose."

Lauren worriedly accepts the gauze. "I'm sorry," she mutters under her breath, cautiously stuffing one of my nostrils.

The pills aren't working yet. My cartilage crunches like broken glass underfoot.

"Sorry, sorry," she repeats, setting the second piece of gauze in the other nostril. My left foot shakes with the pain, urgently tapping the floor. We both hear it. Probably the others hear it too, and I brace for a laugh from the dickhead, then realize he must be the one who was sent upstairs. *Mark*, the leader called him.

One final swipe from the wet wipe and I'm as close to being a masterpiece as I'm going to get. Lauren scoots back to sit next to Tanvi.

"Good job," the leader says detachedly.

Lauren blanches, her cheeks stiffening in reaction to the throwaway compliment. It's the second sign of contempt she's shown, and it's subtle enough that the kidnapper probably doesn't see it. But I do. She's only a kid, but she's no traitor. Not interested in scoring points with the enemy.

It takes a while for someone to reveal their many different expressions. This one, I recognize now that I've seen it for the second time tonight. My mind bounces back to Christmas Eve at Tanvi's house. Helena's nephew, Braden, was staying overnight with his parents. Tanvi and I played cards with him after dinner, followed by something he called the "drama bag game." Someone throws five random items into a bag, and the others have to create a skit using all the items.

Braden was better at drama bag than Tanvi and I were. He owned us. He didn't want to stop playing, and when his mom told him it was time for bed he looked the same as Lauren looks now.

Pissed.

But Braden doesn't have a sister. Those are his eyes staring out of Lauren's sockets. His blond hair, grown long. His limbs fitted into slightly more feminine clothing than when I met him on Christmas Eve — pink chinos, a beige peasant top that gathers at the waist, and crochet high-top sneakers.

Braden has transformed into Lauren. She and Tanvi share a set of wealthy grandparents, the owners of the Molto Troppo chain. Clearly, the kidnappers know that. The Mahajans are well off in their own right, but not like Helena's parents. The kidnappers are after hardcore cash. A double helping.

Mark thumps down the steps as I stare at Lauren, acclimatizing to the change. Any other day I would've clued in sooner; she really doesn't look much different. Lauren's sixth sense must be tingling. She swivels her neck, staring openly back at me. One second all I see is a kid in a bad situation, trying to hold herself together. The next, an eerie smile twists onto Lauren's lips. Ominous, low laughter trickles from her crooked mouth and infects the musty air. The laugh of a taunting bully. Senselessly cruel.

Braden didn't laugh that way on Christmas Eve. It sounds nothing like the kid I played the drama bag game with.

"They will soon fade like the grass and wither like the green herb," Lauren intones, biting down on her smile. Tanvi's face whips toward her cousin, full of questions there's no time to ask because Mark stomps in, disappointment hanging heavy on his bones.

"Nothing up there but dead air," he says grimly.

The quietest of all the kidnappers adds, "Not in the kitchen or back workroom either."

"How can that be possible?" the black kidnapper asks. His tone is genuine surprise. "We were just here. There were no problems."

The leader reaches under his mask to scratch his chin. It's not even fall yet. They all have to be sweltering under the black acrylic.

"The storm must've knocked out the nearest cell tower," he says. "Matthew, check outside, just in case. Worst-case scenario we'll need to load everyone back into the van and drive until we pick up a signal."

The quietest kidnapper disappears into the hallway. *Matthew.* Seconds later the front door slams shut behind him.

"I don't feel good," Lauren murmurs, wrapping her arms in front of her stomach and hunching over, her back forming the shape of a capital C. "This place isn't right." Her malicious smile has dissolved or gone into hiding. She sounds closer to the kid I met eight and a half months ago, but her skin is sallow, her eyes dull.

"It's okay," Tanvi whispers, eyebrows knitting closer together in concern. "We won't be here long."

Behind me, a pocket of cold opens up. Blows on the back of my neck with perfect aim. I snap around, facing the antique wheelchair. The seat bottom hangs crookedly down through the metal frame, making it unusable, even as a chair.

There's no one behind me. Naturally this fossil of a house would be full of drafts. Dust, drafts, and other things civilization prefers to keep out with walls.

"Look, you could let us go," Tanvi says, shifting my attention to her. She peers steadily up at the leader, her brown eyes nearly as impenetrable as black holes. "We don't know what you look like. We have no idea who you are. You could drop us off down the road somewhere. They'd never catch you."

"You think we went through all of this just to have some rich bitch talk us out of it?" the dickhead scoffs. "Not happening. Rest your pretty head and let us iron out the kinks."

The leader stares straight through Tanvi, as if seeing something that isn't there. "It's not up for discussion," he says after two beats. "This isn't a democracy. Like I said before, if you can't keep quiet, the duct tape goes on again."

An electromagnetic pulse can burn out power lines and render electronic equipment useless, sending people back to the Dark Ages. The leader's words have a similar effect, only on sound instead of electricity. Silence sprints across the room in weightless sock feet. My ears ring with the absence of noise.

Refusing to turn and confront the empty space behind me, I watch the remaining three kidnappers from the corners of my eyes. The leader sits in the folding chair closest to the door looking Cal, Tanvi, Lauren, and me over like a shrewd substitute teacher. The other two kidnappers dart around the room holding their phones above their heads, searching for something that doesn't want to be found.

"Luke, take our two unexpected guests' names and the contact info for their families," the leader mutters, his gun reclining comfortably in his lap like a metal cat faithful to only one master.

The black kidnapper reclaims his left hand from the air, his right resting on his gun as he makes a beeline for Cal. *Matthew, Mark, Luke.* My brain leaps for the punchline. When asked, Mom claims to be Orthodox Christian because of her Russian father. But no one in my family is religious. Doesn't matter. Everyone's heard of the four gospel writers. So far, the only name missing is John. He must be the leader.

Aliases.

Somehow Lauren figures out the significance of the kidnappers' names at the precise moment I do. Either that or she's reading my mind. Her pout contorts into a haggard, malicious grin the second I get the joke. The kind of smile someone cracks when they're out to get you and you both know it. They've been biding their time, and it won't be long now. That's what I see. We're on opposite sides of a game, and I don't know how we got there.

Or John lied and the pills weren't tramadol.

Or … the concussion. My brain's twisted in my skull, screwing with my brain cells.

Has to be. Something's revved up my imagination. Sent me tripping. Lauren's not smiling in the slightest. Not anymore, not even according to my chemically altered, temporarily damaged mind. Why would a kid I played with for hours on Christmas Eve be out to get me? She wouldn't. Completely the opposite. She was infinitely careful with the wet wipes and gauze. She's just sick and scared, and I'm temporarily broken.

End of story.

Luke takes Cal's full name and a short list of Cal's people. Anyone who might want to financially contribute to the cause of Cal's freedom. He writes the information in a plain red notebook you can pick up for two bucks at Dollarama. Then he starts on mine, his printing compact and neat like my sister's.

"I think I'm going to be sick," Lauren says, pitching to one side.

"What was in the water?" Tanvi asks hesitantly.

John's left foot raps the floor. Agitation in three-quarter time. "Nothing but H_2O. It's probably just nerves." He focuses on Lauren, the mask that obscures his identity slicing the comfort from his words. "Your grandparents will pay up, and then you'll be out of here. Try to relax in the meantime. We can get you a pillow. You can close your eyes and sleep."

Mark's arms swing savagely at his sides as he gorilla-struts into our — the hostages — midst. Looming over Tanvi and Lauren, he casts a misshapen assortment of dull shadows on the wooden floor. "You were told to keep your mouth shut. You better fu—"

"Mark," John snaps, straightening abruptly in his chair. "Never mind about that. Go look for Matthew. He's been out there too long."

"You told them to shut up. I'm enforcing the rules."

John touches his gun, adjusting its weight on his thighs. "I get it. But we need to move this along. The clock is ticking."

"Fine," Mark says in a tone that spells the opposite. He lumbers into the hallway, emerging with a pillow seconds later. "For the little princess," he declares, lobbing the pillow at Lauren, who makes no attempt to catch it. The pillow sails into her face with a *thwack*, then drops inanimately to the floor.

"Asshole," I protest, fury tweaking at my veins. "She's *sick*." My own pain has begun to fade. A yellowed wall in the process of being painted shaving-cream white.

Mark's turned his back on us. He doesn't look over his shoulder. He doesn't stop or change direction.

Lauren giggles as he goes, the sound curling eely chills into my lower spine. "*We shall not all sleep, but we shall all be changed,*" she whispers. At least, that's what I think she says before her lips clamp shut, her skin nearly as pale as Styrofoam. The phrase triggers a memory that sends my mind sinking into darkness. My father said the same thing in my nightmare the first time I betrayed Tanvi.

I didn't know what it meant then, and I don't know now. We're drifting further into uncharted territory together, and I can't catch my breath.

Five sets of eyes whip toward Lauren. "What?" Tanvi says gingerly, bumping her cousin's shoulder lightly. "What are you talking about?"

Lauren shakes her head swiftly, her eyes rolling slightly in their sockets, lifeboats bobbing at sea. "No no no no no no — get me out of here. We can't stay. We have to go now."

"She's feverish," Tanvi says, staring at John as she raises her voice. "You need to do something."

Luke steps forward, crouching to lay his palm across Lauren's forehead. "There's no fever. Her skin feels normal."

"She's *not* normal," Cal objects. "Something's happening."

John rises, holding his gun. It points at the floor, harmless for the moment but ready and waiting. "Or she's faking it. She was all right a few minutes ago. Nothing strikes that quickly."

"She's not faking it." Tanvi's voice stretches thin, pleading for understanding. "Please. I know my cousin. This isn't some kind of trick she's playing. Something's the matter with her."

Luke swears under his breath as he backs slowly away.

John reaches his free hand up to his head, dropping it just shy of encountering acrylic. "Nobody panic. Like I said, your grandparents will make the payment. Then this will be over with." He glances hurriedly over his shoulder. "Jesus, what's the holdup out there?"

"I'll go," Luke volunteers.

"No, I will. You stay and watch over our guests. Keep your distance from them. I still think she's faking." John stares pointedly at Lauren. "Put the duct tape back on. Everyone but her. I don't want the rest of them giving you trouble."

Luke applies fresh duct tape to our mouths, slashing an air-slit into mine, while John stands apart, overseeing. With only two of the kidnappers in the house, my mind's working overtime. If I knocked Luke over — wrestled his gun away from him — John would still have enough time to shoot someone. Maybe Lauren, maybe Tanvi.

The risk's too high.

"Bind the girl's hands again," John orders. "We can't trust her."

Lauren's head wilts on her shoulders, her unfocused eyes aiming into an unoccupied middle ground. "Turn around," John says sternly. "Let's get this over with."

Lauren might as well be stone. She doesn't react. If I didn't know better, I'd think she was asleep, in the throes of somnambulism. But mostly it's younger kids who sleepwalk, and Lauren isn't going anywhere. The only signs that she's alive are the slow blink of her eyelashes and the rise and fall of her chest, taking in oxygen.

Luke pauses. "It's okay," he says, skirting around the back of her. Pulling Lauren's arms behind her, he tightens a zip-tie around her wrists. She doesn't resist. She's as compliant as a rag doll.

"You can lie down any time you want," he tells her, echoing John who exits the room while the rest of us watch. Luke takes John's place in the folding chair nearest the door, fidgeting in his seat, his fingers coiled around the gun's handle.

They haven't tied our feet. Any one of us could still make a run for it. With the pain in my stomach dulling, I could outpace Luke, although not a bullet — and I'm thinking about it, weighing my chances — when Cal begins to speak. "Yu can led us gow. Yu dohnt have …" I lose the rest of the sentence to the duct tape.

"Just because you're a brother, don't think we're on the same side," Luke growls, his voice dropping an octave. "I don't want to hear it. Shut your mouth or someone's going to pay for it."

Cal and I swap loaded glances. Now? Do we charge at Luke and hope that gives the girls a chance to escape? Would Lauren even try, or would she remain catatonic? Tanvi would never leave this place without her.

Before we can decide, the front door claps open, frantic footsteps slapping into the hall. John stands in the living room doorway, wild-eyed and breathless. He cocks his head, ordering Luke toward him without a sound.

Their heads bend hastily together, John murmuring in a low voice that prevents us from hearing. Luke stiffens at the news, his body struggling to absorb the shock.

"You," John calls, his forefinger tagging me from across the room. "You're coming with me."

Lauren's head falls sideways onto the pillow, the rest of her body slumping along with it. Her eyelids drift shut while John's feet thump the floorboards, moving in on me. "Up," he demands, tearing off my duct tape as I stand.

"Where are we going?" I mumble.

"You'll know when we get there." The gun digs into my side. "Out in front of me." I do as he says, stepping nearer to Luke, who stops me dead with his hands, swings me around, and snaps my arms free with a small bolt cutter.

Nothing hurts anymore. Not exactly. The flutter in my stomach reminds me of birds' wings. Birds trapped in too small a space. I glance over my shoulder at Tanvi while the gun barrel thrusts into my lower back. Something still hurts after all. The thought of leaving her behind. The feeling picks at my esophagus like a scavenger. Only I'm not dead. Not yet.

Tanvi catches my look. Holds it lightly in her own eyes and floats something aside from anger and panic back to me in exchange.

John marches me in the direction of the front door. Tells me to open it. Tells me we're going outside and that he needs my help. "So, I hope the tramadol's kicked in." His tense laugh buckles in the wind. "To your right," he says. "Head for the trees."

I hear the door close behind us, feel the barrel leave my spine. The empty space doesn't feel like freedom. If John's planning to kill me, I'll have to run. Take my chances.

I shift my weight, flexing my leg muscles, calling them to life. The sight of the utility van that brought us here forces my eyes to the left. The van's parked in the front yard, exactly where I last saw it. Less than an hour ago it looked almost new. Now it's a blackened husk. I cringe as I digest the missing windshield, mottled chargrilled exterior, and sagging, melted body. While we've been held captive inside the house, the van has blazed to a crisp. A marshmallow dropped directly into a campfire and retrieved when it was past saving.

But there's no smell. No smoke and no fire to see, either. Shouldn't a freshly burnt-out van stink to hell? Shouldn't we have heard the windshield shatter in the heat?

"It's dead," John says hollowly, and the sound of his missing confidence scares me more than anything that's happened so far. "The weirdest thing is that if you get close to it, the van doesn't even feel warm."

"How can that be?" I ask.

"That's what I've been asking myself." John hurls an arm out in front of him, the light from his lantern swerving. "But the van's not what you're here for. Keep going. Do you see it yet?"

We're in the middle of nowhere, and tonight is made of the kind of thick black a single lantern is no match for, the kind that makes a person feel like they're going blind. But suddenly I understand what John's talking about.

It's up ahead, where the decomposing house's domain ends and a forest begins — a body draped over a low-hanging tree branch. Folded at the waist in the same way people fold a hand towel over a towel rack. The head points lifelessly at the ground, clad in generic black acrylic.

Then I hear it, too. The sound somehow different from the mundane background noise of rain-soaked foliage — the incessant pitter-patter of freshly draining blood against fallen leaves.

12

"Take him down," John commands from behind me. A drop of water from the soggy leaves overhead pelts my cheek. It's muggy enough that a ten-minute run could have me sweating through my shirt. Muggy enough to storm a second time — the first rainfall did nothing to clear the air. Instead I shiver, staring up at the body from five feet away. Blood has soaked through the ski mask. It's draining from his fingertips too, spitting to the ground through the drenched fabric.

"Is he …" I've never laid eyes on an inanimate body before. I'm already standing closer to death than I want to get. It feels contagious, the dark whispering just beyond reach, like it wants us to hear.

"He's not breathing," John confirms.

"Who did this?" My voice echoes on the breeze. Late summer air hurls its weight over me like a cloak, pressing me into the ground.

"Your guess is as good as mine. Just get him down. Now." John doesn't want to touch the body either. Without the gun he's as vulnerable as I am. He doesn't want it to leave his hand — that's why I'm here to do the grunt work.

The gun.

I reach up fast, closing my arms around the kidnapper's legs and feeling for his handgun as I drag him down from the branch. Each of the captors was armed. Matthew or Mark wouldn't have come out here without his weapon.

The body flops back onto my chest, my hands frantically smoothing over his pockets and finding nothing. Then the head lolls against me, a second behind the rest of the body.

"It's not there," John says as I recoil, throwing my head back and to the side, trying to escape the thing in my arms. Stepping back, I lay the body at the ground beneath my feet. Birds flap frantically under my rib cage, desperate to escape. One of them tears into bone — the tramadol floundering under physical exertion.

I bend, my arms folding protectively in front of me.

John peers fixedly down at the body, his gun held aloft. My eyes can't look away from the damage. The longer I stare, the worse I feel. Like a monkey in a test lab, waiting for a horror show I'm not built to understand. The skin surrounding the body's closed eyes is coated in red. His hands are slick with blood. It pools thickly at the bottom of his black crewneck too. If there are bullet holes in the body's clothing, I can't see them. But what else could have done this?

Waiting for me to recover, John says, "Drag him behind the carriage house in a minute — you don't have to lift him." John cocks his head to indicate the shed approximately fifty feet behind us. "It's where they used to store horse-drawn buggies."

The house is older than I thought. Deserted for decades at least.

"We have to get away from this place," I say, urgency cinching my throat. "Whoever did this can't be far. And now they have a gun." Two, if it was Matthew or Mark who committed the murder.

"No one's leaving. The van's toast, and it's a long way back to the main road." John scratches distractedly at one of his arms. "I'm not going to prison for a job that didn't pay off. We're all staying right here and waiting for cellphone service to be restored." He aims the gun momentarily at my heart, quickly shifting its focus to somewhere past me. "Doesn't make sense to be out in the open, anyway. We can protect ourselves from inside the house if we have to. Someone could just pick us off one right after the other if we ran."

They could open fire on us right now if they wanted to, and I stare into the blackness of the woods, imagining that I feel something stare back. A hollow space forms in my skull. A cold spot of ugly questions.

"Take him already so that we can get back inside," John snaps. "I don't plan on anyone else dying out here tonight."

Bending close to the ground, I hook my hands under the body's armpits, tugging it along with me as I shuffle back to the shed. John follows, three steps behind with his gun in the air. The grass is long and wet. I have to keep staring behind me to avoid tripping.

The weight of the body tugs at my stomach, my eyes skittering away from the ski mask, which has become a mask of death. Fifty feet seems like an eternity. When I release the body, my hands feel contaminated with a sin I didn't commit.

"You can wash them inside," John says as I stare at my fingers. He centers the gun on me again. "Keep it together. We'll get through this if everyone keeps their heads."

An unsettling laugh seeps out from under my breath. My neck whips around, my head playing mind games with me, intent on bending me out of shape. "Do you smell cigarette smoke?"

My dad never gave up the habit. Not while I knew him. Most of his friends were chain-smokers too. One of the kidnappers must be also; the smell is unmistakable.

John turns his nose up to sniff the air, but his nostrils are covered by the mask. "I don't smell anything."

With my nostrils clogged by gauze and blood, I shouldn't be able to pick up anything either. But the gritty smell deepens, sinking into my pores. I jump in my skin, someone suddenly standing by my side.

A partial shoulder and blurred grimy denim leg dissolve into nothing when I turn to look at the figure straight on. My father's shoulder in one of the old concert tour T-shirts from his youth, cities and tour dates running down the back. I catch the briefest glimpse of the numbers and letters before they fade into oblivion.

"Stop it," John warns, his eyes following mine. "No tricks."

"I'm not —" I shake my head, cutting myself short. There was never anyone there. We're alone behind the carriage house with the bloody body of Matthew or Mark, and the only thing that matters is making it out of this place in one piece with Tanvi.

John motions for me to walk ahead of him, leaving his back unprotected as we trudge to the house. The quiet is an enemy. It watches and listens as we leave the charred remains of the van behind us and then bolt up the loose porch steps.

The house absorbs our presence. Inside the living room, Luke jumps up from his chair. The rest of the scene is unchanged — Tanvi and Cal slump on the floor with their hands bound behind their backs and their lips duct-taped shut. Lauren lies coiled in the fetal position, eyes closed and face half-buried in the pillow Mark hurled at her before dying or disappearing into the night.

John thrusts his gun into my ribs, pulling me close as Luke stands on my other side, his posture as rigid as a mannequin's. "You won't be doing your friends any good by telling them what you saw out there," John whispers. "They'll only panic. Someone could get hurt."

"What about Matthew?" Luke asks John, his voice hushed.

"No trace of him. Mark's down. Tucked out of sight, behind the outbuilding." John hesitates, selecting his words and tone carefully. "We need to stay the course. Keep alert through the night and work out a way to organize new transport."

Luke's left knee vibrates through his black pants. "Man, Matthew's no killer. Why would he do this?"

One mystery solved. The body was Mark's. Matthew is MIA.

"Not in front of him," John admonishes with an irate sideways glance. "Secure his hands again."

"I need water," I remind him. Death clings hotly to my palms. "And a bathroom." Before I'm sick. My gut's twisting and churning, the memory of the tree-hanging body shadow dancing in my head. I cock my head to indicate the other hostages. "They'll need something to drink too." My eyes linger on Tanvi. The familiar curve of her lips and the dramatic arc of her cheeks weigh me down like an anchor.

"One thing at a time," John tells me before turning to Luke. "Take him up to the bathroom. Bring a bottle of water. I'll watch the others."

Luke hands me water, then plucks the nearest lantern from the floor, the gun never leaving his grasp. "Better make this quick," he says as we head into the hallway and close in on the staircase. Sharp, slender pieces of wood poke out of the bottom step at acute angles, threatening to stab anyone in their orbit. Half of the bottom step has rotted away. The remaining half wobbles and groans when I place my weight on the wood. My stomach lurches along with it. I instinctively reach for the banister. It quivers under my hand, like someone not used to being touched, but then holds its ground.

The rest of the steps feel sturdier than the first. I climb them gingerly, half-expecting the staircase to dissolve into dust, taking me with it. Ascending into darkness with the majority of the lantern light illuminating the steps behind me, the back of my neck prickles.

"It's the first door at the top," Luke declares. "And it's as nasty as the rest of this place."

Reaching the second floor, I spy the doorway of the nearest room. It's ajar, the darkness within dimmer than the rest of the corridor.

"Go on," Luke says impatiently.

Stepping forward, I stretch out my hand, pushing the door open wide. Something scurries along the decomposing floorboards, disappearing into a gaping hole next to the toilet. Several fragments of drywall have torn away from the walls. The toilet lid has been left

down, and the walls sport green peach fuzz — a hundred and some-thing year old wall in a freakish state of adolescence.

Closer to me, a wall-mounted porcelain sink juts out of the wall, promising running water that it can't deliver. My nausea subsides as I hesitate in the doorway, my eyes scanning to locate the source of the swishing noise tickling my ears. Could have been a mouse diving into the hole. Could have been almost anything. This hulk of a house has given up trying to keep wild things out. Anything and anybody is welcome.

I snap like a twig without seeing it coming. My composure sloughs away from my skin and bones, gathering on the floor along with the drywall and then scurrying into the shadows of the shittiest room I've ever seen.

No higher reasoning involved. It just happens. I lose it. My body twists, the floor complaining underfoot. My right hand smashes the water bottle into Luke's eye, my left belting him in the Adam's apple, stealing his breath.

He wheezes and rasps, his windpipe gasping for oxygen. Lunging low, he drops the lantern. It clatters on the floor. Arms grab me around both legs, his head connecting with my chest. The force tackles me to the ground. I collapse against the toilet, my shoulder banging it hard on the way down. I barely feel it. Barbed wire puzzle pieces in my stomach shudder and shift, reopening wounds and erasing every-thing else. Mark's dripping body. The kidnapping. Mom crying at the hospital, promising Natalya and me she was done with my dad. Tanvi's hands sly and playful on my waist, itching to make me laugh and give away our hide and seek spot behind the open bedroom door to her friends. Gone, gone, gone, gone.

Straightening slowly, Luke raises his weapon. "Motherfucking ass-hole," he says hoarsely. The gun barrel lines up with my frontal lobe. "Why'd you do that? You looking to get yourself shot?"

The lantern has rolled against the wall, beneath the sink. It lies on its side next to the crumpled, leaking water bottle.

"What's going on up there?" John roars from downstairs.

Luke kicks roughly at my shoe. "Get up."

I shake my head. No, I'm not looking to get shot. No, I can't get up. I'm a pile of broken glass.

Luke takes a step back, into the hallway. "He fell!" Luke shouts, voice cracking. "But it's cool. We're all right."

"Now get yourself up," Luke tells me. "And don't try that shit again or I'll take out your kneecap. I don't want to kill you, but that doesn't mean I won't hurt you."

The words whiz by my ears without landing. The swishing too — whatever furry thing is indiscriminate enough to pick this hellhole as its motel room. Something small and fast brushes by me in the dark, and revulsion must be primal because I automatically stagger to my feet.

Luke reaches for the lantern, stepping back fast. "Get your water."

I stare at Luke, not wanting to bend again. If I do, the pain will howl.

Then I think of Tanvi a floor below me. The way our eyes used to find each other in a crowd of friends or group of strangers. Suddenly, no matter where we'd been the moment before, we'd exist in the same mental space from across the room.

I imagine her eyes on me now, in this shitty nightmare of a bathroom where Luke's ready to take out my kneecap in retribution, and I do it. I bend and pick up the bottle, careful to preserve what's left inside. Just enough to wet my hands over the sink. I dry them on my jeans and plead, "Don't take what I did out on anyone else, okay? They didn't have anything to do with it."

"You think I'm some kind of monster?" Luke's eyes disappear behind the lantern light, twin black craters. "You think I'm gonna — what — go down there and beat on one of the girls?" His voice bounds downhill. "I'm not a monster. I'm just doing what I have to do here."

I bob my head like I believe him. With his ski mask still fixed in place, there's no visible evidence of the punch to the neck I delivered, but Luke's left eye is bloodshot and a long, spidery cut stares out from underneath his lower lid where the plastic bottle crunched open.

We eye each other up in the dingy shadows, whatever's rustling around in here with us tugging at my peripheral vision. Luke's taller than me but with a similar build. In the moment he's stronger than me — relatively undamaged — but either of us will do what we have to. Anybody looking to get in the way of that should think twice.

"That body outside was bloody," I tell him, my voice revealing more fear than I mean to. "Its fingers and eyes, even, but there were no bullet holes."

Beyond the bathroom, something thuds. A solid object dropped onto wood floor or hurled against an upstairs wall. Luke flinches, glancing swiftly behind him into the dark corridor and then back at me. "Get out there," Luke commands, slipping further into the bathroom to switch places with me.

I inch out into darkness, my eyes on my feet so I won't flip over any surprises. If there's something else in the house, it's bigger than what we spotted in the bathroom. When I hear the thud again it's closer, and it reminds me of our old apartment. The walls and floors were as thin as two-ply tissue. You could hear every step from next door or upstairs. Cupboards slamming. Toilets flushing. And repetitive unidentified noises like these.

Lantern light spills from behind me as Luke trails me into the hall. Something drags across the floor. Stops. Is propelled vigorously forward again. I freeze. Listen for what direction the sound is coming from, my eyes scouring the corridor. Four closed doorways, not counting the open bathroom. Paint, or maybe wallpaper — so intricately cracked from ceiling to floor that it reminds me of henna tattoos — lines the slowly disintegrating walls.

"What's the racket?" John shouts from the ground floor.

Luke's lips part to answer, his reply existing only in my gaze and the part of his mind that's shifted its focus to the ceiling. He holds the lantern higher, his other hand acting in synchronization, raising the gun.

I follow the direction of the light, shivering in the fast-disappearing heat. My body knows what's happening before I do. I've heard this sound before, in places it had no right to be. My bedroom. Tanvi's. Keion's car.

The hairs on my arms and the back of my neck stand to their full height, like corn stalks ready to be harvested. Above us, halfway down the hallway, an old hairbrush clings to the ceiling as if suspended by strings. The silver brush handle fishtails a little as it glints light back to us, the sound of its movement like a coin twirling on a table-top. My breath lights up the air too, turning it smoky white the way everyone's breath looks come Tealing winter.

Luke yanks the lantern away from the brush, shining it at the far end of the corridor. The noise amplifies, the brush jiggling agitatedly against the ceiling, defying gravity. "You see that?" Luke asks.

I peer at the empty scrap of hallway where he's focused the light. The walls aren't like henna tattoos after all. More like hundreds of swirling, intersecting scars that will never heal, or a state road map that won't lead you home.

"Someone was right there," Luke adds, his voice thin and cold like ice coiled around an electrical wire. "Looked like an old white woman in a nightgown."

But no one's there now, and I don't want to see what he's talking about.

John hollers up from the first floor again, and Luke shouts back, "We're coming down." We turn together, our steps frantic but not fast enough. Unmoored, the hairbrush skates rapidly along the ceiling, closing in on us.

My breath curls up deep in my lungs and stays there, not wanting to meet the air. Dense blackness spreads out ahead of me — I might as well be in deep space — and my hand reaching for the banister is an act of faith. Despite every crazy thing that's happened in the past few minutes, it must still be there.

Something drops from overhead, narrowly missing me. It strikes the top step forcefully instead, then the second and the third, clattering halfway down the staircase like an angry Slinky. Luke shines the lantern over my shoulder. We stare at the antique hairbrush lying deceptively lifeless in the middle of the staircase.

"*Run*," Luke says into my ear. My right hand lands safely on the banister. The temperature's plunged in the last thirty seconds, and for a moment I understand what Lauren meant with a clarity that chafes at my skull like coarse wool. I'm not the same person who walked out the front door with John minutes ago. I don't know who I am now. Everything's changed; it's changing still. Being rewritten by something stronger than what I can see and touch.

What it wants is anyone's guess.

Holding tight to the banister, I careen down the steps, the pain in my gut momentarily forgotten and Luke a hair's breadth behind me.

13

Sitting on the floor next to Cal with my hands still untied, I watch John and Luke hover in the living room doorway, their faces strained and their voices trampling each other's sentences. The finer points of their argument remain indecipherable, sinking into the shadows. John makes sure of that, subduing Luke time and again.

Luke motions repeatedly in the general vicinity of the staircase, John's gaze flickering intermittently in my direction.

"One of them is dead," I whisper, Cal staring straight ahead, pretending my lips haven't moved. "The other's missing."

Cal's eyes bulge, teeming with questions I don't have answers for. His gaze flies to Tanvi. She stares back at us with the concentration of a hawk, trying to tune in to our wavelength from across a physical divide. Seeing her sitting cross-legged, with Lauren's feet nestled in her lap as Lauren sleeps on peacefully — more peacefully than you'd expect would be possible in a place like this — I notice one of Tanvi's knees is skinned. Her long hair is knotting at the back.

I shift my stare to John and Luke, their arms jerking and spines held taut, their guns skittish extensions of their right hands. Their control over the situation is fading fast, and they know it.

"Something's wrong with this house," I continue, careful not to look at Cal. "Upstairs."

It hurts to talk, and I don't know how to explain without sounding like a straitjacket candidate. I need more tramadol. I need to lie down. Rest. Just for a few minutes. Until I can regain some of my strength. Slowly, I ease my back nearer to the floor, straightening my legs out in front of me. An old memory I didn't realize I'd forgotten washes to the surface as pain bullets through me like a tearing seam, my spine meeting solid ground.

My grandmother and her white candles. Years ago, she used to suffer from migraines. Her prescription would dull the pain, but never annihilate it. For that she used a white candle, letting it burn down to nothing as she chanted:

> Pain take flight and disappear,
> Sickness lay down misery and hear,
> My plea to energy and light,
> Vigor and wholeness hold me high,
> Turn my eyes to the endless sky,
> In the light, love's strength revealed,
> In the light, let me be healed.

My grandmother's honeyed voice flows through the folds of my gray matter, rhythmic and soothing like an old radio song played low. Smooth as water. Steady as stone.

I swim motionlessly toward the sound, where the pain is milder and more distant. From that place John and Luke are far away too, their disagreement of no real consequence.

It's a trick of the mind, but I need it.

Only for a little while, I promise myself, eyelids sealing me away from the world.

Under a graying sky littered with storm clouds, my father leans over my body, watching for a cue that I don't know how to give. My arms and legs are brown from the sun and pudgy with baby fat, my father's face unlined like when I was a kid. The smell of cigarettes sticks to him like flypaper, but the smile he beams me is white and warm. Bright as rhinestones.

"You're okay," he tells me. "Don't give up now. It's just beginning."

My mouth falls open, but no sound emerges. My arms flail uncontrollably, precision beyond my grasp.

"No excuses," he says, smile listing and then capsizing entirely. "You need to stop feeling sorry for yourself and fight, damn it. No one's coming to do it for you."

"What the fuck do you know?" I spit out, recovering my voice. "You're an asshole. That's all you've ever been."

My father laughs in my face and yanks at my arm, forcing me to sit upright. "Doesn't mean I'm wrong, Mikey-boy." He claps me on the back and then arcs his hand around the back of my neck, his grip firm but not harsh. "You don't have to like me; you just need to listen."

"Screw you," I tell him, throwing out both arms to shove him away.

"That's it," he says, grin returning to his cheeks as he loses his footing and stumbles into the distance. "I knew you had it in you."

My eyelids peel back, allowing the lantern light in. Someone's leaning over me, sure enough, but it's not my dad. Lauren swats her blond hair away from her lips, blinking slowly as she withdraws. The dilapidated living room knits spiderwebs between my ears and over the ventricles of my heart, slowing my mind and body in tandem.

I roll delicately onto my left side, lining both arms up next to me, one piled on top of the other. Balancing my weight on my forearms, I carefully leverage my upper body into a sitting position. It's not the agony I expected; while I've slept, the pain's been halved.

Peering behind Lauren, I clock the empty space where Tanvi should be. "Where's your cousin?" I gasp. My head pivots on my shoulders.

Cal's guzzling from a water bottle. Across the room, Luke sits on the chair nearest the door, his knees spread wide and his hands dangling between them, the gun appearing as weightless and harmless as a plastic toy.

"She had to go to the bathroom," Luke says firmly. "John took her."

My pulse revs. "How long have they been gone?"

"No time at all. Relax. They'll be back in a second." His eyes and tone are as nonchalant as if I just asked him for directions.

Cal shakes his head in aggravation. "I wanted to go with them. But they'll only take one at a time."

Luke's head rears, his shoulders stiffening. "Listen up, I'm tired of this backtalk." He raises his gun, centering it on Cal.

"It isn't backtalk," Cal says, his voice sagging under the weight of an effort not to sound confrontational. "We're just trying to reason with you. Somebody's dead, right?" He looks from me to Luke, seeking confirmation. "What went down outside?"

"Somebody's dead?" Lauren squeaks.

Luke ignores the questions, his attention pinging to Lauren regardless. "You said this place wasn't right. How do you know that?"

"I didn't say that." Lauren's mouth collapses into a frown, a thin crevice of dissent digging into the space between her eyes.

"Yeah, you did," Luke insists. "Before you fell asleep. You said some other freaky things too."

"*What?*" Lauren appears mystified.

"She was feverish," Cal interjects. "She doesn't remember. Leave her alone."

Lauren bites down on her lip. Turning to face the cross resting on the mantelpiece, her eyes search for something without moving.

"You really don't remember, do you?" I ask, touching her arm.

She shudders. A sound my ears can't twist into any known words dislodges from her diaphragm. Her mouth jerks crudely around the vibrations, like the connection between it and her brain has been partially severed.

A buzz of static electricity jolts through my fingers where they connect with Lauren's arm. My hand whips away from her, cold rocketing through my body like a flash freeze.

Footsteps thunder over our heads. Sprinting across the ceiling and thumping onto the stairs.

Tanvi charges into the living room, tangled Medusa hair shielding her face from view and temporarily changing her into something feral. Luke leaps from his chair, grabs her shoulders, and shakes her. "Where's John? Where's John?"

"He's back there." Tanvi casts a terrified look over her shoulder, wholly herself again. "Something got to him. In the hall upstairs. It snatched him up and hurled him back. I ran."

Luke releases her, Tanvi stepping deeper into the living room on shaky newborn deer legs. Cal folds his arms around her, hands smoothing over Tanvi's hair and steadying her.

My heart's still leveling out — too grateful for her safe return for jealousy to get a solid grip.

"John!" Luke hollers into the darkness, opening his lungs the way a razor blade is capable of opening a vein. "John! Answer me!"

Silence engulfs the house as each of us listens for a sound that doesn't arrive.

"Jesus Christ," Luke intones, raising both hands to his head, desperation and anger clawing at his throat. The gun handle presses against the fabric of the ski mask, the weapon so much a part of him that either he doesn't notice or doesn't care. "Everybody then, everybody with me. We're going upstairs to find him." Luke's eyes pin Tanvi to the wall, intensity holding her there. "If you did something to him, you better pray that I forgive you."

Lauren laughs maliciously from behind us. Every one of us hears it.

When I spin to look at her, Lauren's lying on her back with her eyes closed, the pillow crammed under her head like the last few minutes never happened.

"I'll stay with her," Tanvi volunteers, confusion plucking at her brow. "She's not well."

"No one's staying. Get her up. This is happening right now." Luke coughs into the stale air. "Grab a lantern too. You're going first. You're going to lead us up."

"She can't go first," I object. "She has no weapon. We don't know what's up there."

Luke cocks his head at me, his words setting like cement. "You think you're tougher than she is, then you go first, M. Fine by me."

I grab a lantern while Tanvi hurries to Lauren's side.

"She's not just sick," Cal says quietly to Tanvi. "Something else is wrong."

Luke's voice torpedoes across the living room. "We all know something's fucking wrong. Just. Get. Her. The. Fuck. Up. Or I will."

Lauren stumbles to her feet, her eyes clinging to the ground. Tanvi wraps an arm around her cousin's shoulder, squeezing reassurance into her young body. They hasten toward us together.

We fall into rough formation, me out front with the lantern. Cal next. Tanvi and Lauren following close behind him, hands clasped. Luke's the caboose, gun in one hand and lantern in the other, no free digits available to hold the handrail.

"Watch the first step," I warn, purely for the benefit of the other hostages. "It's loose."

We tackle the stairs. Quickly and without incident. The old hairbrush has vanished, and the silence of everything but our footsteps feels wrong, like someone's toying with us.

Cal and I hesitate as we reach the second floor. Between the two of us, we could take Luke down, but not before he gets a shot off.

If whatever we're facing here is worse than Luke — who didn't kill me when he had the chance — we might need him. My mind tumbles downstairs, slinking out the doorway and behind the carriage house where Mark's breathless and bloody body reclines in the muddy grass.

"Open one of the doors," Luke instructs, his voice like curdled milk.

I check the bathroom first, Cal at my shoulder, breathing audibly. "Clear," I shout back.

Four doors left. I head for the one at the far end of the corridor. The doorknob resists my pressure. "This one's locked."

Staring over Lauren's head in the hallway, Luke's dark clothing transforms him into a shadow. "Force it," he demands.

"I'll do it," Cal tells me. He knows I'm weak now.

Stepping out of Cal's way, I crowd in close to Lauren and Tanvi. Lauren's lips vault into a smile that remains absent from her eyes. "Wash your hands," she whispers, spit gathering on her lower lip. "Purify your heart."

I don't recognize the spiteful eyes that bore into mine. There's nothing childlike about them. Swallowing the bitter taste in my mouth, I glance at Tanvi next to her. Both her hands mold themselves supportively to Lauren's shoulders. Lauren doesn't protest, doesn't react.

Tanvi blinks quickly, her return look approaching apologetic. *She doesn't mean that. She's not herself.*

She means it.

She can smell it on me. The things I've done. And the stench of death from Mark's body, too.

Then Cal charges at the door, right foot kicking vehemently into the wood. The door groans but refuses him entrance. He tries with his shoulder, thudding leadenly but fruitlessly on impact. Switching back to his foot, the door flies open on the third attempt.

I push past him, holding the lantern high to reveal what's left of a modest bedroom. Most of it ragged, torn, filthy, faded. Twin bed flush against the wall. Dressing table topped with a rectangular wood-framed mirror. Mahogany wardrobe. Small floral-pattern armchair tucked into a corner. Unlike downstairs, framed pictures still decorate these walls. A sailboat floating in a lonely harbor. Portraits of people who have been dead for too long for anyone to miss them.

"Open the closet," Luke says, peering in from the hallway.

Dust particles take flight as I tug anxiously at the wardrobe handle. It's roomy enough to store a body inside, but John isn't here, only the hairbrush from the stairs. I slam the door shut, not wanting to confirm its presence. As I turn to exit the room, lantern light tumbles over one of the decorative pillows piled on the bed. Something thin and flat peeks out from behind the cushion. I reach for it, pulling it free from the pillow. A cloud of disrupted dust spews irritably from the cushion. It's a house nameplate, the kind that would've swung from a post somewhere near the end of the road as a marker. SHANTALLOW.

The sign slips from my grasp and drops onto the bed, Luke and everyone else staring at me from the hallway, watching it fall. Shantallow. My shock falls quickly away too, fading fast because just as a glass can hold only so much water, a mind can absorb only so much shock. The rest of it disperses who knows where. The word I heard from Tanvi's mouth in my sleep months ago is a place that doesn't want us. Beyond that, I don't know …

"Keep going," Luke orders. "Next room."

Cal's out in front, closest to the next door. The doorknob turns easily in his hand. Trailing him by less than two feet, I shine the lantern into the room. It's bigger than the first, a double bed with an enormous headboard positioned near the uncovered window. On a clear night, moonlight would stream through it, bounce off the mirror, and bring shadows to light.

Tonight there's no moon, only the light we bring with us.

A hefty roll of fabric juts out from under the bed, strangely solid. Long too, stretching almost the length of the box spring above it.

"What is that?" Luke says urgently. "Pull it out."

I spin to hand the lantern to Tanvi, my heart out of whack. Its normal rhythm forgotten. The things we say with our eyes are beyond words. It doesn't matter how afraid we are — like people who've fallen through a hole in the ice and been carried away by a fast-moving current. We're here now, under water, swimming for our lives.

Cal and I step swiftly toward the bed, bending to yank at the fabric. It's more than just a spare blanket or bedspread. It's heavy, something encased within the folds. Something fleshy and tall.

In our grip, the fabric slides reluctantly out from under the bed. Luke and Tanvi have gathered behind us, the concentrated light from both lanterns spotlighting the lumpy mass. A small horizontal slit in the material reveals lips and teeth.

An intact mouth, petrified into an expression of terror.

14

The room bears down on us. One of the furniture legs rocks unevenly, like its being pushed. My eyes instinctively scan the surrounding space, looking for an invisible culprit. Hatred for this house burns in my veins as the air turns cold.

A squeak from the ceiling forces my gaze up. The chandelier over the bed swings erratically. The noise of old chain and fixtures in motion grates like nails on a chalkboard.

"Open it up!" Luke screams, refocusing our attention on the body.

Rolling over the fabric, we search for the ends to pull apart. There aren't any. The blanket's been sewn shut. Luke drops to his knees next to us, thrusting one hand deep into his pocket. Leaning over the blanket, he slices into the fabric with a pocketknife. The slit expands into a gash. Then a hole, big enough to force a human head through.

Wrenching the fabric away from skin, Luke cradles the man's head in his hands. "Get him out of this," Luke shouts breathlessly. "Get him out!" Cal snatches up Luke's knife, continuing to cut the man free. I pull at the hole with my fingers, ripping the material to shreds.

Together we peel what's left of the blanket away from the body.

Most of us have never seen John's face before — a white male in his early thirties, eyes shut as if he were just kicking back on his couch, catching a few winks. Short brown hair and a snub nose. I could've bagged his groceries without ever really noticing him.

"Is he breathing?" Tanvi asks.

"I think so," Luke says. We stare at John's chest, watching it expand. Luke lightly taps John's face. "Wake up, man. We have you."

Unlike with Mark's body, there doesn't seem to be any blood. No obvious signs of physical trauma. No response from John, either, and my mind pounds with questions. Who would do this? How? Why?

"He could have a head injury," Tanvi says, swallowing her lips.

The damn chandelier goes crazy, shaking with the force of an earthquake. Rage pools in Luke's eyes, his jaw snapping and his teeth biting the air. He's hit his limit and hurtled past it. He leaps up on the bed like a man on fire, throwing his hands over his head and catching the chandelier with fingers. Holding it still, defying its will.

As he hops down from the bed, Luke's eyes spring back to Tanvi.

She peers unblinkingly down at John, her cheeks sharpening as she evaluates his condition. "We probably shouldn't move him. He's on his back, which is good. But we need to raise his legs at least a foot above the ground. And loosen his clothing."

Tanvi and I both learned CPR at school. Probably Cal did too. But John's still breathing, and there's not much else we can do for him from this forsaken place.

Cal swipes two anorexic-looking pillows from the bed, tucking them under John's feet. They're not enough. The three of us stare expectantly at Luke, fresh shock stranding us in the moment of helplessness.

None of us will volunteer to leave this room — alone — to get more pillows from the adjacent bedroom. We could be next.

Only then does it dawn on me that Luke set down his gun and lantern to cut John from the blanket. My eyes drill into the hastily cast aside weapon behind us on the floor.

Luke follows my gaze. His shoulders stoop, his body somehow heavier as he exhales. He claws jerkily at the bottom of his ski mask, tears it free from his skin, and hurls it to the ground. "I'm done," he declares, misery scratching at baby-faced features I already recognize. His neck's begun to turn purple where I punched him. "I'm not holding you anymore. You all do what you want."

The revelation feels ancient, like I saw it coming a long time ago. Craig, Gavin, Greg, whoever the fuck he is. Last time I saw him he was sitting on my neighbor's stoop. I would've let him into my house. Did he start planning the kidnapping way back then because of things I said that night?

But there's no time for outrage. That already feels ancient too.

I slide backward, fingers reaching for the gun.

"Lauren!" Tanvi calls suddenly, backing into the hallway with one of the lanterns. "Lauren, come back here!"

I haven't seen Lauren since we walked into the master bedroom. Occupied with John, we never realized she was missing.

Cal and I tear after Tanvi, rushing into the previous room to search for her. The cold is everywhere, bleeding our breath from our bodies in long wisps. Thumping from behind closed doors sends us spinning into the corridor. "Lauren?" we yell repeatedly, the cracks in the walls like gnarled veins. They scratch at my eyes and twist inside my head, carving trenches of loathing. "Lauren, where are you?"

We run for the bathroom, discovering it empty except for the furry thing that lives there.

It steals into the hole next to the toilet as we avert our eyes. Tanvi whirls into the hallway, Cal and I right behind her. She jiggles the doorknobs of the two remaining doors. Both locked.

"Downstairs!" Tanvi exclaims, her eyes stricken with growing horror because the worst things can happen in seconds.

Luke hollers something raggedly from the master bedroom. We sprint for the stairs, a tapping noise from the ceiling trailing close

behind. I don't look up. No one does. See no evil, hear no evil, run like someone's life depends on it.

Tanvi stumbles on the final step, finding her footing before the rotten wood can hurl her to the ground. The three of us land safely on the first floor, Luke's unintelligible words fading behind us. Something hits my right calf, thudding to the wooden floor.

Bolting for the living room, sudden warmth seeps into my fingers and face. Like flipping from January to August in a handful of seconds. Curled up on her side alone in the middle of the room, Lauren has her eyes closed, her lips parted, and her mouth relaxed. Her hair spirals wildly out against the pillow scrunched under her head.

"Lauren!" Tanvi's strides are long and swift. She crouches beside her cousin, one of her hands sweeping firmly along Lauren's arm. "Lauren, what are you doing?"

Motionless, Lauren looks as innocent as a fairy-tale heroine waiting for the magic moment to wake. While she sleeps, she's the kid I met at Christmas. While she sleeps, there's no reason to fear her.

"Lauren!" Tanvi's fingers caress her cousin's cheek, her voice urgent but her touch gentle. "Come on. Time to get up. We're leaving."

Cal stoops next to her, adding his voice. "Lauren, wake up. We gotta get out of this place."

Standing by the fireplace, I watch Tanvi's and Cal's increasingly desperate efforts to rouse her — shouting hoarsely, sprinkling her face with water, attempting to sit her up. Nothing works. Lauren flops in their arms. Living, breathing dead weight.

"We'll have to carry her," I say.

"He's right," Cal agrees firmly. "I can carry her out."

And I can't, not for long or with any speed. My ribs groan in frustration. I don't need him reminding me of all the things I'm not.

"We need to get the van keys," he continues. "They're probably upstairs with John."

I gnaw at the inside of my lip and shake my head. "It doesn't matter if they are. Someone scorched the van. I saw it for myself." I watch Tanvi's heart sink as she digests the information. The revelation pulls at her cheeks and jaw.

Then I glance down at Lauren, wondering if some part of her is listening. "We need the gun." John's weapon wasn't in the blanket along with him, we would've seen it. There's only one gun left within our reach. I should've grabbed it upstairs when I had the chance.

Snaking my hand around one of the remaining lanterns, I jet into the hall, shouting out ahead of me, "Luke, we're leaving!" My left foot collides angrily with the hairbrush on the floor. I kick it into the darkness. The brush coasts smoothly away, like a puck on unblemished ice, mocking me with its feigned innocence.

Cal appears in the living room doorway at the sound of the brush skimming along the corridor. "What was that?" he asks.

"Nothing important." I train my eyes on the decaying staircase, its fringes blurred by predatory shadows. When something has to be done, there's no route around it. I picture myself ascending the staircase with one hand on the banister and then returning moments later with the gun held tightly in my other hand. If I can see it, the vision can come true. It's no different from running hills. "If he doesn't come down in a second, I'm going up for the gun," I add.

My breath is shallow with doubt.

People don't lose their lives or minds running hills. Shin splints and Achilles tendonitis don't lay you out in the grass behind the carriage house with blood oozing from your eyes and fingertips.

Cal doesn't tell me he'll come upstairs with me. We both know he has to stay close to Tanvi and Lauren.

"Don't come after me if I'm not down in a few minutes, all right? Send someone back after you get out of here." I stare at Cal hard, watching him nod.

"You'll come down," he tells me. "You're a runner, right? Be quick, and you'll be okay."

I nod in appreciation. He's a good guy. It doesn't make things easier when it comes to whatever's going on between him and Tanvi, but it makes it hard to hate him.

My right hand outstretched to meet the banister, I head for the stairs and don't look back.

15

Halfway up the staircase, an unexpected sense of calm washes over me, exhaustion burning through the nerve endings of my fear. I don't want to die here. I'll fight however I can. Those are the choices I can make; everything else isn't up to me.

Listening for noises from above, I call out to Luke again.

Silence crackles from the second floor.

My running shoes thump against the steps, the lantern steady in my left hand. For a second my eyes threaten to betray me, a hazy figure beginning to form in my peripheral vision.

A scream pierces the air. As solid and sharp as an incisor breaking skin. Tanvi in trouble.

I race back down, my legs moving in slow motion, heart galloping as if it can make up the shortfall.

Landing back on the ground floor, time stutters back to a normal pace. A thousand milliseconds to a second. Sixty seconds per minute.

Flinging myself into the living room, I see Cal sprawled dazedly on the floor near the doorway, as if someone cold-cocked him and laid him out. Tanvi's a couple of feet from the wheelchair, her body twisting turbulently and her fists punching air, her long hair fanned back behind her, running upward into the air like a reverse waterfall.

Lauren sleeps on, seemingly oblivious to Tanvi's screams. I careen past her, reaching for Tanvi's hair, trying to wrestle it free. Something pushes my hands away, shoves its block-like weight into my shoulders, forcing me backwards.

I stumble and charge at it again, tripping over Lauren's feet. My chin knocks straight into Tanvi's shoulder. We begin to fall together, the grip on her hair holding her up for a moment before it releases, allowing her to drop to the floor.

She falls on top of me, most of her weight landing on my arm, but enough of it compressing my chest to make me whimper. Rolling away from me, Tanvi's hands fly to her hair. I stay crumpled on the floor, catching my breath, corralling the fresh pain into a corner of my mind where it can't control me.

Cal regains consciousness, his eyes bleary and his hands on either side of him as he sits up, processing the scene.

"Fuck the gun," Tanvi rasps, clasping her hair tightly against the side of her neck. "We're going now, without it."

I blink quickly, eyes deceiving me as the shadowy figure from beside me on the stairs glides into the living room and solidifies into flesh.

Pushing my weight onto my elbows, I stare the form down. It can't be him. Only the house weaving its deceptions. My dad must be thousands of miles from here, drinking tequila on the beach.

"I don't want to leave him here," Luke says in a low voice, not a vision or trick after all. Just a case of mistaken identity. One of Luke's sleeves is torn, his black clothing is caked with dust from his chandelier scuffle, and his neck wound glimmers resentfully in the lantern light. "But I'm not staying. There were voices upstairs in the room with me. Not even whispering — straight out talking, arguing." Luke's left hand compulsively rubs his abdomen, washing with unseen soap. The gun protrudes from his right hand, aimed at the floor.

Rushing to his feet, Cal declares, "We thought you'd disappeared." He lurches to Tanvi's side, throwing his arm around her and pressing a kiss firmly into her hair. "We're getting out. Something attacked us."

Luke's grip on the gun tightens. "What did you see?"

"Nothing." Tanvi's eyes are stern but frantic, like images of people who have survived natural disasters. The same shock sits firmly behind my eye sockets, like a heel grinding your head into the floor. "But it's here."

I stagger to my full height. "What time is it? How long until morning?"

Luke shakes his head. "My phone's dead. Battery drained to nothing a while back, and I don't know what happened to the others' phones, but we dumped all of yours where we picked you up."

"It doesn't matter what time it is, Misha." Tanvi's gaze bulldozes into me, threatening to knock me off balance. "We go *now*."

I turn toward Luke. "You have a gun — at least give her your knife."

How can we fight what we can't see coming? It's impossible. And so far none of the guns have made any difference. But cops put on bulletproof vests every day, knowing someone could shoot them in the head. You do what you can.

Luke's neck tilts, his head slanting in contemplation. Then he treads decisively toward Tanvi, hand diving into his pocket and reappearing with his pocketknife. "I'd give you the gun, only I'm probably the only one here who has ever used one outside of a video game."

Tanvi's eyes sharp-focus on the weapon in his other hand. "It's a Glock, right? So no safety. Just pull the trigger." Regardless, she pockets the offered knife, nodding in thanks.

"Got anything else we can use?" Cal jokes numbly.

My gut cries out for tramadol, my eyes winging around the room — past the folding chairs, LED lanterns, ghoulish broken wheelchair, and wooden cross — and zoning in on the first aid kit. Someone left it next to the stack of paper cups beside the fireplace. I pad unsteadily toward it, wrestling another tablet from the kit, popping it between my lips, and pouring a flood of water down after it.

Cal scoops Lauren into his arms without breaking a sweat. Luke, Tanvi, and I each take a lantern. The four of us file swiftly out the front door, Luke hesitating before closing it behind him. Descending the porch steps, I think of John helpless upstairs — his face painfully ordinary — and Mark lifeless a stone's throw away. They should never have brought us here, and they've paid for it in full.

But what's happened in this place isn't solely about retribution. If it were, Lauren wouldn't be suffering too. She's only ten years old. She doesn't deserve any of this.

Tanvi gasps as she stares at the burnt-out van. Our journey home would've been simple if the van had been left alone. Somebody doesn't want it that way.

"We follow the driveway until we hit the main road," Luke instructs. "I'm guessing it's a forty-minute walk."

"Where are we?" Cal asks him, nearing the van.

Luke's face creases in regret or embarrassment. We're walking out of here together by choice, but that's not how most of us arrived. "Middlesbrough. Near Side Road Four. Lot of land out here, not a lot of people."

Only an hour outside of Tealing. If we're lucky, someone will motor by shortly after we hit the side road and call a cruiser for us. We could be home before the sun's high in the sky, all of this relegated to a bad memory.

"When we get there —" Luke begins.

The pain in my abdomen gnaws away at my jagged bones, waiting for the tramadol to take effect. Breathing hurts, walking hurts. The very act of living is laced with pain. The last thing I should do is crouch, but I can't help myself. An idea jiggles at my mind the way a burglar jiggles doorknobs, looking for someone stupid enough to have left their door unlocked. I drop to the ground, groaning and struggling to see under the van. Wet grass dampens the bottom of my jeans, my hand straining to hold out the lantern while the rest of my body struggles to maintain its balance.

"What is it?" Tanvi asks over her shoulder.

Turning back, she squats next to me, her head tilted within inches of the grass. Focusing her lantern light alongside mine, Tanvi's neck jerks, her body jolting and her legs scrambling backwards away from the vehicle, like she can't un-see what's beneath the van quickly enough. Her right hand plunges into the grass, keeping her from toppling over.

Contorting my body past my pain threshold to angle in closer, I'm seconds behind her, eyes scarred by the mass of charred flesh they slammed into. A human-shaped chunk of steak grilled beyond useful-ness, until it was little more than blackened bones.

My body skitters away, half-slipping and half-flying to my knees, and then my feet, my jeans soaked from the kneecaps down.

"No," Luke groans from behind me, where he squatted in the grass without me being aware of it.

The anguish whipping through his throat burns my eardrums.

No one should see the human body destroyed with such contempt.

It's inhuman. Unforgiveable and unforgettable.

"Is it him?" Cal sputters, the only one who can't see the body for himself because his arms are filled with Lauren. "The fourth guy who was with you?"

"Let's go," Tanvi cries, because the truth is no one could say. The body's unidentifiable.

Shaken and silent, we clump together in the center of the Shan-tallow drive — a skinny dirt road infested with sprigs of scraggly grass and patches of weeds. The unforgiving black sky hangs low and heavy over our heads, rumbling belligerently as we leave the van in our wake. Rangy trees close in on us while we walk, lanterns held out against the darkness, my mind poisoned by the things I've seen.

Was the burnt body an accident? The torching of the van intentional, but the murder a mistake?

Matthew might have been hiding, trying to save himself from Mark's fate. Why didn't whoever or whatever killed them finish off John too? Why did they let us go?

The hideous questions seep into quicksand inside my skull, playing on a loop, toxins infiltrating an artery. The image of the body under the van will never disappear, never really fade, only drill down deeper, finding dark corners to hide in.

Tanvi's head swings dazedly in my direction, her eyes touching down on mine. *Don't think*, her gaze says. *Keep walking.*

Her attention flips to Lauren in Cal's arms. She looks at home there, at ease like a three-year-old toted from the back seat of a family car to her bedroom without ever waking up.

"When we were here before it wasn't anything like this," Luke says, breaking the quiet. "There was no one — nothing — here. It seemed perfect, somewhere we'd never be found. The place hadn't been disturbed in a long time. We saw some beer bottles in the shed, coated with decades worth of dust. That was it."

"What were you going to do if you didn't get paid?" Cal asks.

"John said their grandparents would pay." Luke's eyes drop to Lauren. "Said he had no doubts, and that they could afford it." His eyes tumble further, into the inky dirt and snaking grass at his feet. "Wasn't right. I'm not saying otherwise. But it was nothing personal, and it was never supposed to be like this."

Clearing his throat, he continues. "Listen, when we get to the side road, I'm going to go my own separate way. You all will do what you gotta do, I understand that." His gaze hangs on me the longest. "I know the area will be crawling with cops once someone picks you up. But I have to try to get clear if I can."

Neither Tanvi nor I respond. The serious unfinished business I have with this guy — my questions about whether I triggered this entire hideous, sorry night — have to wait for some other time. I

temporarily fold my extra guilt into a shape tiny enough that I can carry it without slowing me down.

Cal mashes his lips together, chewing over his thoughts. "We should be quiet," he mutters. "We don't know what's out here with us."

From then on we walk in silence. There should be nocturnal animals foraging in the nearby trees and underbrush, twigs snapping as they go. Crickets chirping. Owls calling to each other, sounding as otherworldly as ghosts lamenting their passing. But we hear nothing except our own movements. My ears ring with the absence of sound. Even the wind has stopped dead.

The hot, stagnant air feels shabby and claustrophobic against my skin. My fingers sweat against the lantern handle. Strangely, my gut feels virtually unscathed, although only a few minutes have passed since I swallowed the second dose of tramadol.

Substances shot into a vein take effect quickly. No liver metabolizing required.

I've never taken anything stronger than Aspirin or Advil. Never been high. I'm not now, either. Just intact. Nearly back to how I felt physically before the gospel writers broke my nose and punched a set of dents and cracks into my rib cage.

Adrenalin doing me a favor. Or maybe we've been out here longer than I think. Without any way of telling time, it's hard to know. The sky isn't dropping clues. The moon and stars don't like this place any better than we do; they're staying away. No sign of sunlight on the horizon, either.

The trees crowd in nearer with every step, their leafy canopy eclipsing the dim light leaking in through cloud cover and the dirt road beneath us dissolving into feral land. "Are we going the right way?" I ask, panning to Luke with my lantern.

"Can't be," Tanvi says, puzzled. "The van wouldn't have been able to pass this way."

Luke hesitates in his tracks. We all do, casting our gazes agitatedly back to the direction we've come from. The tall, close-knit trees assembled behind us are indistinguishable from the way that lies ahead, offering only enough room to forge a footpath through. How did we get this deep into the woods without noticing?

"We must have taken a wrong turn somewhere." Luke twists to survey the surrounding forest, Cal adjusting Lauren's weight in his arms and a malignant realization breaking the surface of my consciousness.

Behind us in the all-encompassing darkness, one body has begun to decompose, another lies blackened and faceless, its identity erased, and a third's heart still beats, not knowing it's been abandoned. Three victims of Shantallow. All strangers to me before tonight.

But the most familiar aspects of the night — the ones I've seen time after time in my dreams — are undeniable. Tanvi and me. In the woods. Terror rolling us off in waves, threatening to drag us under and bury our bodies someplace they'll never be found. In the nightmares we were always alone. Paused in a clearing, preparing to run.

The details don't line up perfectly, but we're here. Somewhere off Side Road Four in Middlesbrough, within the orbit of a cadaverous house that should've been torched to the ground a long time ago. My imagination didn't invent Shantallow. It's been here waiting for us all this time. After over a year of visiting this place in my dreams, at last Tanvi and I have arrived.

In that moment, Lauren laughs faintly. Hollow and stiff, like a sound forced rather than offered.

She knows.

I just caught up to the truth, and somehow she knows it. The way an animal senses an imminent earthquake — birds filling the sky before the ground wrenches open and devours everything in its path. Lauren's tuned in to a different wavelength.

Mine.

Lunging forward to peer into her face, I'm met with simple calm. Nothing more than a sleeping child.

"I heard it," Cal confirms, eyes darting from side to side. "But it didn't sound like it was coming from her. She never moved a muscle."

Luke raises his gun, whirling to point it behind him in a slow arc of motion that targets half of the forest. "We all heard it. Like when I was upstairs with John. Voices coming out of the walls."

Tanvi quickens her pace. "Don't listen," she urges, her face skeletal behind the lantern light, eyes and cheeks sinking into an abyss of shadows. Riveted, I can't stop staring, my dream memories interlacing with reality — a dream I could only ever escape by waking up. "We have to keep going. We must be getting close to the road."

Hurrying onward, my ears strain for the faintest sound: leaves crunching under Tanvi's volleyball shoes, Cal's measured breath, and the things around us that don't allow themselves to be heard until they're ready.

"Are you okay?" Tanvi whispers, falling into lockstep with Cal. "I can take her for a while." Studying her cousin, Tanvi stretches her free arm out to grip Lauren's hand.

"She'll be all right," Cal says, answering the question Tanvi didn't ask. "Soon as we get picked up, she'll be as good as new. It's this place …"

Nodding stoically, Tanvi slowly releases her hold on her cousin's fingers. Freed, Lauren's hand swings rhythmically through the air, matching Cal's steps.

"Did you hear that?" Luke asks. "Sounded like a car."

The faint whirr of something that could easily be an engine. The sound snakes through the trees and lingers in my eardrums, swelling with hope. "I hear it," I confirm.

The four of us begin to run, Cal, Luke, and I slowed by the branches and slick leaves of the forest floor. Tanvi sprints ahead, her black hair unfurling behind her like a cape. "Wait!" I call.

The trees shutter behind her, leaving only the narrowest gap between them. Tanvi's lantern light flickers and dwindles, the rift between us growing by leaps and bounds. In the distance, the light bobbing in Tanvi's hand is small enough to be a firefly. I train my eyes on its glow, propelling myself forward, weaving and jumping through the trees and over scraggy ground.

A low-hanging branch slaps me in the face, scratching my forehead. I wallop it back and push on — afraid of losing her, panicking.

Then I see her, standing sandwiched between two sinewy trees and pointing triumphantly ahead, her arm as straight as a Popsicle stick or curtain rail. "I found the driveway again," she says, her voice like liquid gold. "Look."

Sure enough, the distance between the trees widens ahead, bare patches returning to the ground, approximating the remnants of a dirt road that veers sharply left. Our exit strategy. The way out of Shantallow — a secret my dreams never shared.

Even the stark light from our lanterns isn't enough to disguise our relief. For the first time in five months, Tanvi almost smiles at me, her eyes softening and her cheeks suddenly weightless. For the first time in five months, I'm not only the Misha who hurt her. I've become someone neither of us knows yet. The person who survived this night.

I hold her gaze gingerly, the new feeling settling lightly on top of the others — fear, disgust, confusion — until we turn away in sync.

"Hurry up!" Tanvi calls, pivoting to shout to the others. "We're nearly there."

Luke's voice bounds back to us from within the woods, a knife's edge of impatience tangled with optimism. "Hold up. We're coming."

16

The five of us wind along the muddy path, powered by four sets of legs. Following the dirt road around a sharp left where it immediately stretches, widening seductively. Fresh wind rushes against my neck and arms, echoing the sensation of freedom within reach. "Everyone stays together," Cal lectures.

We advance like a restless four-legged animal, Lauren our sleeping head.

My mind conjures a mental picture of the rural side road before we reach it. Two slender lanes of gravel dividing an ocean of trees. No lights. No tarmac. But a symbol of civilization regardless. Safety.

A guy in an old pickup truck will come bumping along the road with no inkling that he's about to become our hero. Or a woman who works shifts somewhere, like my mom. She might be too suspicious to stop, but she'll call the police as she drives away, glancing at us in her rear-view mirror. The cops will arrive within minutes and this will be behind us, without any of us understanding why it happened in the first place except that bad things happen all the time; the world is ripe with destruction and full of dark places. Then my eyes catapult to the shriveled black mass that lies nestled at the foot of Shantallow like a loyal dead dog — the once white van, scarred by fire. Dread courses through my bloodstream, my cheekbones and lips protruding in a silent scream.

"That's not possible!" Tanvi cries. "We never turned around."

The battered, threadbare dregs of a house — balding, broken, cracked, and crumbling — loom behind the van like an abomination born of ash. A past that won't allow itself to die, preferring to fester like gangrene. Profoundly pathetic, reveling in its own monstrousness.

A gunshot severs the air. I swing to look at Luke, my teeth feeling like fangs. Like I'd bite through anything to escape this fucking place, and then sleep for a hundred years, trying to forget it.

Luke's right arm is frozen in front of him, the pistol aimed at the house beyond the burnt-out van, and the darkness has stolen his bullet the same as if it were bone. That's what it does. Takes everything it can get and then grabs you by the hair to take more.

"Stop it, man," Cal warns, his face bands of exhaustion and his torso hunched toward Lauren in his arms. "You're wasting ammo."

Luke's laughter erupts like a case of hiccups, high and choppy, tinged with hysteria. "Ammo? You think these bullets can help defend us? It doesn't look like they've done jack shit." He wags his gun at the van. "Didn't save him. Didn't save Joel upstairs."

Joel. My brain swallows the name, files it in a folder the cops will want to see along with everything I remember about Luke himself.

"Yeah, that's right, his name is Joel," Luke continues. "Doesn't matter now anyway, does it? If help comes for him, they're going to find out his real name."

"Help will get to him," I mumble, turning my back to the house and the van, making them disappear. The mismatched eyes of the house gape vindictively down at me with an intensity that burns through my spine, commanding me to acknowledge it. "We're going to get out of here. We just have to start over."

Tanvi nods mechanically, her eyes light years away and the lantern shuddering in her hand. "We were sloppy," she says. "We lost track of which direction we were walking in." And time. We lost time and went down without a fight. Let ourselves be led docilely back to this spot, like a flock of sheep. Each of us falling into some kind of daze or hypnotic state, drinking it down like it was freedom.

"This time we won't," Tanvi continues, the declaration as dry as kindling in her throat. "We'll make sure." She stares at the van, chin crumpling for a second before she pulls it taut and steps nearer to Cal. "Let me take her. You're tired."

Cal gathers Lauren in closer to him, like a security blanket he's not ready to give up. "It's cool, T.V. I'm all right. Let's just go."

Luke straightens his spine. "I can carry her. Got a little sister at home. I've probably spent twenty percent of my life carrying her on my back." He holds the gun sidewise, the tension in his arm easing. "Someone else can take it. Doesn't make any difference anyhow. It's like bringing a toothpick to a fencing match. The gun isn't what we need."

Luke shakes his head at me, pre-empting my offer to volunteer for something I'm not sure I can accomplish. "Don't even bother, M. You're not going to make it ten minutes down the road with that kid in your arms. And if you collapse, no one's going to carry you. You'll be lying in the woods praying a blanket doesn't swallow you up like a boa constrictor."

Cal spins abruptly and begins walking again, without any further discussion and with no light to guide him. His steps are heavy and cautious, the way anyone moves when they're determined to push past their limits but not commit any stupid mistakes doing it. Tanvi jogs after him, raising her lantern as if in greeting to the dirt road. Luke remains where he is, eyeing the grizzled old house, his mouth fighting an eerie smile. "You coming or what?" I say, refusing to face Shantallow again, images of the seared body under the van blazing through my neurons.

My feet shuffle over the mud and grass, my gaze locking on Tanvi ahead, trying to eclipse the grim picture with something good, something beautiful that's been unlucky enough to land in the worst of places. Luke coughs and catches up to me, gun attached to one hand and lantern to the other, like an action figure with accessories included.

He laughs under his breath as we walk, cheeks twitching and the wind kicking up another notch while thunder rumbles in the distance.

"Stop it," I bark. "Hold your shit together." We have to concentrate. Follow the driveway out to the side road. We can't afford to get lost again. The storm's gathering its forces, preparing to return.

Luke bites back the sound trapped in his esophagus. Clearing his throat, he glances slowly over his shoulder at the scene of destruction we've left behind.

"Don't do that," I tell him, parroting what Tanvi said earlier. "Ignore it." Like with Lauren's phantom laughter.

"Why?" Luke asks, eyebrows jamming together.

"Because it wants us to look."

The fine, threadlike cut underneath his lower eyelid puckers, Luke whistling through his teeth. "Is it happening to you too?" His gaze returns uneasily to the road. "Like what happened with the kid?"

My grip on my lantern tightens. "No." At least, I don't think so.

But something's happening. The darkness is all around us, and it wants in.

The trees are closer now, dirt road still visible under our feet. A couple of paces ahead of us, Cal's and Tanvi's voices are flat and hushed, whatever they're saying to each other un-decodable by my ears.

"What about you?" I ask.

Luke grins unevenly in the lantern light, showing off a perfect set of teeth. Clamping his mouth shut, a frown rises to replace it. "Those guys back there, I wouldn't call them my friends. Not most of them. But this" — his eyes pop — "this is unreal. It can't be happening. Not how it seems. Man, I just keep thinking I'm going to wake up."

And if he did, would he go through with the kidnapping or walk away?

Forget it, doesn't matter. There's no reset button for this day.

Thunder booms like cannon fire, closer now. Close enough to feel in my stomach, like the beat of a drum. The sky seethes, sheet lightning penetrating the trees in imitation of blinding sunshine. Somewhere behind us, Lauren giggles manically. Never mind that she's nestled in Cal's arm, not five steps ahead.

"Fuck you!" Luke sings in response, his stupid smile back in place, stretching his cheeks too far, warping his face into derangement.

A lone drop clips the end of my nose. The ceiling of black unzips, releasing a torrent of rain. Within seconds I'm soaked to the skin. Rain washes into my eyes, my lashes struggling to push it back. Digging my hands into my armpits, I bend my head, water sloping down the back of my neck, rolling under my shirt along with the rest of the rain, pasting the fabric to my skin.

Tanvi whirls to look at me, arms knotted in front of her breasts, hair matted sleekly to her cheeks, and eyes deflated into slits. Satisfied that Luke and I have kept pace despite the downpour, she hurries forward, bent like a tree that grew in chronic wind. I see her expression again and again in my mind as we walk, thunder exploding through the trees and lightning violently illuminating every mossy tree trunk and fallen branch.

Through it all, Tanvi's face.

The storm casts off the forest's earlier silence with a force that sends us staggering, fighting to keep our balance in the onslaught of rain. What's left of the route out to Side Road Four threatens to wash away. From somewhere behind us, inflamed voices surge against the thunder. Closing in fast. Unearthly shadow voices that don't belong in our world and that quicken our pace.

With Lauren's extra weight, Cal begins to lag behind. I could outrun him and everyone else, make it out to the road and send back help.

The thought tilts in my brain, messing with my equilibrium. It's what Tanvi wanted in my dreams. I didn't like the idea then, and I don't like it now. My foot twists sideways on the sopping ground as I slow down, righting myself.

We have to stay together. I'm not leaving this place without Tanvi or Lauren.

As I fall back behind Cal and Tanvi, Luke grins zealously, charging past me and diving deeper into the trees. The cacophony of voices shriek and cry, congealing into delirium. Female and male. Young and old. Inflamed, all.

Rustling noises beat at the woods behind me. Something advancing. Swift and certain.

Suddenly, Cal trips. Lauren bounces out of his grip, landing at the base of a gnarled tree trunk. Cal's shoes skid out sideways, his body falling down close to hers, legs splayed out in opposite directions like an open pair of scissors. Rushing to Lauren's side, I squat beside her, examining her face for signs of consciousness or injury. Holding one hand close to her mouth, warm air meets my skin. She's still blacked out. Still breathing too.

Tanvi drops down next to us, repeating Lauren's name while the other voices rage on — drowning her out like scalpels and skewers, ripping at flesh and twisting in muscle, intent on making someone bleed. Scooping one hand under her Lauren's head, Tanvi protects it from the wet ground. The fear in her eyes is not for herself. We're all scared — hearts racing and fingers shaking with it — but the deepest fears are the ones you fear for other people when you hit the limits of your ability to help them.

There's only one thing left I can do.

Gathering Lauren's pale, sleeping form into my arms, I stand. Familiar pain flaps erratically inside my abdomen. Tanvi turns to check on Cal. She helps him up as I begin to jog, not allowing myself to wince, blocking out the voices as I go. Not letting myself register how much nearer they are now, practically chafing at my heels.

Luke cuts in front of me, his arms outstretched and his smile absent. *It's okay*, he mouths soberly, reaching for Lauren.

It's not.

He's been halfway to crazy since we boomeranged back to the house, and he's one of the people responsible for our presence here. We can't trust him.

But Cal's loping unevenly next to Tanvi — struggling with an injured foot — and given my condition, Luke's chances are better than mine. If anyone can get Lauren out of here, maybe he's the one.

Luke hands me the gun. I take it, releasing Lauren into his grasp just as something brushes my ankle. Luke sprints nimbly away, a flash of lightning illuminating his path.

The thing fastens itself around my right foot, impersonating a hand. Fingers that are not fingers pull my weight out from under me, flipping me to the ground. Flinging my arms out to break my fall, I feel cold, wet leaves skim against my chin for an instant before I'm swept into the air. Dangling like a mouse plucked up by its tail. Head swinging close to the ground, legs jutting straight toward the sky. Squirming and howling in the non-hand's grasp.

The light from my lantern gleams carelessly up at me from where it fell. I kick at nothing, shouting raggedly, thunder blocking out my protests with its relentless detonations. Yanking my head up close to my feet, face numb, I reach for the counterfeit fingers. Strong and immoveable as steel chains. Untouchable.

Whatever's holding me shakes me forcefully in its grip. My head and chest tumble, forest floor rising swiftly up to meet me. My brain rattles in my skull. Starbursts form in front of my eyes, pretty and ethereal, swirling into kaleidoscope patterns.

No matter where you go, there you are.

It's something my grandfather used to say, with the smell of butterscotch candy permanently on his breath, and the concept coils through me while I stare at the crisp, whirling colors overlaid against a backdrop of drenched leaves and mud, brain throbbing in my skull. Wrong way down. Swinging, swinging. Shutting my eyes, seasick with motion. Nothing else matters. Here I am. Only here and now, everything else stripped away.

No matter you go there, where are you?

Pill bugs roll themselves into balls if you poke them with sticks. Protecting what's essential. Shielding my head with my arms, I try again to save myself. Holding my head and torso near to my legs, breathing hard. Shivering and hyperventilating in the center of the storm, losing sense. Fighting for something I can't name.

Lightning crashing and the world rocking on its axis, I hold on.

Something brushes against my cheek, cold but not unkind. Gentle, almost. Flinching, I recoil. Body twisting like live bait on a hook.

The tension around my right foot eases. I drop roughly to the forest floor, twigs scratching my hands and exposed arms where I land, smooth plastic polymer resting at my fingertips. Slipping my fingers around the gun, I jolt to my feet. A stoop-shouldered woman stands less than six feet away, one of her arms occupying the same space as a tree. She's middle-aged, maybe. In the dark and deluge it's difficult to tell, and the last thing I want to do is look at her. But it doesn't matter what I think I want. Something inside us always wants to look.

She's bone dry in a shapeless short-sleeved dress and a hat that almost resembles an old swimming cap, her face tilted away from me. Slowly, she turns to look, relishing the moment. My legs tremor under me. Already I'm turning to bolt, running to escape the sight of her.

Half of the woman's face has caved in, the milk-white bone of her cheek partially exposed and her eye bulging from the tragically sunken tissue. The marred side of her face is swollen and misshapen, blood oozing from her ear onto the white neckline of her dress. Damage that a blow to a single side of the head with a brick or shovel might deliver, leaving the other half relatively unscathed.

Not an accident. A murder.

Scrambling through the woods without my lantern, my breathing is decibels too loud. Like a beacon calling to bad things.

If I could find somewhere to hide. Hunker down behind a thick tree, cover myself in leafy, silty camouflage, and hold my breath like a competitive diver. If I could do that for long enough, whatever's after me might lose interest.

But Tanvi. Where is she? My gaze scours the woods as I half-trip and half-sprint, mouth opening despite the danger. "Tanvi!" I howl into the pitch black, shocked that my brain let go of her even for a second. "Tanvi!"

I stumble over something light, accidentally kicking it out ahead of me. Without thinking, I stoop to pick it up. A lone shoe. Child-sized. Lauren's crochet high-top sneaker.

"Tanvi! Cal!" I cry, a single high-pitched voice mimicking me from the darkness, mocking my fear. *Tan-vi. Caaaal.*

Something thumps my back, digs into my skin like it's trying to reach bone. Pitches me forward. My left hand drops the shoe and touches down, preventing me from falling. Lauren's disembodied laugh snakes through the trees, gusting cold on the back of my neck. One step behind me.

I twist and fire, fingers squeezing the trigger like I've done it twenty times before. Trying to kill something with no life in it.

But someone yelps. Falls.

Someone solid and real, lying among the weeds and leaves a stone's throw away, shouting desperately up at me. "Don't shoot. It's me!"

Striding forward, my eyes scrunch Luke and Lauren into fuzzy, unlit focus. Him on the ground behind her, one of his feet held apart from the rest of his body, like a size-ten broken wing.

"You got me," he says, gravel crunching in his tone. "You got me in the fucking foot, man."

I never saw him. Never heard him. Just the damn psychotic laugh of the same young girl lying curled in front of me, fast asleep.

"She okay?" he asks quickly.

"Yeah. She's all right." I stare past Lauren, at the black running shoe I sank a bullet into. In the dark all I can see is the torn fabric of the hole near the ankle, not the wounded tissue underneath. "I didn't mean to … something was … right behind me. It …" I can't string the words together. Can't hold my thoughts upright in my head.

The shadow voices are quiet, watching and waiting. My skin prickles with the knowledge of their presence. Any second now, they'll strike again. We're not safe here. "It had me," I rasp. Spinning abruptly, I face a crowd of tall trees, their trunks as straight as soldiers' spines. Strong, undefeatable. Like this place.

And in this nightmare place, I might as well be eight years old. Too weak to defend anyone. Rotten with uncontrolled fear of the things that might happen while I'm forced to watch. Eyelids peeled wide like a banana with its skin rolled back.

"M, listen to me." The authority vibrating in Luke's larynx sharpens something inside me that was going slack. "You gotta help me up. We have to keep walking."

Tanvi! my mind shrieks. *Don't forget about Tanvi.* We can't go on without her. "Where are the others?" I demand.

"We'll find them." A volley of thunder punctuates Luke's declaration. Lightning blazes through the trees seconds behind it, my eyes squinting after it, making the most of the light. Searching for Tanvi every place she isn't.

Bending, I grab one of Luke's hands and haul him up next to me. He winces as he leans against the nearest tree. I offer the gun carefully, afraid I'll accidentally sink another bullet into him. He was right — the gun's useless. Worse than useless: dangerous only to the people we want to protect.

Settling Lauren in my arms, both crochet high-top sneakers inexplicably back on her feet, I rise cautiously. The pain's stickier now.

Like molasses made of teeth churning through my rib cage. We won't reach the side road in a hurry, but if we don't reach it soon, there might not be anything of us left.

The rain's blinding. I can barely see. Hardly walk. Luke limps behind us, leaking pained noises the thunder intermittently overrules.

I shout Tanvi's name out ahead of us, step after step, minute after minute. Not smart, probably. The more noise we make, the more easily anything can find us. But the speed of sound is faster than we are, and I have to find Tanvi. The odds that something's happened to her multiply with every passing moment.

"Tanvi!" I yell, panic rising in me afresh. "Cal!"

"*Hey*," Luke says.

Ignoring him, I move faster. Lauren's weight tears at my abdomen, immediately halving my pace.

"*Hey*," Luke tries again. And the truth is it's easier talking to him than not, despite what he's done. His voice reminds me I'm not alone.

"What?" I snap.

"You know my real name, right?" When I don't respond quickly enough he says, "It's Greg. The nicknames were Joel's idea. He thought it was funny."

Recriminations simmer silently between us in the dark. "How could you do this?" I ask, the blame hot on my tongue. "You know me."

"Yeah, so well that you don't remember my name," Greg declares. "Look, you weren't supposed to be at her place tonight. You broke up with her months ago, right?"

"Is that when you started planning it? The right I was running my mouth off like an asshole? Did you do this because of me?"

"Not exactly. Joel's wife works with the little girl — Lauren's — mom." Greg's voice catches, weary with the effort of walking and talking at the same time. "Me and Joel started talking about it one night. Not seriously at first. I remembered what you said about the rich grandparents, too. Joel knew the two girls would be at the Mahajans' tonight."

Guilt burns in my veins. I played a role in this. Planted a shadow of an idea in Greg's head. Placed Tanvi in unimaginable danger that I haven't been able to twist her free from.

"You got some payback already — I'm the one who's shot." Greg sounds so matter-of-fact that another layer of unease slips on top of the countless others piled on my shoulders. "If something happens out here, tell my mom it wasn't her fault, all right?" He pauses, his tone shifting. "It wasn't that she didn't raise me right. I know what's right, and I know it's not this. But what I did tonight, it's not on her. She's a good person."

I stop walking and adjust Lauren's weight in my arms, trying not to think about my own mother and the things she doesn't know about me. Things that aren't her fault, either, and that I wouldn't want her to blame herself for. "I'm right in front of you," I tell him. "Odds are if something happens to you, I'm going down too."

Light streaks through the trees, Greg digesting my words. "Maybe, maybe not," he replies pensively. "The kid will probably survive us all. Once we're dead her eyes will snap open and she'll skip straight out of here."

I shiver and glance down at Lauren's sopping blond hair, plastered against her face so that only her nose and a fragment of her mouth are visible. "Wake up, Lauren," I plead, an equal portion of me hoping that she won't. If she opens her eyes she's just as likely to say something sinister I don't want to hear as she is to be the kid I met last Christmas.

Pausing again, I lean back against a tree, lecturing myself. Telling the soft, crumbling parts of me that I can walk on like this for as long as it takes, that it doesn't really hurt much. I'm beyond pain.

Greg catches up to me, the same tree supporting his frame. It's an old hemlock, I think. Not poisonous like it sounds. The mighty ones, like this, have big, high root systems that can bring down other trees if they fall.

Everything is interconnected. Sometimes we just can't see it.

Glancing sideways at Greg, I admit, "I don't know how much longer I can do this." If I bend to set Lauren down, picking her up again will be too difficult. I can't leave her here, but I can't make it much further with her in my arms.

Greg's head dips, rain running clear off his chin and nose like an opened tap. He's angled his right heel away from the ground, keeping the pressure on his toes instead. "I can't walk much longer, either. We can stop any time. Wait for whatever's going to happen next."

Not what I want to hear. Frowning, I slam my eyelashes shut. Think of Tanvi sitting cross-legged on my bed, brushing her hair back into place with her fingers. After she'd gone, my room would still smell of her shampoo. Especially my pillow. I'd fall asleep to the scent of grapefruit or sweet grass and shea butter.

I shout Tanvi's name into the woods, my fingers numb from Lauren's weight. If the rest of me were as deadened as my hands, I'd be better off. Lauren's small-boned, not even as heavy as your average ten-year-old. Any other day, carrying her would be no challenge. But I've hit the ceiling. Beyond that, I'll find only rips and tears. Dissolution into pieces.

"You gotta do what you gotta do," Greg tells me. "It's no good all of us being stranded out here when you might be able to make it to the road by yourself. You can set the girl down. I'll sit with her. Wait for help." He raises the gun as if ready to pass it off a second time.

I shake my head, raindrops leaking between my lips and rushing down my throat. "Hold on to it," I counter. "You wait here. I'll send someone back for you."

"Right." Greg laughs in my face, his eyes lit with doubt and irritation. "You're never going to make it holding on to her, M. But you do what you want. I'm taking a breather."

His laugh clings to me as I walk away, my footsteps uncertain and every breath lined with strain and ache. The more distance I put between us, the more tinged with madness Greg's laughter becomes, until I yearn for two more hands to clap over my ears. Finally, the thunder steals between us, erasing any sign of Greg's presence.

When I reach the overgrown driveway minutes later, I could swear I hear it again. His hyena giggle like a manic cackle of frustration from deep behind me in the forest.

He knows what's in store. Sees it coming.

I know it too, yet I keep going. Rounding a bend that will likely return me to Shantallow. Yelling Tanvi's name into the rain like a little boy lost or the last survivor of a sinking ship, staring up at the sky and counting stars, waiting for the ocean to take him.

17

Tanvi's voice trickles out of the darkness, rainwater curdling in my stomach at the sound of another sick joke. At first the noise is faint, easily ascribed to my imagination. As I continue along the bend in the path, it amplifies into a roar. "Misha!"

A body comes barreling out of the trees. Every inch soaking wet. Tall for a girl. A torrent of dark hair hanging in her face, rendering her eyes a secret. In the distance, behind her, Cal limps forward, zombie-like, lantern light bobbing beside him.

"Thank God you still have her," Tanvi declares, hurtling forward to peer into Lauren's sleeping face. "I don't know how we lost you. It was like you just disappeared."

"I've been looking for you all this time." My voice splinters as it hits the air. Gratitude for Tanvi's living presence balances with regret that she didn't make it out to the side road. No one's coming for us. We're all we have.

"Where's Luke?" Tanvi gapes behind me as if he might materialize.

"Out there somewhere, waiting for us to bring help." I start to explain, Cal joining us and Tanvi cutting me off, extending her arms and silently assuming her cousin's weight.

Suddenly Lauren's voice whispers in my ear, warm and as sickly sweet as treacle, "You must destroy them totally. Make no treaty with them and show them no mercy."

Thunder claps over our heads, frenzied shadow voices chanting and shrieking from the woods behind us. "What do they want?" Cal yells, shaking his head and pressing his fingers into his hairline nearly hard enough to draw blood. "Why can't they just leave us alone?"

There's only one way to go — the direction the voices herd us in, bearing down on us from just a few paces behind. Hidden by the trees and the dark, their anger and lunacy runs through me like a live wire as we hobble along the path, surviving by seconds and inches.

I've been winding my way around the same bend for too long already. When there's only one way left to run, that's where you scurry, and when we reach the gospel writers' charred van — the abandoned old house jeering victoriously down at us from behind it — I wait for a shock that doesn't come. Shantallow's been lying in wait since the minute we walked away from it earlier, positioned at the end of every dirt path we'd ever find.

Sagging at the waist, I stifle a chuckle that sticks to the walls of my diaphragm like sand inside a swimsuit. *Ha-ha-ha.* Sound hiccups out of my body. My lack of control triggers a faulty reflex mechanism, short-circuiting. Laughing breathlessly, my eyes water and my ribs quiver painfully.

Tanvi and Cal stare at me with sharp, stricken faces. Meanwhile the voices close in, forming an invisible circle around us, a noose tightening. There's nowhere to go — we're surrounded. "The sun will be darkened, and the moon will not give its light," a mangled male voice growls, its timbre unholy and twisted with hate. "The stars will fall from the sky."

"Don't listen to them!" Tanvi screams. Kneeling to set Lauren down in the wet grass, she arches her body over her cousin's. With Lauren shielded as best as Tanvi can manage, Tanvi closes her eyes and fastens her hands to her ears, sealing herself off from the outside world.

Cal turns away from me to lower himself by her side. Planting the lantern in the dirt, his hands encircle his head like a helmet. Before I can move, something tugs at my shirt, flipping it up to expose my lower chest. Hot breath warms my drenched neck. My teeth chatter in my jaw, heart thwacking and accelerating, threatening to explode. Slamming my eyes shut, I plug my ears with my palms.

Inside my head, the woman from the woods grins brokenly at my fear. The rain pounds on, lightning exploding through the delicate skin of my eyelids. My arms and legs set like granite, unmoving. Pressure cups my head, wanting to crush my skull. Still, my eyes fight temptation. I won't look at her broken cheek or the eye that no longer fits smoothly within her socket. I won't listen to their insane ravings and lies. You can't make me.

But of course they can. They can do anything they want.

Scared as I am, anger itches in my bones. The human soul doesn't want to cower. The injustice burns in my fingertips. Memories sharpen and then lose focus, ceding to others. My parents slow dancing in a dimly lit kitchen, dishes drying on the countertop rack. Mom covering up a black eye. Balancing on top of my dad's shoulders at a free summer concert during one of his more sober periods, his hands holding my lower legs in place so I wouldn't slip. He knew the words to every song. He swayed his hips as he sang along.

Fingers grip my shoulders from behind. Softly, then firmly. Squeeze into tissue. Something brushes my arm. Takes my hand in its own. Four fingers. One thumb.

It shouldn't feel so real, so solid. Another trick. This one pries the fingers of one hand forcefully from my ear. My eyes jerk open and stare into hers.

Tanvi. Cal at her side, having taken temporary possession of Lauren. The voices have stopped, or maybe been temporarily displaced by the living.

Tanvi swivels to squint at the house, her face taut with rancor.

"I can't make it out like this," Cal says, looking only at her. "If I can wrap up my foot and get some of those painkillers into my system, rest a little, I'll have a better chance."

"We can't go back in there." Tanvi flinches, fresh raindrops skating down her forehead and losing themselves in her hair.

Shivering in my wet second skin, my eyes fasten on hers. "It had me in the woods. It's not just the house we need to worry about." I don't want to set foot inside any more than she does — malevolence colonizing every corner, infecting our minds with hopelessness. "We're too tired, and most of us are injured. We can't keep going. In the morning at least the visibility will be better."

"We can stay on the porch," Cal suggests, his syllables worn down to nubs. "We'll stay dry, and the second we see the sun come up we're out of here. We're all gonna get out. But first I need to go into the house and grab the pills and first aid kit."

Tanvi's fingers skim his arm in silent acceptance. I turn away like I don't see it, heading for the house and giving the van a wide berth. Cal and Tanvi follow quietly.

"Stay out here with them," Cal instructs as he climbs the porch stairs to hand me the lantern.

He doesn't need to say it, but I nod, shoes squelching on the porch's ancient wooden planks. "Leave the front door open," I tell him. "I'll keep one foot inside." Half in, half out. That's as much protection as I can offer.

"The first aid kit's by the fireplace," I shout after him as Cal edges reluctantly past me, into the bowels of Shantallow. Tanvi lowers herself and Lauren onto the middle step, refusing to take more than partial shelter under Shantallow's roof. She stares over her shoulder at the last spot where Cal was visible in the main corridor, eyebrows knitting into an anxious furrow.

"Keep talking, Cal!" she yells, rain coating her lower legs.

"There's still one lantern in here," he shouts back, the distance and dense black air between us muffling his words. "Wait, the —"

"What?" I prompt.

"Nothing. I have what I need. I'm coming back."

Can it be that simple? Tanvi and I glance at each other in wonder. Then the lantern light dims in my hand. Flickers. Dies.

In the absence of light, the sloping porch roof instantly becomes claustrophobic. A closing casket lid. My fingers feel for the battery compartment, fiddling with the cluster of batteries, trying to force more life out of them than they're willing to offer. There's no resuscitating them. They've given up for good.

Cal bolts out of the house, pillow under one arm, first aid kit tucked under the other, his hands clutching a loaf of bread and a stack of paper cups. Stumbling into my shoulder in the darkness, he exclaims, "*Shit!*"

"I'll go back for the other lantern," he offers, his inflection more thread-like than whole — straw trembling in the wind.

"No!" Tanvi objects. "Forget it. We don't need it."

I grab the doorknob, closing the front door firmly behind him. "Did you see anything?"

Cal's lower lip slips. "Not exactly." He bends to deposit the collection of supplies on the porch, lining them up against the wall of the house. Sinking down next to them, he clicks open the first aid kit. "The ..." He retrieves the roll of elastic cloth bandage and begins wrapping his foot. "The cross from the mantelpiece was missing."

My weight shifts, the porch squealing in response.

Tanvi's silent from the steps.

"You okay, T.V.?" Cal asks.

"Yeah," she replies, her voice low. "You guys can sleep, if you want. I'll keep watch. I'm not tired." Her foot drums the bottom step.

"No one's sleeping," Cal declares. A sound like Tic Tacs rattling in their package agitates across the length of the porch. He must have the tramadol bottle in his hand. "You want a couple, Misha?"

Sliding down on the floorboards, I position myself between Tanvi and Cal. When you take your eyes off people, they disappear. From my spot near the door I'll be able to keep an eye on them both. "I'm okay," I tell him. With no clue when I swallowed the last pill, I'm better off sucking up the pain and keeping my clear head.

"You're definitely not okay," Tanvi says, the razor-sharp point in her voice making me flinch.

I was never okay to begin with. We both have all the proof we need.

"You looked like you were ready to collapse when we found you," she continues. "If your ribs are broken, you're not supposed to lift more than ten pounds. I'm glad you did, but they say you're not even supposed to vacuum with a chest injury. Does it hurt to breathe?"

"The ribs might just be bruised," I say, her question disappearing between porch floorboards as the innocent meaning behind her original comment sinks into my cells. She wasn't slamming me. If anything, that was concern.

A few feet away, Tanvi struggles to her feet, hefting Lauren onto the porch with her. Cal reaches for the pillow he brought out from the house, repositioning it so that Tanvi can settle her cousin comfortably on the worn planks, her head nesting on synthetic fibers.

"How's your ankle doing?" Tanvi asks, sitting down by Cal's feet and Lauren's head so that she's at the epicenter of our group.

Suddenly a woman screams from nearby in the forest. Blood-curdling and cut short.

Next to me, Tanvi's breath catches. My hands freeze at the end of my arms, dangling into darkness. Our silence stretches like an elastic band tugged to breaking point. In the strained quiet the rain begins to ease, its rhythmic tapping on the porch roof slowing and softening.

"That sounded like an actual person," Cal blurts. "Maybe there's somebody else out here with us."

My leg twitches, floorboards grumbling. The woman from the forest's exposed cheekbone gleams in my memory. "I saw something — someone — earlier in the woods," I say, beginning to explain about the dead woman.

A second shriek slices the air, rapidly subsiding into a whimper. More animal than human. Something with its paw snared in a trap, bloody and broken.

Tanvi rocks back and forth, her head bobbing and the reverberations from the motion veining out along the floorboards. For a long while none of us speak. We listen for the rain and the screams from the woods that break nature's silence, time after time, in an irregular cycle. The repetition should desensitize us. But that's not how it works. Anticipating the noises is as harrowing as their arrival.

Finally my mouth dries up and my joints stiffen. "I need water," I whisper to Cal. "Hand me a cup."

Cal doesn't stir. Tanvi cranes her neck toward him, immediately scooching closer on the floorboards. "Hey," she says loudly, grabbing his leg. "Cal!"

He jumps in his sleep, some newly woken limb bumping into the first aid kit. "What?" he cries. "What's happening?"

"Nothing." Relief sugars Tanvi's tone. "It's okay. I just wanted to make sure you were all right." Not like John or Lauren. Cal's only been lulled into dreamland by the tramadol. "Pass me a couple cups."

He does as she asks, Tanvi holding one out to me. I advance warily down the porch steps, extending my arm into the rain where the cup can catch it. The storm has become more drizzle than downpour. It takes forever to gather a single gulp.

From somewhere behind the tree line the woman sobs and squeals. I recoil, my right foot jumping backwards, heel smacking the porch's bottom step. Forcing my shaking hand back into the air, I hold my ground. When I drink, the water tastes warm but clean. Everything else might be rotting, but the air remains breathable, the water drinkable, and the trees healthy and infinite. Maybe because the unnatural things that live here don't touch them.

"Do you want water?" I ask Tanvi.

She drifts down the steps to hand me her cup, thanking me when I return it to her lined with a couple of teaspoon's worth of rainwater minutes later. Cal's wordless in the shadows, likely fallen back to sleep. Before retreating under the porch roof again I search the sky for hints of morning — the comfort of impenetrable obsidian sky yielding to somber blue.

"What do you see?" Tanvi asks from behind me.

"Nothing." A hundred coats of black paint overlaid against the night sky, smothering the moon and stars.

Settling myself in my previous space on the floorboards, I think of my mom and Natalya. The police would have found my car outside the Mahajan house. Cal's too. Keion would've jumped into his cab to search for me.

Tanvi's voice steals out from the darkness. "Why were you outside my house tonight?"

It's not how it looks. That's what I would've said before. But from here, I can't lie to her. We've come too far for that.

"Sometimes I drive by," I admit. "Not a lot. And not to stalk you." I could add I'd never hurt her, but who would believe that?

Leaning forward, I pull my chin in toward my chest. Breathe in and out. Feel the weight of last spring settle into my back and limbs, burning my skin with regret and self-accusations.

"This is the place from the nightmare, isn't it?" she says. "Only we're not alone here like in the dream."

I nod, momentarily forgetting that Tanvi probably can't make it out in the dark. "I dreamt about it more times than I can count," I confess. "I was having the nightmares before I met you. The very first time I saw you, I recognized you from the dreams." Although I've never told her that before, it's easier than talking about the ugly things I did.

In my imagination she purses her lips, refusing to look at me. "You should never have kept it from me all that time," she says.

A metallic ping from the driveway steers my eyes in the direction of the van. The sound of a stone — or something similar — hitting the hood.

"It's nothing," Tanvi murmurs unconvincingly after a ten-second delay. "What do you think it all means? Why are we here?"

"I have no idea. Sorry." Once the word has slipped out others bloat in my mouth, forcing their way onto the sagging porch. "I'm sorry for everything. I never should've —"

"Don't," Tanvi snaps. "I don't want to hear it. We need to concentrate on getting through this, and none of that is going to help."

"But you have to know that I'm never going to let anything like that happen again. I know I can't be with anyone. Not like when I was with you. I can't handle it." There are some advantages to starless night; I'm not sure I could say these things aloud if she could look me in the eye. "It's too much to lose. It fucks me up in a way that's not normal."

"That's your idea of how to handle your massive anger and insecurity problems?" Tanvi's bitterness ruptures the darkness and gleams hot. "To be alone from now on?"

From now on. The phrase cartwheels in my head, merging with the final memory of her in my bedroom, down on the floor surrounded by broken glass. If she'd swept her arms and legs out along the hardwood, making the same vigorously graceful swinging movements used to create a snow angel, there would have been blood.

I never want to feel that way again. Sick with myself for a handful of seconds of noxious gratification that would never have plagued a normal person in the first place.

"That won't fix anything, Misha," Tanvi continues. "You think you can just go on pretending that you're this amazing guy — obsessing over looking and acting the right way twenty-four-seven — when in reality you don't have a life."

"I have a life." A future. Despite my meltdown last spring, I never let my grades slip. Senior year they'll be better than ever. I've dropped cross-country, swapping it for one of the less time-intensive school clubs to make sure of that. There's every reason to believe that come next September I'll be enrolled at the University of Toronto's Faculty of Applied Science & Engineering. I'll study hard. Graduate. Land a job that gives me more money than I need.

"But it's fake," she counters. "Like an airbrushed photo. If it was real you wouldn't have to try so hard constantly."

"People *try* in life, Tanvi," I argue, resentment crusting my tone before I can stop it. "Maybe just not the people you know. Maybe things come easily for them."

"Because they have money? Is that what you're implying? They don't all have money, Misha. Anyway, money doesn't necessarily make everything easy. And if I don't understand what it's been like for you growing up, maybe it's because you never told me. Not really. You always skimmed the surface. I never really knew you until the end."

"Don't say that. You knew the best version of me. The person I want to be."

"But that you've given up on now to hide away? How does that make any sense? *Shit.*" She stops herself short. "I don't care, okay. Pretend to be whoever you want. It doesn't matter. Just don't sit here telling me you're sorry and expect me to forgive you — that's never going to happen."

"I don't expect you to forgive me."

One of her shoes scuffs against the floor. The rest of her betrays no sound.

Tanvi leaps restlessly to her feet. "None of that matters anymore." She glides past with a swiftness that generates a current. The gust brushes my face as Tanvi hurries down the steps to hold her cup aloft into the rain. "The only thing that does is getting home."

"We will."

"We all keep saying that, and here we are." Tanvi stares up into a sky that remains stubbornly night. "It should be getting light by now."

I've thought the same. We've been here for an eternity.

Tanvi pivots, jumping in her skin with a force the darkness can't hide. Pointing at the porch stairs, she gasps, "Did you see her?"

The dilapidated steps protrude from the spot directly ahead of me. My eyes laser into unoccupied space, fingertips tingling in fear. "I don't — I don't see anything," I stammer. Not this time. It was the woman from the forest who tugged at my shirt before. Her hot breath on my neck. Her that I can't see in front of me now. But that doesn't mean she isn't here.

"Alice," Tanvi whispers, her voice like a feather caught in a squall. "She was right there on the steps. So close. You could've taken a couple of steps and touched her."

"Alice," I repeat. *Alice who called Tanvi directly after she had the nightmare, despite having left the land of the living months earlier.*

"I know." Tanvi's wrists hug her waist as she approaches the porch, her foot landing tentatively on the bottom step. "I know that's not possible. It's this place, playing with us again. But ..."

"But?" I prompt.

"She didn't look like somebody who would be here. She looked like her usual self, only worried, concerned." Tanvi's right leg rocks against the step, the other refusing to join it. "Not scary or threatening. I think she might even have been in pajamas. A pair my nonna gave her for Christmas years ago. They had raccoons on them."

Raccoon pajamas. I nearly crack a smile at the innocuous picture.

BAM.

A vintage concert T-shirt snaps into place behind my eyes, forcibly dislodging the pajamas.

Raleigh, NC

Atlanta, GA

Virginia Beach, VA

The vision of city tour stops itemized on worn cotton races along my brain circuitry, Alice's message to Tanvi sprinting in sync, setting my prefrontal cortex alight. *When the time comes, don't let the darkness inside you.*

"I think I saw my father too," I admit. Three times at least. Behind the carriage house where I laid Mark's body on the grass, inside on the staircase, and back in the van before we arrived. "But he couldn't be here either."

Could he?

Closing the distance between us, Tanvi climbs the steps. Stands on the spot where her aunt stood. Lays her palm flush against the adjacent post, feeling for any trace of Alice's warmth while my mind twists and flips — like a fish yanked out of water — before exploding into realization.

18

My eyelashes are sticky and refuse to open. My teeth and tongue taste of ash and dry earth. The air hangs heavy and stale, like a windowless room with its door locked for days. Infinite quiet fills my ears. The sound a cactus makes growing in the desert, spines knifing out from its skin, keeping the plant safe from all but a select few predators.

Forcing my right arm to move is about as simple as breaststroking through quicksand. But I do it. It's the only way I can pry open my eyes. Clamping my fingers to my eyelids and separating them.

Once that's accomplished I can't understand what the problem was. My eyelashes glide open and shut with ease, narrowing their angle to protect my retinas from the sun's tenacious gleam.

A field of lush green grass cradles my back. I comb my fingers through the cool, narrow blades as I sit up and stare at a familiar two-storey house. The sun's rays bounce magnanimously off its fresh white paint. A smaller outbuilding abuts the main structure like an eager sidekick. Pale blue shutters flank the house's upper windows, their inner aspects touching the porch roof. A triangular peak divides the roof in two, elevating the house's appearance from unremarkable to medium-picturesque.

I know its face, but I can't place it. Can't think what I'm doing here, either. My mind's clouded by a web of fog.

A dark-haired boy no older than nine jogs past me, fists up in front of him, thumbs together at the knuckles as he bends his head to his hands and blows. A whistle rings out — loud and clear — breaking the silence. Charging toward the house, the boy's hands part, the blade of grass caught between them fluttering to the ground.

"Wait!" I call after him.

I run too, trying to follow. Questions agitate in my throat. *Where am I? How did I get here?* My legs jerk in slow motion, falling further behind with each second. The house's front door thuds shut before I can reach it, the boy disappearing inside.

Gripping the doorknob, I find it unlocked. Muffled voices filter through the main corridor as I troop clumsily inside. A man and a woman arguing. The noise of their exchange guides me into the kitchen, where a middle-aged man stands in the middle of the room with his sleeves rolled up to his elbows and a woman in a shapeless light blue dress leans against a spotless counter, empty save for a large white mixing bowl.

Neither of them notices me. I'm the shadow of a speck of dust.

"You've heard the strange things she says," the woman insists, her eyes hooded and fearful. "You've seen her tremors and twitches. They're worse with every passing day. So are her headaches. She needs to see the doctor. She never sleeps anymore. She wanders the hallways jabbering to herself. She frightens me, Thomas."

"You know she doesn't want to see the doctor," the man contradicts. "She's said as much. She's a very devout girl. We should be pleased and proud. Not many young people are as pious these days."

"It's not piety. It's something else." The woman's voice drops like an elevator with its cables snipped. "She's unnatural. My mother is frightened of her too."

A third voice gusts through my body from directly behind me. I stagger forward, the presence lumbering along with me to stay close. Whirling to look at it, I struggle to hold my gaze. A teenage girl, her long brown hair tied back with ribbon, grins with unsettling saccharine sweetness. Her top and ankle-length skirt are simple and austere, bony shoulders jabbing up under the white fabric. Underneath her smile, the girl exudes a chilling dissatisfaction. Her pupils glint with deception and something else I can't pinpoint. Something I want to turn away from.

"You can see me, can't you?" I say. "What is this place?"

"Who is frightened?" the teenage girl asks, staring past me as though she doesn't need me to move aside to do it.

The man frowns and tilts his head. "Why, no one's frightened, Josephine. You must have misheard."

"It's only that I'm frightened *for you*," the woman corrects, gathering her bravery in close like a shawl. "You've been feeling poorly for so long, Josephine, dear. We wouldn't be doing right by you if we didn't insist you see Doctor Stewart."

Josephine bites her lip, her eyelids puffy and traced with vaulting purple veins. "I would never break the fifth commandment, Mother. I don't want to displease you. But what a waste of time that would be for Doctor Stewart. I feel perfectly well."

"Now, that's not so." The woman reluctantly pats her daughter's hand. "All your spells."

Josephine's eyes begin to roll back in her head. She stops them dead, refocusing her gaze as her lips manufacture a second smile. "I've been chosen, Mother. I'm being tested. If you would pray with me, you'd understand. God would tell you the same way he's told me. God can heal all afflictions."

Josephine's parents shrink under the weight of their deference, their exchanged glance sparking with trepidation. Her mother ventures, "Well, of course he can, but —"

"Worship the Lord your God, and his blessing will be on your food and water," Josephine declares, her right fingers jerking at her side. "I will take away sickness from among you. Pay attention to what I say; turn your ear to my words. Do not let them out of your sight, keep them within your heart; for they are life to those who find them and health to one's whole body."

She bows her head reverently. "Don't you see, Mother? Who are we to question the word of God? I am happy to be tested. Honored."

Josephine's eyes flick up to mine. They burn like battery acid. "You should be honored also." Leaping forward, she knocks me to the floor.

She's stronger than she looks, and I'm caught off guard. A bug on a windscreen taken out by a windshield wiper. I go down quick and clean. Falling and falling, never hitting ground. Sinking through black soup and blue skies. My head rolling over my feet, accelerating until I've forgotten how to breathe.

Dead maybe. Or something like it.

What's *like* dead? That's the question, isn't it?

When I stop plunging, I'm standing deep in the woods, crowded by trees as tall as skyscrapers. They form ceilings and walls of shade, labyrinths within labyrinths. They camouflage secrets. Bury lies. Hide you away from the world, if that's what you want.

But I don't. Not now. I don't want to see what happens next.

Josephine's long hair dances in the wind, her dress billowing up around her knees. "I will pray for your soul, Mother," she cries.

"I don't understand." The woman from the kitchen stares bewilderedly out from under a form-fitting hat. "Where's the child you spoke of? The one you said you heard sobbing for her mother."

"Am I not your child, Mother? Would you have come to soothe me had I been crying in the woods?" Josephine's lips flatten into a treacherous line. "See that you do not despise one of these little ones. For I tell you that in heaven their angels always see the face of my

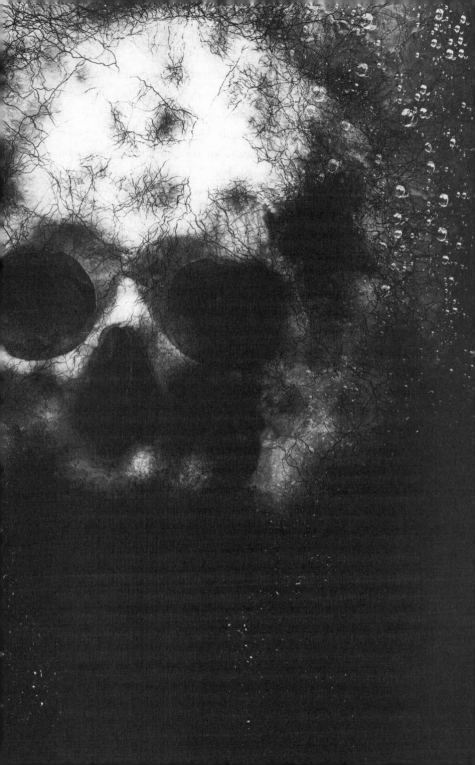

Father who is in heaven." She reaches behind the wide trunk of the nearest tree, her fingers snaking around the handle of a shovel.

"What are you doing?" The woman turns to run.

Josephine swings, the shovel crunching into her mother's shoulders from behind. She crumples to the deadfall with a groan. The girl doesn't hesitate; she shows less mercy than a spider that wraps its prey in silk and then waits for it to die. Josephine's weapon of choice isn't sharp or clever, but it does the job. She belts her mother repeatedly, her forehead creasing in concentration with each blow. Within moments Josephine's mother is a motionless, pulpy mass, one side of her face caved in, the breeze whistling morosely through the trees.

Too late, I realize I should've done something to stop the murder. My body doesn't obey me anymore — I'm like a portrait in a frame — but my helplessness doesn't entirely excuse my lack of intervention.

"Why?" I ask furiously. "Why do this?"

Josephine's shovel digs resolutely into the brush and soil at her feet. "If your hand causes you to stumble, cut it off; it is better for you to enter life crippled, than, having your two hands, to go into hell, into the unquenchable fire." She whistles while she works, cheerfully digging her mother's grave.

Once she's rolled the remains into a shallow pit, Josephine hurriedly covers them with brush and dirt. Batting the filth from her twitching hands and the front of her dress, she sets out for home, and I lurch along with her. Repelled by her presence but unable to resist.

Before long we veer onto a dirt path wide enough for a horse and buggy. Ahead a sign sways gently in the breeze. SHANTALLOW.

Faint recognition ripples through me. *No matter where you go, there you are.*

"Where have you been?" demands the nine-year-old boy as Josephine trudges through her front door, disheveled and ashen. "Where's Mother?"

"Gone. I tried to bring her back. She wouldn't come." Josephine's hand grazes the boy's cheek. "I'm sorry, Walter. But she isn't righteous like we are. I'm afraid she's run off with another man."

"She wouldn't," the boy denies, face reddening. "She's devoted to Father. You take it back."

Josephine sighs tiredly. "You're too young. I shouldn't say such things. Forgive me."

Black mist ascends slowly from the floor. Enveloping my feet first. Then cutting me off at the knees. Swallowing me whole and regurgitating my form in a hallway, near the top of a staircase where Josephine faces off against a small, white-haired woman. At the bottom of the stairs, a wheelchair that must be hers squats emptily in wait.

"You've been trying to turn Father against me," Josephine hisses. "Don't deny it."

The old woman clutches skittishly at her robe, her pale, watery eyes pleading with the girl. "He only wants to search for your mother. There might have been an accident."

"There was no accident. She abandoned us." Josephine's lips appear nearly blue in the dimly lit hallway, her pupils dilating wolf- ishly. "She was faithless and immoral. I pray for her. You should too, Grandmother."

"You shouldn't speak about your mother so." The old woman's voice splinters. "You're a wicked girl. What other sort would utter such lies about the woman who gave birth to her? I don't know why your father has let them go unchallenged, but I won't. Not any longer. You may have bewitched him somehow, but your father needs to hear sense. Your unearthly stares and your ways of twisting the word of God have unnerved me for long enough."

Josephine gurgles with laughter. "What makes you think Father would believe you over me? I'm his blood. You're only a useless old woman." She grasps her grandmother's shoulders, propelling the woman stealthily backwards so that the two of them hover at the very top of the stairs.

"Stop!" the old woman cries, clawing at her granddaughter's arms, and then her hair. "You are my flesh and blood too. I beg you." Her fingernails dig into Josephine's skull, Josephine jerking under her touch but holding fast to her grandmother. "May the Lord judge between me and you, may the Lord avenge me against you, but my hand shall not be against you."

"Don't hurt her!" I warn. I can't allow it to happen again.

But my feet are stupid. They move like bricks. Heavy and imprecise. Sliding my body between Josephine and her grandmother, I'm somehow as skinny as a paper clip. Like no shield whatsoever.

Josephine hesitates. A spindly branch of blood forms on her forehead as the old woman shrieks, "That's the word of God. We must obey it. You shall not murder. If you love me, you will keep my commandments."

The blood streams into one of Josephine's eyebrows, staining it vivid red. "How dare you try to use his words against me when I love and worship him a thousand times more than you do?" Josephine scowls, shaking her grandmother into submission. "Do not yield to them or listen to them. Show them no pity. Do not spare them or shield them. You must certainly put them to death. Your hand must be the first in putting them to death."

She releases her grandmother with a violent shove. The old woman's head cracks against the wooden steps, her body thumping after it. Sliding freefall down the staircase in a jumble of lifeless limbs. The wheelchair squeaks in agony as her kneecap collides with one of the spoked wheels.

"Father!" Josephine wails, contorting her face into a mask of grief. "Come quick! There's been an accident."

Darkness descends without warning. Falling fast and furious, but weightless as snow. I stumble along the corridor, trying to escape it. In this place where I can't run, the void breathes cold on my heels and the back of my neck. It trips me to the ground, ingesting me in a single gulp.

For a moment the entire world burns black with absence. If you're drawn to light, does that make you a moth? I need help. Intervention.

Fluttering toward something that might be a candle or an electric spark, my mind recovers lost words and chants them like a prayer:

> Moon and stars, forever shine,
> Moon and stars, friends of mine,
> I close my eyes and trust your light,
> I close my eyes and say goodnight,
> Watch over me while I am gone,
> Watch over me until the dawn.

Suddenly I blink down at a large wooden table. It's littered with fabric swatches, colorful spools of thread, and tools I don't recognize. I'm dizzy and confused, adrift. Then I see the man from the kitchen. Josephine's father. He's perched on a stool, bent over a woman's hat, fussing with the faux flower affixed to its side. His hands shake turbulently as he glares at them in frustration.

Josephine appears in the doorway, her face mottled gray and thin. "Can't I help? It's been days since I've spent any time working alongside you."

The man's eyes brim with unspilled tears. "I've been struck down, Josephine. I can't still my hands, nor my thoughts. My mouth stings with the point of a hundred needles. Why has God cursed us?"

He's as sick as she is. The two of them suffering from something I don't understand. The worst kind of sickness. One that folds back in on itself like a collapsible map, stealing sense and obscuring truth.

Josephine scurries to her father's side. "Father, no. You mustn't say that. He's only testing us. Pray with me now." She kneels on the floor beside him, clasping her hands together as her father struggles for breath.

"You pray for me, child," he gasps, slumping in his seat.

Oxygen stutters in his esophagus, eyes closing and his body rapidly resigning itself to failure.

"No!" Josephine surges to her feet, embracing her father as he leaves the world of the living. Her cheek on his shoulder, her eyes shut against the new realities of her existence. Orphaned, alone in the world except for her brother.

Darkness hovers above me, lapping the ceiling like storm waves. I brace myself against its descent. But this time darkness doesn't fall. I remain steadily in place, watching with dread.

Josephine lets go of her father, leaving him sagging on his stool like someone who's only fallen asleep on the job. Staring up at the ceiling, her hands scrunch into quaking fists. She howls in protest. Rage and heartache splice into an inhuman scream. Her fists strike the table with a vehemence that makes it leap.

Those same hands, pale and freckled, pummel air as she rasps, "You, shadowy spirit, I command you, leave this place. You don't belong here."

She means to hurt me, if only she could. But her hands can't reach me anymore. I'm miles beyond, while standing right next to her.

Josephine's eyes glow with outrage. Narrowing her gaze, she backs out of the room, her back hunched like an angry cat. "You presence mocks me, serpent. You are not welcome here." She stomps upstairs, her gait uneven and her right hand making the sign of the cross.

I look on as Josephine and her brother drag their father's body up to her parents' bedroom, pulling a sheet solemnly over their father's head. "We need to tell someone he's passed," Walter says, his eyes pink-lined from sobbing as he and Josephine sit cross-legged on the floor beside the bed. "We should ride into town and fetch Father Carey."

"Shhh," Josephine intones, her eyes tender the way I've only ever seen them with her brother or father. "We mustn't tell anyone. We only need to pray. God can bring him back for us. He will. I know he will. It's another test. *Everyone who lives and believes in me shall never die.*" Blanching, she suddenly clutches her stomach.

"Your pains again?" Walter coils his arms around his knees. "If you leave me, I'll have no one. You can't leave me here, Josephine. Promise me."

"I would never leave you."

Walter frowns, the dark pouches under his eyes aging him by years. "You would if God wanted you to. You do everything he wants."

"Yes, but he wouldn't want me to leave you," his sister assures him, a deliberate gentleness smoothing any edges from her voice.

"How do you know?" the boy asks.

Persistent banging from downstairs commands their attention. Overhead a black cloud begins to bubble, preparing to boil. "What are you waiting for?" I roar up at it. "Take me away." No one in their right mind would choose to be here. Witnessing horror after horror, helpless to intervene.

"There's someone at the door," Walter cries.

He clambers to his feet, Josephine shrieking after him, "Wait! Don't answer it."

I shout along with her, warning whoever's on the other side of the door. "Get away! It's not safe here."

Josephine glares defiantly into the hall, as if she can see me. "You will not stop any of this," she declares. "The deeds are already done."

Gathering her skirt, she stands carefully. Fighting to keep her balance as she shambles down the steps that reunite her with her brother while she conceals something within the folds of her skirt.

A lanky young man in a flat cap stands uncertainly next to Walter in the corridor. "I'm sorry to bother you, miss," he says. "My name is Henry Adler. I'm looking for the Farwell house." He bends his head, his cheeks flushing. "I arrived by train. Hopped on the railway traveling west and I'm afraid I may have jumped off too late."

"The railroad tracks are miles and miles from here," Josephine declares, eyes landing on Henry's patched knapsack and then the beads of sweat dotting his forehead.

Henry nods. "I've been walking since morning. I'd be real grateful if you could spare some water."

Josephine ignores the request. "The Farwell house is all the way over on the east side of Middlesbrough, I'm afraid. We've never met before, so I don't suppose you're part of the Farwell family?"

"No, miss. Charlie Farwell and I were in the war together. I've only come to pay him a visit."

"Charlie lost his left leg in the Battle of Vimy Ridge," Walter chimes in.

"Yes, he did." Henry frowns, biting the inside of his cheek. "Although victory was ours, we lost thousands of men in the battle."

He doesn't see the hammer reeling toward his head, catching him an inch above one eyebrow. Hobbling backwards, Henry collapses against the front door. Josephine charges again. Her reflexes are sluggish, her balance poor. The hammer bashes into Henry's ear. Blood oozes onto his neck, dripping onto the floor and fanning out under him in a semicircle of crimson, his eyes slapping shut as his body slides to the ground.

"You didn't have to kill him!" Walter screams. "He just wanted water. We could have given him all the water a person could drink."

"He's not dead." Josephine extends a crooked finger, aiming it at Henry's chest. "You see, he's still breathing."

Walter scrambles closer, bending over Henry's prone body. "There's so much blood. We have to fetch Doctor Stewart quick."

"We can't do that. Think of Father. If anyone sees him, they'll want to bury him. We must wait for God's miracle." Josephine's right leg quivers, her eyes lost in thought. "Fetch me some rope from Father's workshop. Quickly now."

Her brother dashes into the room behind the kitchen, emerging with a thick length of rope. Josephine ties Henry's hands taut behind his back. Then binds his feet. His bleeding slows, but he doesn't regain consciousness.

"You shouldn't have hurt him," Walter laments in a small voice. "He was in the war. He fought for our country."

"I did what I had to do," Josephine snaps. "Don't you understand that he would have asked for Father? He would have wanted him to bring him into town or the Farwell house. He would have ruined everything. We need time. Days. A miracle can't be rushed."

"But what do we do now?" Walter's posture deflates, shoulders rounding and knees buckling.

"We wait." She reaches out to ruffle her brother's hair. "Have faith."

Returning to the scene of her father's death, Josephine fashions a sleeping bag out of two heavy blankets. She cuts a mouth-sized hole in the fabric. Then she and Walter stuff Henry Adler's unconscious body inside. Finally, Josephine sews the fabric above his head closed. "No matter what he says when he wakes, we can't let him go until the miracle's taken place," she instructs her brother. "It will be easier to resist temptation if we don't have to look him in the face."

"Untie him!" I urge, unable to do it myself. My fingers melt into air.

"Leave us, serpent," Josephine replies calmly. "I will never heed you."

I would gladly go, if I could. Instead I'm forced to watch as she fasts for days, waiting for her miracle, spoon-feeding Henry Adler through the cloth when he wakes once, distraught and shouting garbled words that don't form sentences. There is no second awakening. Her father, Thomas, doesn't stir either.

Josephine weakens rapidly, sliding in and out consciousness to the sound of her own half-uttered prayers. Meanwhile, the venomous black cloud oozes into every room of the house, its size multiplying with each passing day. The cloud's inky vapors drip from curtains and the corners of ceilings, pooling on the mantelpiece and kitchen counter, swishing around the tips of my ears, teasing me with the promise of release.

In her last moments, Josephine kneels beside her father's bed with her palms smoothed together. "Glory be to the Father, and to the Son, and to the Holy Spirit," she whispers. "As it was in the beginning, is now, and ever shall be, world without ..." Her eyes close fast, and don't reopen. She slips gently forward, her head landing sideways on the bed, her knees still bent under her. Walter finds her in this pose when he pads into his parents' bedroom with a tall glass of water his sister wouldn't have drunk anyway, just as she refused all the glasses before it — waiting for a miracle, in a place doomed by a sickness transformed into evil.

Walter's glass shatters on the floor. Into a thousand tiny pieces no one could ever hope to reassemble. His face collapses into ruin, his inconsolable cries piercing otherwise empty rooms. Slowly, he descends the staircase, wandering brokenly out the front door as if being led by a greater power, golden sunshine stealing him from view. Shantallow's sole survivor, a nine-year-old boy.

Then I'm all alone. A shadowy, paper-thin sliver of myself left blinking at the darkness washing surf-like through the house. It plugs my ears and streams into my eyes, half-blinding me as I think I spy someone else — leaning in the doorway with an unlit cigarette between his fingers, staring back at me with a brazenness that curls his upper lip. A man out of place, out of time, and the darkness warm and heavy, like the air before a summer storm. Wrapping itself around me like the weight of a hundred ambivalent hands pulling me toward day.

19

But it's not day. Not remotely. Just the same grisly shade of night my eyes have been stumbling over since the lantern went dead.

"You're awake," Cal notes from the porch steps.

"Yeah. So are you." Last thing I remember the tramadol had him down for the count.

Tanvi and I sat in silence for so long after she saw Alice — my mind running wild — that I must've dropped off against my better judgment. Now my neck wrenches to the right. Peering at Tanvi's and Lauren's sleeping bodies stretched peacefully out next to each other on the porch, my lungs chug oxygen and relief. The two of them are both okay. In the time that I was asleep, disaster didn't strike.

"It's been quiet for a while," Cal confirms. "The rain's stopped too." Tearing something between his fingers, he slides a freed piece between his lips — the bread he took from the house. "We need a plan for tomorrow. We have to make damn sure we don't end up back here. I say we forget the road and head straight through the woods."

"Tomorrow isn't coming. We can't wait for that." Memories from my nightmare poke holes into my consciousness. Not just a dream. A window onto the past.

I'm not sure I even believe in that. My maternal grandmother might. My father definitely wouldn't swallow it. Not when I knew him. He would've fanned the air at the suggestion and rasped, "That's some ripe bullshit."

But it was so real. As horrifically real as anything else that happened tonight.

"What?" Cal chokes. "What do you mean tomorrow isn't coming?"

I shake my head. Words won't explain. We're souls — or whatever you want to call us — stuck on a sheet of flypaper.

"That's fucked up, man. You can't put something like that out there and then clam up."

Scanning Tanvi's body in the dark, I will her to wake up. Cal won't understand. It's a bridge too far, even with the things that have happened here tonight. "Something tragic went down here a long time ago," I begin, remnants of sleep bleeding into my voice, "and I don't know how, but now it's trapped us."

Cal shakes his head. "Something happened, no doubt, but —"

"I saw it when I was asleep. The family who lived here. The daughter was insane. Delusional and violent. Sick with something. Her father too. But she killed at least three people."

Cal exhales warily as he trains his eyes on my chin. "Listen, this place has been messing with all of us. But whatever you saw was just a dream — your head trying to make sense of all the craziness."

"Maybe." I only say it so he won't write me off. We need to stick together. Trust each other. Form a united front. "How long has she been out?" I cock my head to indicate Tanvi.

"Not long. She was getting emotional. This night, you know … and *you*. Man, don't get me wrong, I'm not trying to get into it with you, this isn't the right place for that, but" — he straightens his spine and drops his voice — "I don't know what you're doing here. You were a complete fucking asshole to that girl, and then you come creeping around her house."

I lower my head. "I know."

"So when this is over you need to leave her alone. Have some respect. You understand?"

"Yeah." The part of me that wanted to slam a fist into him earlier is mute and lifeless. "Coming from me, it'll sound like bullshit, but I didn't drive by to mess with her. I never thought she'd find out I was there."

"Your unlucky day," Cal declares wistfully. "Unlucky for all of us."

"Do you think the cops know who took us?"

"I doubt it. If they start digging, certain people might suggest it was you."

That never occurred to me, but he's right. With no ransom phone call to guide the police the kidnapping could look like the work of a jealous ex-boyfriend with a history of posting revenge porn.

"Everybody who knows T.V. saw the photo," Cal continues.

It always comes back to that. The things I shouldn't have done. Like I'm some feral animal on the inside. Different from the people who would know better.

Something pinches the back of my neck, trying to get my attention. Something that's not entirely here but doesn't want to be forgotten. "Was it bad for her after the photo?" I ask under my breath.

Isn't that what I wanted? For Tanvi to eat shit for breaking up with me? But if that's who I am, why isn't it less complicated? Why feel like I drowned a sack of puppies whose cries I still hear in my sleep months later?

"Bad enough. The dickheads came out of the woodwork. Could've been worse, but she's tough." Cal turns away, staring into the fortress of trees. "I don't know why I'm telling you this."

I don't know why I do anything, when it comes down to it. Is there any space inside me that's only mine? Is every last piece of real estate either handed down from my father or a reaction against him?

I think of what Tanvi said last night about my life being fake like an airbrushed photo. That's not what I want for myself. I want change to be as real as this night.

"My dad has surgery in the morning," Cal says, jumping subjects. "Now he'll have to reschedule. He hates that."

"Your dad's a surgeon?" The thing prickles at my neck. Not a bug I can swat away. Something that won't be ignored.

"An otolaryngologist," he replies. "ENT."

Ears, nose, throat specialist. Cal's dad probably bumps into Helena Mahajan at the hospital on a regular basis. They live in the same world. The one I only have a visitor's pass for so far.

"My mom's an ophthalmologist," Cal adds. "They're so cheesy together. Always referring to themselves as double trouble."

Meaning his folks could've paid his ransom after all. Not as much as Helena's parents could afford for Tanvi and Lauren, but the kidnappers would've netted a healthy bonus. I'm the one weak link.

Fingernails scrape along the side of my neck. Ruthlessly enough to break skin. I gasp, one hand flying protectively to my neck.

"What is it?" Cal asks anxiously, craning to stare at me. "*Serpent.*" His tongue curls spitefully around the syllables, suddenly feminine.

Both hands shoot to his mouth. They scoop inside his lips, fishing for whatever grungy residue remains. Not his word, not his voice. *Hers.* Brittle and vicious.

Cal's eyes pop with fear. He leaps up from the steps and bends at the waist, his head extending away from the rest of him like a garden hose nozzle, ready to vomit the presence through his mouth and eject it into the world.

Tanvi hurtles forward, thumping his back. "Cal," she says starkly. "Cal. *Cal.*"

I stand too. Press my hands firmly into his shoulders to calm him down. "Fight it," I tell him, squeezing one arm between him and Tanvi, edging her away. If we're losing Cal to this place, he shouldn't be anywhere near her.

Straightening, he chokes out a single word. Tries to. *Help.*

Beyond the steps something moves. My eyes collide with it full force, my body still restraining Cal.

A figure in black. Emerging from the woods. Mechanically dragging his injured foot behind him like he has no particular affinity for the appendage. His face reminds me of a tarp, giving nothing away about the contents it covers.

"Greg!" I shout.

He doesn't break stride. There's no hint he even heard me. His expression remains as emotionless as any major appliance you plug into a wall socket.

Tanvi's gaze pans past Cal, connecting with Greg quickly approaching the steps. "Luke!" she calls. "What happened in the woods?"

Standing tall and wooden, he breaches the porch stairs. Edging Cal into the post and pushing me aside along with him. Tanvi leaps back, avoiding contact. Greg reaches for the front door. One of his feet thrusts inside as he hurls it open.

Stumbling forward, I heave my arms around his chest. Lock them into place like a deadbolt, trying to stop him. He's not Luke or Greg anymore. Something else has slithered under his flesh and marched him out of the woods. It's in control. If it succeeds in carrying him into the house, he might never come out again.

Greg's head pitches back in revolt, struggling robotically against me. One of my hands clips his. Ice crystals crunch under my fingers — an obscene cold that shouldn't be possible this time of year. My body recoils in shock.

Cal advances as I retreat. Our bodies plow headlong into each other, canceling each other's efforts. Falling back onto the porch with twin wallops of misery. The door slaps shut behind Greg, the entire porch vibrating in response.

"We need to go," Cal barks, regaining command of his voice. "Right now. We'll send someone back for him."

Tanvi screams from behind us: "Lauren's missing!" Racing down the steps, she banks right, the wind whipping up her hair like a mainsail made of a thousand strands. Cal and I scramble after her. Three sets of eyes scanning a perimeter composed only of shades of black.

Tanvi reaches the van first. Drops to her knees and peers under its scarred remains. "She's not here!" she shouts. Steps behind, I follow hot on her heels, sprinting back in the general direction of the house. Tanvi tugs futilely at the locked carriage house doors, their weight groaning and resisting as I catch up.

"There's no way she could've gotten by the three of us," Cal calls from several feet back. "We would've seen her. She must have gone back into the house right before Luke went in." *While we were distracted with Cal.* Another dirty trick.

Tanvi whirls around in the darkness, the starless night oppressive and unshakeable, feeding on our fear. "Then I'm going in." Her eyes snap to mine as I begin to run with her, our movements mirror images. "Don't try to stop me."

There's no time to tell her what I saw in my sleep. It wouldn't help anyway.

Cal accelerates out ahead, widening his lead. The telltale slowness from his injury has vanished. He hits the porch steps first, on fire with tramadol and adrenalin. "Wait for us!" Tanvi calls after him. Glancing over his shoulder, he pauses with his arm raised, deciding his fate. His fingers close on the doorknob. Pitching the front door open, he launches himself headlong into the house of horrors.

I speed after him, second into Shantallow. Inside, feeble light from the remaining living room lantern sifts into the corridor and lower half of the staircase. I hesitate in the entranceway, longing for the safety of a light in my hand. But Cal's already nearing the top of the stairs. His feet scuffle noisily as they rise and fall, alerting me to his location before my eyes can find him.

Tanvi's shoes scrape against my heels when she dashes in behind me. She's not slowing for anyone or anything. I can't either.

Ascending into rapidly fading light, my left hand clings to the railing, the other stretches out in front of me like a shield. "Lauren!" Tanvi shouts. "Can you hear me?"

"We're coming!" Cal blares from the second-storey hallway. "We want to help."

Bone-white arms lunge out of the dark inches in front of me. Aiming for my head. I duck instinctively, left elbow slamming painfully into the banister.

Something dark whips over my head, skimming my hair. It cracks into Tanvi behind me. A direct hit. She groans. Drops like a bowling pin.

Spinning to catch her, I'm too late. She falls backwards down the stairs. *Thumpety-thump thump-thump-thump.* Bones bashing against worn old steps. The large wooden cross from the mantelpiece slides down next to her, racing toward bottom.

"Tanvi!" I spurt downstairs after her. Snatch up the stone-cold cross with a hand that doesn't want to touch it. Hurl the unholy thing into the hallway — as far away from us as my arm can force it — and then crouch beside her. Tanvi blinks dazedly up at me, blood trickling down the side of her face. Her hand reaches for it, feeling for the stain of wet. Wincing audibly, her fingers shift to her shoulder.

"Are you all right?" My throat chokes like engine trouble. "Let me —"

"I'm — I'm okay," she lies, voice betraying her. "We have to find Lauren. Help me up."

I slip one hand supportively under her back and grasp her right hand with my left. Looking her over in the murky light, I can't see well enough to discern where she hurts the most. I pull her slowly up along with me, my ribs screaming silently in protest. "Did you break anything?" I ask. "Let me get the lantern."

Tanvi shakes her head, wide-eyed with shock and determination. "No, let's go." She grabs the end of my shirt impatiently, lifting an ankle to maneuver herself back onto the bottom step with a fragility that stops me dead. Her left shoulder and upper arm scrunch in close to her torso like a work of human origami stomped under a steel-toe boot.

"Not in the dark," I insist. "We need the lantern. We have to see what's coming."

"Get it, then," she says grudgingly.

I dart for the living room, ears scanning for feet on the stairs the way they shouldn't be if she listens to me and waits. But I'm no time at all. The instant I appear Tanvi begins to tackle the steps again. "Cal! Lauren! Where are you?" she yells.

We land on the second floor, Tanvi rushing to the right and me hurtling along with her, pushing the lantern out ahead of us. Light seeps along the corridor and into the same bedroom where we found John earlier. My heart rate spirals, my blood pressure vaulting sky-high as my mind shrieks, *Freeze.* Three shadowy figures lurk inside the illuminated room — two on their knees, hands pressed stiffly together as if locked in prayer. The third lingers just inside the doorway, watching the others from unblinking eyes.

Cal. Paused with fear or fascination. Our appearance breaks his spell. His gaze flips to Tanvi, eyes narrowing in the glare of more light than he's been exposed to in hours. Greg and John kneel with their backs to him. Spines held perversely straight, eyes shut tight, and lips mouthing unspoken words that look like gibberish.

Puppets. That's what they are.

If we could sever their strings somehow ...

But Tanvi's twisting on her heels, zooming in the opposite direction. I keep up, the pain in my nose and abdomen turning clear. Panic acting as local anesthetic, canceling out everything except what might be ahead of us.

Freeze. Run. Fight. The three stages of fear. My brain cycles through them repeatedly in quick succession, like someone skimming a dial through radio stations, unable to find the right one.

Behind me a door wallops shut. I gawk over my shoulder. Cal's been sealed inside the bedroom with Greg and John. I hear him jiggle the doorknob, then pound the door urgently with his fist, hollering for help. My eyes snag on the nearest wall. *Step on a crack, break your mother's back.* There are too many to count. Long and deep. Misshapen. Like a network of irregular scars.

One wriggles frantically against the wall. Then a second. The swirling scars of the corridor walls twitch with life. Hundreds of rangy black worms writhing, trapped in the throes of desolation. My empty thumb and fingers jet to my eyes, rubbing reassurance into the closed lids.

They're not real. Only cracks in soiled hundred-year-old wallpaper.

I bump into Tanvi's shoulder. Cringe at her sharp intake of breath.

What are we doing? If Shantallow wants to wrap its savage arms around Lauren and keep her close, how we can we fight it? We're only human. The sum of too many parts as breakable as eggshells.

A door at the end of the hallway creaks opens a sliver. Gingerly, almost. Tanvi's head twitches as if she means to look at me. Then she advances. My feet follow closely in her tracks, lantern lighting our path. Showing me precisely where I don't want to go.

Tanvi's palm presses into the doorway, easing it open further. My fingers clutch her good arm. *Don't do this.*

I can't look. And can't not.

We've never been inside this particular room before. My eyes don't take in the dusty old furniture or anything else. They can't see past Lauren levitating in the middle of the room, her ankles bent forward at sharp angles and the toes of her sneakers scraping eerily against the flooring while her heels and arches fly free. Her mouth contorts into a snarl, her eyes squinting cruelly into the light. A spiderweb of crystals, wispy-light like cotton candy, erupts on her cheeks and forehead.

I tighten my grip on Tanvi. *Stay back.*

She slips through my fingers like silk. Bullets to her cousin. Flings her arms firmly around Lauren, battling — with all her will and muscle — to tug her toward the floor.

Lauren's giggle rasps in the back of her throat. Low and nasty like someone fueled by hundred-year-old hate. My stomach flips, rejecting the perverse resonance. Lauren's left hand snakes out of Tanvi's grasp. Reaches for Tanvi's head with fingers spread wide and tall, tensed like spiders' legs. Her movements are pure animal, swift and unforgiving — left hand brutally clawing Tanvi's scalp from back to front.

Tanvi screams blue murder. I've never heard that sound in her throat. Never heard anyone living scream with a shock and horror that sets the hairs at the back of my hands on end and punctures my chest like a scalpel.

The lantern falls from my grasp. It rolls back into the hallway. My right knee buckles as I run. Lauren laughs wildly. No hero to the rescue. Only me.

I grab for her arms. They flail rabidly at the air, blurring my vision. One of her feet kicks into my calf. *Fuck*. I groan and sag, throwing my entire weight and strength around her.

"Don't hurt her!" Tanvi protests. "It's not her fault."

"*It's not her fault*," Lauren mimics, her breath foul like a teeming dumpster in the July sun. The reek overpowers the packing stuffed into my nostrils. Makes my eyes swim.

"Just hold on," Tanvi pleads. "Don't let go of her."

We embrace Lauren from opposite sides, neither of our grips loosening. But our combined efforts aren't enough to plant Lauren's feet on the ground. She sways in the air like a kite caught in a current. What's left of her is ice and frenzied hate wrapped in ten-year-old skin. I snap my face away to avoid her putrid breath, her body twisting and limbs thrashing, battering us wherever they can reach.

"Lauren, stop!" I command. "Make her stop." *Josephine*. The girl from my dream, in the middle of her second reign of terror. *Make Josephine stop*.

"She hates you," Lauren seethes, the words crunching between her teeth like shattered glass. "You disgust her. She never loved you. She always loved another."

My calf muscles tense. My tongue turns to cotton in my mouth. I blink rapidly, my eyes latching onto Tanvi's hair, heart sinking.

"It doesn't matter," I mumble, directing my words at Josephine. "You can't have this girl. She's not yours."

"You don't matter," Lauren spits back. "No one cares what happens to you. You're worthless like your father. You will always be worthless. Everyone knows it. They smile in your face and mock you behind your back."

"Don't listen to her," Tanvi says. "That's not Lauren."

I know it. Doesn't mean she's wrong. Doesn't change the fact that no matter what I do, I will always have to be alone.

Lauren's knuckles crash into the bridge of my nose. Shattering already broken cartilage to smithereens. My left arm drops, releasing my hold on Lauren's shoulders. I back up, doubling over in agony. Whimpering like a child. Tanvi struggles to restrain her cousin, my right arm smarter than the rest of me, still clutching hard to one of Lauren's hands, limiting her reach.

The meager light from the hallway lantern streaks harshly across the floor, casting everything from the knees up into a grimy gray gradient. Raising my head, my eyes leap to the blackest corner of the room, where the closed window blind intercepts any stray light from outside. A body surfaces from the darkness, never fully gaining form — caught between worlds — disappearing before I can bring it into focus. In another time and place, I'd blink and decide I'd imagined it.

I can't do that now. I've seen him too many times tonight to dismiss him as nothing. Things I thought I knew have inverted to reveal themselves as lies. *There's no such thing as life after death. My father is somewhere in Mexico, lost to the nearest dive bar. He doesn't give a damn what happens to me or my sister.*

"Dad?" I whisper. Only his arms — unmistakably bone white — and the sleeve of his shirt are still visible.

Rocketing forward, I hurl my arms back around Lauren. Tanvi cries quietly into her cousin's shoulder. She heaves and shivers from the other side of Lauren's thin body, where my arms border hers. "I don't know what to do," Tanvi murmurs despairingly. "I can't leave her in this place. Maybe you should go. Get help. She's too strong —"

"I'm not letting go," I tell Tanvi. "We'll both keep holding on." Until when? Like Josephine waiting for her miracle that never arrived? But this is different, isn't it? The three of us don't need a miracle. We only need Josephine to loosen her grip, return what was never hers to take.

Tanvi gasps, her head swinging sharply to the right. "I felt something. Was that you?"

"I didn't do anything."

Tanvi's gaze whips into the far corner of the room, Lauren making use of the distraction to twist her narrow fingers around Tanvi's neck and squeeze. Tanvi coughs in distress, eyes bulging as I wrestle Lauren's hand into submission again. "*Alice,*" Tanvi says. Her eyelashes open and close in wonder as she regains her breath. "She's come back."

I can't see Alice the way I've seen my father, but something's changed. I feel it in my gut. A layer of oppressiveness has been sucked from the room and swapped for something better. Hope, maybe. Imperfect goodness. The knowledge that we're not alone here.

"In any way that matters you are all alone," Lauren counters, reading my mind and speaking in a voice deeper than it should be for her ten years. Mean and scratchy as steel wool. "You always have been. You will die here alone." She laughs shrilly, thrusting her head closer to Tanvi while we fight to keep Lauren wedged between us. "He hates you. He wanted to hurt you. It brought him joy. Nothing makes him happier than your misery."

"That's not true." Denial booms in my stomach like a bass drum.

I've kissed Tanvi everywhere there is to kiss a person. Listened to her heart beating through her chest, her nipple so close it was out of focus, my hand fitted to the curve of her hip like a second skin. I made her promises I thought I could keep. Laughed with her like we were kids. Combed the tangles out of her hair after we showered together. Wanted things for her. The best things. Wished — with everything I had inside me — that I could rewind history and bring Alice and her parents back, if that would make her happy. I've been happy when she was happy and sad when she was sad.

And I have wanted to hurt her. I've made her cry and broken her down, on purpose. Because I could. I had that power.

Do you know what it feels like to really hurt someone you care about? Never the way you imagine. When someone's pain is what you want, you can only ever lose.

How do you see that up close for years but never learn it? How am I so broken?

"And you will know the truth, and the truth will set you free," Lauren intones with false solemnity.

Her body's colder than anything living. Colder than Greg's, even.

Her hate is crisp and raw, too. It seeps through her body and clothing, my skin absorbing it and begging me to shrink away from her.

"I believe in God," Tanvi begins, "the Father Almighty, Creator of Heaven and earth."

I don't know what I believe anymore. Except that my father is in this room with me. He's been here since we arrived. Not to torment me, but to offer me what he could. Strength. Warning. His pale arms on the stairs, alerting me to what was coming. Him waking me from sleep. Him peeling back a veil to reveal the tragedy that befell Josephine's family.

He never went to Mexico. He died in a ditch or an alley some-where — a location I will never know the name of because no one missed him enough to search. The world was better off without him.

My mom, sister, and I were the closest people to him in this life, and he hated us. Or made us believe that he did. I am who I am in large part because of him. But he's here now, and my emotions — hot and cold, angry and shamed and carved open — churn under the surface, kicking up through collagen and tendons and breaking through.

"Alice wants you to know it's your fault," Lauren says to Tanvi. "You left her all alone in the world. She died alone. Because of you."

"It's a dirty lie," I erupt, and between my damaged ribs, my twice-broken nose, and the meat-locker chill of Lauren's body, it's killing me to hold on. It must be leveling Tanvi too — her injured shoulder squashed against her cousin's chest — but she just keeps praying. Words rolling rhythmically off her tongue like ancient poetry.

I can't let go. I won't let her down again.

"Happy shall he be, that taketh and dasheth thy little ones against the stones," Lauren croaks.

I shiver, chilled to the bone. "We're not giving her up. It doesn't matter what you say or do." My voice gathers rust, crumbling into grit.

"Let the dead bury the dead," Lauren intones, strength knitting itself into the fabric of her words. One of her hands breaks free. Her thumb digs viciously into the hollow of Tanvi's neck.

Tanvi chokes and forces it away with both fists. Lauren lashes out like a wild animal. Her teeth tear into my shoulder — where the neck of my shirt's askew — feet scissoring in every direction. We fight to subdue her. Time after time, Lauren's cracked, jagged nails gash into exposed skin and her elbows jut sharply into our flesh. Whenever we tire and accidentally loosen our grasp it's like beginning the battle from scratch. Lauren never weakens. She's inexhaustible. Stronger than either of us. Together it's all we can do to restrain her. We'd never make it down the stairs with her, let alone get free of this place.

"Why fight me?" Lauren asks slyly. "When you know you don't have the strength?" She snickers, steam leaking from her mouth. "Your prayers are worthless. He doesn't hear them. He only hears mine."

"We aren't your enemies," Tanvi murmurs, tongue stumbling with weariness. "My cousin isn't your enemy, whoever you are. She's only a child. Fearfully and wonderfully made." It must be some kind of biblical quote — something that would be meaningful to Josephine — and I listen to Tanvi hesitate, her breath shallow as she adds, "Innocent."

My mind ricochets to my dream. *The boy running with the grass whistle between his hands.* "Innocent like your brother," I suggest. In a corner of my memory, his glass shatters on the floor; he cries out for everything he lost. "Innocent like Walter."

"Don't speak his name," Lauren hisses, a whiff of rot escaping her mouth. "You aren't worthy to speak his name. You know nothing."

I've angered her. Made things worse. My brain scrambles for a way to undo the harm — so that she won't take her fury out on Lauren — but then Lauren stills, her limbs slackening. Her cold body resists us with listlessness instead of violence. Heavy and immovable as a tractor-trailer without any wheels. Her toes make unbroken, motionless contact with the floor at a slant that even a prima ballerina couldn't sustain.

We hold on and hold on. For longer than I can measure in a place where time never appears to pass — but I catch glimpse after glimpse of my father in the dark, and when Lauren falls to the floor I can't allow myself to imagine it's over. To believe that and be proven wrong could snap me in half.

Hope can be an enemy too. Make you trust when you shouldn't. Make you lose.

Even when you promise you'll steel yourself against it — harden your heart — it persists. Only to burn through you like acid when it suffocates.

But you have to have hope. That's what everyone says. Never lose it. Never give up. As though hope is a magical, bottomless well that will get you through anything, and I don't know — but maybe they're right after all, because then I hear Lauren breathing, in a rhythm all her own. Quick and uneven like a child about to cry.

"What are we doing up here?" she whimpers.

20

Tanvi squats on her haunches, wobbling with exhaustion. Smoothing Lauren's blond hair back from her face, she studies her cousin intently. I hunch down next to them, seeing only a little girl. The same contours and innocence in Lauren's face as I first registered in Braden's. This could easily be a trick too. Shantallow's capacity for deception and cruelty could be limitless and infinite. Fatal for every last one of us.

"Hold my hand," Tanvi says softly, pulling Lauren up with her. "We're leaving."

In the brief seconds between thought and action, footsteps rampage through the hallway outside. The three of us hesitate in place, bracing for the worst. Tanvi steps protectively in front of Lauren, right arm outstretched to shield her. I reel toward the door to pull it shut — hide us from whatever's on the hunt.

Fingers curl around the edge of the door before I can close it. They force the door wide open with a bang, Cal standing in the hallway with blood oozing from both his ears.

"They're insane," he mutters, vacancy glossing his eyes. "Gone fucking gone gone gone. Kept saying the same — the same the same — things over and over. Couldn't even see them in the dark, but their voices were buzzing. Like there were a hundred of them instead of two." Cal claps his fingers over his ears, his eyes darting from side to side, half gone himself.

We all are. The human brain can only cope with so much. Push us over the edge and the ability to distinguish past experiences from present ones shrinks. The amygdala ramps into hyperactive mode like an overtired toddler running in circles and screeching, ready to claw the eyes out of anyone who dares come near them.

My nerves are miles past shot. Nothing but frayed edges and fear of my own fucking shadow left. I'm like a ghost of myself that's somehow retained its skin and bones. Shaking like a junkie in withdrawal. Heart outpacing itself, like a cold engine revved into extinction.

Without Tanvi and my dad, I might not have made it this far. I might be curled into a ball on the floor, rocking myself into oblivion.

But here we are: Tanvi, Cal, Lauren, and me. The four of us with our minds and bodies badly bruised by trauma, yet still more or less on our feet. Ready to run again.

Light from the abandoned lantern spills through the gap between Cal's feet in the hallway. We'll scoop it up and take it with us. Hold it up against the darkness like something holy and walk toward day. It has to be out there.

Has to be.

But before I can move, Lauren weaves past me, charging toward Cal in the doorway. He jumps aside to let her out. Tanvi and I shoot forward to follow.

We almost make it through. Our bodies are inches from the door when it crashes shut in Tanvi's face, delivering the two of us into near darkness. A thin scab of light creeping under the doorway allows my fingers to find the doorknob. It rattles and turns under my hand, but refuses to open.

Cal bashes against the door from the other side. Over and over again, groaning and swearing in frustration.

"Let me try!" I holler through the wood. You'd think it was heavily fortified steel or that my body was made of straw. The fucking thing doesn't budge.

"Lauren, are you okay out there?" Tanvi asks in high-pitched alarm.

"We're okay." She raps insistently on the door three times in quick succession. "I hate this place. Break the door down."

We don't like it either. Cold settles on my shoulders. Something wet dabs my right hand.

"Tell them to go," I say under my breath.

Lauren may have gotten free, but Josephine hasn't left.

Tanvi's face shoots questioningly toward me in the dark. Behind my ear, Josephine laughs poisonously. Her hands that aren't hands swoop up the front of my shirt. Razor diagonally into my skin as Tanvi and I watch in horror.

"Cal!" Tanvi shouts. "Listen to me, I need you to get my cousin out of here now."

"We can break the door," he argues. "Between the three of us we —"

Her urgency axes through his plea. "No! Please. Just get her out of here. Get her to safety. We'll be right behind you, I promise."

"T.V."

"Do it!" she demands. "Do it right now, for me. I need to know she's out of danger." She drops her voice, whispering into the door. "If you don't do it now, it could take her again."

"No!" Lauren screams defiantly from the other side of the door. "I'm all right now. We're not leaving you."

"You heard what she said — we have to go," Cal commands, reluctance dragging at his voice even as he holds it taut. Lauren's scream recedes into the distance. The sound of someone being hauled down the corridor against her will. The scab of light from under the door ebbs along with it, black soup gulping down its leftovers.

In complete darkness, every particle is a potential threat. Patches of black fuse with other patches, forming phantom shapes in the void. Something thuds. Creaks. Fingers as weightless as feathers tousle my hair. I duck, my hands out in front of me, feeling my way forward.

"You still there, Misha?" Tanvi asks, her voice like a star, a light to guide to me.

"Still here." And so is Josephine. Her breath cold on my neck.

The window blind snaps up, frail light altering the room but not taming it. The fuzzy edges of furniture come into view, hostile and time-worn. Tanvi stands in front of the window, hair wild like a raging waterfall and body bent at the middle, hands fastened to the bottom of the window, struggling to yank it open.

I weave around the bed to help her. Something jerks at both my feet. Flips them off the floor and drags me backwards in a rush of motion. Flings me frantically against the far wall. My shoulders and head thwack against the wall, the sound triggering a familiar dread. *He's shit-faced drunk again and my mom will pay the price for it.*

Only this time it isn't him. Isn't her, either. I'm Shantallow and Josephine's punching bag, and it never tires, never sleeps.

Tanvi tears toward me, flying past the bed.

"Stay back!" I warn, locking my hands around the back of my head and pressing my spine into the wall. Shielding myself as much as I can. "The window — just get the window open. We have to get out. The girl who lived here was insane — she killed her family."

Tanvi doesn't ask me how I know. Her head tilts on her shoulders as she stares at me. Then she runs. Bounds back to the window with her arms out in front of her. Something stops her short before she can reach it. Pushes her hard. She drops to her knees. Crawls in the direction of the light like a crab scuttling for water.

I do the same.

Pressure sledgehammers my back. Crunches me into the floor.

Glass shatters, the sound sharp and delicate. Grainy fragments rain down on my hair and the back of my neck. I shuffle forward, shards slicing my palms. Standing quickly, my eyes shoot to Tanvi at the window, an upended bedside table on the floor in front of her.

"Come on, come on," she urges, sliding her body halfway through the window, dangling precariously over the sharp fragments of glass that cling to the bottom of the pane. "I can see Cal and Lauren out there. Running for the woods. Someone's chasing them."

Stretching my arms out in front of me I sprint for the window, calf muscles firing like they're powered by nitro. Something kicks my right knee out from under me. The floor swoops up to meet me, flattening my chin with a whack, pummeling my kneecaps. The pain screeches through my nerve endings, begging me to quit moving and give in. Anything to make this stop.

"Get up!" Tanvi shouts from the other side of the open window, her feet planted on the sloping porch roof.

My legs won't move. Tears form in the corners of my eyes. Or maybe it's blood. But she's waiting. *Get up get up get up*, I tell myself. *Don't make her say it again.*

Only when I manage to force myself to my feet it's the worst kind of déjà vu — the one you knew was coming but couldn't stop because there's no other way. My knee buckles under the force of a new strike. First one kneecap, then the other. I stare ahead as I start to plummet. Spy Tanvi plunge her arm through the window and reach for me. My feet skip forward on air, searching for traction where there isn't any. Then my hand snaps out to meet hers.

The gap between our fingers widens into an abyss as I go down. Grunt like an animal as I fall. My battered body cringing under the hurt. Too much to take.

Tanvi kneels on the porch roof, her head hanging through the bedroom window, her voice urging me on. "Misha!" Her arms lunge into the dark room with me — ladders to another world. Pushing myself to my knees, I crawl, glass piercing my palms. My kneecaps groan underneath me, my mind willing them to hurry.

If I get up, it will only happen again. Even on my knees I feel Josephine at my heels, ready to knock me sideways.

"*Misha*," Tanvi repeats, her voice softening under the weight of something I don't understand. "Now. Run to me."

Behind me, the air is strangely light. Not wholly under the spell of Earth's gravity. As I stand and break into a sprint, it propels me forward. One of my legs charges through the open window, the sole of my shoe landing firmly on the porch roof. Over my shoulder, something luminous blazes from inside the bedroom. Hazy and burnished coppery gold like the setting sun. I turn to look as I tug the rest of my body to safety, eyes squinting against the blurred glimmer of two forms, their frames united in a dual task. Somehow holding Josephine off and hastening me outside.

My eyes skim to Tanvi's. The awe in her face amplifies my giddiness into euphoria. But there's no time to linger. She turns to scramble down the sloping roof. Lowering ourselves off its shortest point, we hang on by our fingers for only a moment. Then release.

Landing in the damp grass at the front of the porch, I grimace. I need a triple dose of tramadol. A stretcher and someone to carry it. Everything hurts in a way my brain can't contain, the pain bleeding into every thought and even the smallest actions. But Tanvi's no better off than I am. And I'm not going to the house to get more pills.

Tanvi's already begun to jog, unevenly and slowly like an old woman weighed down by severe arthritis. "Come on," she calls, listing to one side as we descend into the forest. "We need to catch up to them."

Narrowing the distance between us, I glance at her sideways, Tanvi's expression invisible in the dark. "They had the lantern, but I can't see any sign of them," she says, thick, disheveled strands of her hair clumping together to wall her from her view even if the moon should miraculously break through the clouds and train its spotlight in our direction. "No light anywhere."

The tree canopy is too thick. I can barely make out my own hands. Rain-sodden leaves splash droplets of water on our shoulders and heads as we pass under them. Tanvi's pace slackens, her footing on the forest floor precarious. I fall into line behind her, the gap between trees narrowing. We'll never catch up to Cal and Lauren like this, but neither of us is capable of moving any faster. The trees themselves could practically beat us in a race.

"My knee." Tanvi winces, stopping to massage it with her palm.

Mine's busted up too. The right worse than the left. But her injury seems more acute, by the look of her gait. Doesn't want to take weight. A meniscus tear or ligament injury, maybe.

"You should go find them," she advises in the same tone that a newscaster would announce tomorrow's weather. "I'm too slow."

"Don't be stupid — I'm not leaving you here."

"There was someone trailing behind them," she argues stubbornly. "I think it was John — what if he catches up to them? We don't know what he'll do."

"I don't care. You really think I'm going to abandon you in this forest when you can hardly walk?"

She doesn't reply, only peers fixedly at me in the blackest night I've ever seen, warm bitterness clinging to her body like a wet blanket. It heats the air between us, charring it into acrid resentment.

"I'm sorry — I know you're worried about your cousin," I add. "But I can't. Cal is with her. He'll take care of her."

"Unless something happens to him." She reaches for her knee a second time, gingerly working it over with her fingertips. "I saw something back there in the room for a second. Your dad. Not distinctly, but that was him, wasn't it?"

I clear my throat as she turns to stumble onward. "Yeah. With Alice. I saw her a bit too." The vivid, blushing light emanating from them both. "Before tonight I didn't know he was dead. It seems so obvious now. Someone who knew about his money probably took him out years ago." Or just some dangerous asshole he bounced the wrong kind of look at. He never knew what was good for him. Didn't know when to stop.

"I'm sorry," Tanvi offers uncertainly — maybe because until now I've only ever had shitty things to say about my father.

I bob my head. "It must have been him sending the nightmares all along, trying to warn us away from this place."

A noise midway between a grunt and chuckle of exhaustion bubbles from Tanvi's throat. "That didn't exactly work."

"No." Only made me exponentially more curious when I saw her on the Ghims' lawn that very first time. But if I didn't know it before tonight, I know it now without question — I would've fallen for Tanvi without the dreams. Not an act of fate, exactly, because in fate you don't choose. But wherever, whenever I saw her, something inside me was always going to inch forward, breathless and dizzy, and lean toward her, hoping she'd lean back.

All the dreams did was set me on a path I would've stumbled upon myself eventually.

"When the time comes, don't let the darkness inside you," Tanvi declares, her voice porous, like I can hear the wind rustling through the syllables. We're so spent and shattered that it's a wonder we can talk at all. "Do you remember — it's what Alice told me that night on the phone. Like she could see this coming down the road."

"I remember." My nose aches like it's been bulldozed by a demolition team. The barbed wire puzzle pieces inside my chest slash at me sideways, readjusting themselves under my skin. "From where they are, there must be things they can see that we can't." Possibilities, likelihoods. Mortal danger.

"Do you think they're still here?" she asks. "In the forest with us?"

If I could click off my higher reasoning and concentrate with my instincts, maybe I could feel something. But I can't. My instincts are fried to a crisp. The intense pain crowding in on me prevents me from sensing anything much beyond it.

"Maybe — I hope so." All I know is they were here to help us. We ignored their warnings, and they broke through the barrier to stand by us anyway. But if they could snap our chains and wrestle us free from this place, they would've done it already. Their power here must be limited.

I remember that I haven't told Tanvi my most recent dream. "When I was asleep, my dad showed me what happened here years ago." I briefly describe the murders and Josephine's insanity, Tanvi slowing again, bracing herself against a tree with her head bent.

"But the girl's not the only one here," Tanvi murmurs. "All those voices … and the woman you ran into out here. The old woman Cal saw upstairs, too."

"Her victims. Maybe other family members too." Her father, her brother. "They all seem unsettled." Not at peace. "The whole place feels like it's been tainted."

Tanvi inhales deeply, like a cigarette smoker or someone fighting a panic attack. "It sounds like mercury poisoning. You said her dad had some kind of workshop here where he made hats?"

"Yeah. Are you okay?"

"That's where the phrase 'mad hatter' comes from," she continues haltingly, bypassing my question. "It used to be an occupational hazard. Something to do with felting. Hatters would inhale the mercury vapors used to treat animal furs. Prolonged exposure gave them tremors and twitches. But there are lots of different symptoms — headaches, weakness, respiratory problems, mental deterioration."

Scientists got it too, I remember with a flash — a memory byte from ninth grade science class. Michael Faraday, Isaac Newton, Pascal. They all suffered from mercury poisoning.

Something gasps from behind us, the noise evolving into a series of truncated shrieks as I spin to look. My toes curl in my shoes, trying to hide from something they can't outrun.

But there's nothing to see. Not yet.

When I swing my gaze back to Tanvi she's collapsing in slow motion, her fingernails snagging on the tree trunk as she falls. As I catch her in my arms, she slumps like dead weight but whispers my name. Conscious but weak.

"It's okay," I lie, depositing her softly on the damp ground. "Put your head between your knees."

She does as I say. "I'm so light-headed," she croaks. "Shaky and dizzy."

Could be anything. Concussion from her fall on the stairs, exhaustion, dehydration. It almost doesn't matter. There's no cure for any of those things in this forest. There's only death.

My left foot kicks against something compact and solid as I maneuver to sit down next to Tanvi. My fingers fold around it, confusion punching my ribs. *The gun.* Greg must have left it here in the woods. Whoever was in control of him had no use for it.

But it makes me feel simultaneously better and worse when I balance the Glock on my lap, a cold wind sweeping cruelly in toward us, rounding my shoulders and making me shiver. The deadfall around me blooms with sudden frost. Crunching an icy twig under my palm, I swivel to face Tanvi. Her chin rests snugly against her chest, her breath white against the cold. She's out like a light.

"Tanvi." I touch her hand, the ground freezing underneath my legs. "Wake up." A fleck of white lands on my middle finger. Then another. A third catches in my eyelashes as I stare slowly up at the sky. Into darkness blanketed by heavy snow.

It amasses swiftly on the ground. Carpeting the forest in lies. This is no Christmas card scene, no matter how idyllic it looks.

I shove the gun hastily down the back of my jeans. My knees crack like old bones as I struggle to my feet, the shock rampaging through my brain like a heat-seeking missile that doesn't know its target. Invisible fingers tap my chest where a coat lapel would be, if I were wearing one. I scrunch up my eyes as I tilt my gaze toward

Josephine's tormented mother, or whatever slice of her has remained.

The falling snow doesn't touch her short-sleeved dress or hat, and my legs quiver as the exposed milk-white bone of her cheek jerks into a smile. The slant of her grin makes her eye bulge worse, its exposed sinewy red underpinnings cheerfully regarding me, waiting for me to give in and scream.

But my voice is gone. Covered in snow and ice, bone and blood.

Dad, I try to say. *I need you.*

I can't hear the words in my mouth. Shantallow has stolen them; rendered me silent.

Josephine's mother tosses her head back and howls, mocking me in my helplessness. The sound perforates one of my eardrums — the hearing in my right ear instantly withering and a sharp ringing taking its place. I bend to sweep up Tanvi, my knees buckling and ribs crumbling to dust. A tumultuous choir of overlapping voices wrenches at my better ear as I fall backwards, landing on my ass.

A branch snaps low behind me. I swivel in the snow, reaching for the gun. Somebody's shambling lethargically through the trees, closing in on us. "Stay back," I warn. "I'll shoot."

He doesn't stop. Curving my finger around the trigger, I notice the familiar way he's dragging one foot. "Greg, stay where you are!" I aim low, firing at his kneecap. Bull's eye. Greg kicks backwards, slips like a cartoon character lurching on a banana peel. Then he rights himself and continues, eerie animal growl caught between his teeth.

He can't hear me. There's no rational way to get through to him. I hold up the Glock again, shoot at his other leg. He sinks to his knees, moaning low.

"Stay down," I plead uselessly. "Stay down, stay down."

Miraculously, he doesn't move. Only continues to moan in the dark.

The voices are louder now. Near. The woman's disappeared, but she won't have gone far. She'll be back. With reinforcements.

I push off the ground with my hands, careen back to Tanvi.

Gathering her in my arms, my body revolts, forcing me down again. I can't lift her. The pain won't allow it. I've been overriding it, one way or another, all night. Not anymore.

But we have to get out of here. They're coming.

I skirt around Tanvi, reaching for the hand attached to her uninjured shoulder. Then I drag her through the snow by her arm — hoping I don't dislocate it — her head and body bumping ruthlessly along the ground, scratching against the fallen leaves and branches that lie underneath. My chest spasms in misery. My feet stumble. The trees at our sides outrun us and sprint back to taunt me, lining our route again and again.

A distorted male voice, forlorn and furious, wheezes, "He has cursed and forsaken us." The sound spirals in the air, seeming to come from every direction.

Scanning the perimeter, I accelerate, only to slow again as we reach a wide, circular clearing. The first one I've seen tonight.

My hand tugs as I step forward. I glance over my shoulder, down at Tanvi, her body no longer dead weight. With the tree cover broken, open air above us, and ambient light reflecting off the snow, my eyes make out hers. They stare steadily back at me, glazed with shock.

I release her hand. It sweeps through the snow at her side as she rolls onto her knees. "What happened?" she asks, trying to stand.

Her legs tremble as I reach to help her, her head yanking in the direction of the voices as they surge behind us in a monstrous synthesis of anguish. "They're still coming," she mumbles, more to herself than me.

Panning her gaze around the clearing — the air thick with snow-flakes the size of quarters — her eyes spring back to mine. "This is the place, isn't it?"

From our dreams. I nod slowly. Her lip is swollen on the left side, her forehead scratched and bleeding. Like I've seen too many times in my sleep. The only detail that was missing was the snow.

"Don't say it," I tell her, my eyes burning.

I can't do it. I won't.

Tanvi folds her arms in front of her chest, rubbing warmth into her skin. "It's what I always say, isn't it? That you have to go on without me."

I nod brokenly. I've broken so many times tonight, but now I'm bottoming out. My heart pulling away from my chest in pieces, my brain imploding with what I'm about to lose — the person I lost months ago to life, but can't stand to lose to the possibility of death.

She's supposed to have the chance to be happy with Cal. Or some other guy who will love her in all the right ways. Sit on her nanaji's porch with him listening to his animal tales until he's a hundred and two. Have a family of her own someday, maybe. Or not. Start an epic new business and take the world by storm. Whatever she wants, every good thing she deserves. A life beyond this hellish night. A life far beyond me and my fucked-up problems that should never have gotten near her to begin with.

If I stay and the worst things happen, we'll face it together. But if I walk away and leave her behind — *live* while she never escapes this ground — the guilt will cripple me, and her absence from the world will destroy whatever shell is left.

How could it ever be worth it to survive without her?

"And you tell me you won't, right?" Tanvi blinks quickly, her eyelashes filling up with snowflakes. She takes three fragile baby steps forward before freezing in her tracks, bending her head to stop it from reeling. "Listen, I can't walk, let alone run."

"It doesn't matter." My words disintegrate as they hit the air. "Cal and Lauren are way ahead of us. They could already have reached the road and sent back help."

"I hope so. But we don't know that. John might have attacked them. Cal would try to protect Lauren. She could be all alone out there now. We can't assume they made it. For all we know they've circled back to the house again. You saw what Josephine did to Lauren. At least two of the kidnappers are dead because of this place." Her right foot plows frantically through a snowfall we shouldn't have seen for months. "Look at this — *the things this place can do.*"

Tanvi digs her fingernails into my arm exactly the way she does in my dreams. "We need better odds, Misha. You're fast, and I can't run now. You have to be the one."

"And if I say no?"

"Don't." She drops her eyes, stares unfocusedly at the unlikely blanket of white at her feet. "It doesn't make any sense. You cheated on me like I was nothing to you. Posted my naked picture on the Internet to humiliate me, but now that we're not together you're going to just lie down in the snow and possibly die here with me instead of doing something to try to keep us all alive?"

This is different, I almost say. But it's not. It's easier to fight to the death for someone you love than to keep yourself from hurting them. That's the truth about being me.

"You're not allowed to tell me no now," she adds, her glare zooming up to catch me. "You still owe me."

I blink the water and grit from my eyes, peer straight ahead, struggling to see into the army of tall trees waiting for us on the other side of the clearing. The forest ahead is darker than where we came from, and I understand why she wants me to go. I get it, I do. She's lost too many people already. She'll do anything to ensure Lauren's safety.

I want Lauren to be safe too. But Tanvi matters more. Tanvi is everything, and she wants me to go.

I watch her lower herself carefully into the snow, staring demandingly up at me, her knees and the underside of her legs scraped raw from being dragged through the woods.

"I have to tell you something." I choke on the damn sentence like the constantly drunk asshole that I'm not, but could have been someday if I hadn't spent most of the past four years fighting it. "When you came to my house after I posted the photo —"

A guttural howl cuts me off, a multitude of screams falling in behind it. We're running out of time.

"I remember," Tanvi prompts.

"When I held you back and you fell." My fingers knead my forehead. Dig into my hair. My eyeballs drown in the things I've done, and the thing I'm about to do — for her, because it's what she can live with even if I can't. "For a second, I felt glad. Stronger than you. Like my dad must have felt every time he hurt my mom."

Tanvi's eyes hang on mine, unclouded and unyielding. She's the strong one. She can take the truth. It's the weakness inside me that wants to run or look away.

"He's not that person anymore," she says, closing her arms around her bare legs, one of her running shoes digging trenches in the snow. "You don't have to be either."

Tears freeze on my skin. Crack when my jaw quivers.

She's more generous than she has to be, and I still love her. Probably always will, in some way. But this is not a story about undying love conquering all. We were never going to get back together. If I can move quickly enough — and if I'm extremely goddamn lucky — it's the story of our survival.

"I don't want to leave you." I try one last time. "Don't make me do this."

Tanvi stretches out her foot and taps my shoe with hers, just like she did the second time we met. I didn't know if I'd ever see her again, and it's just the same now. "You're going to make it," she tells me. "You're going to bring back help. Everything's going to be all right."

"You promise?" I try to smile, Shantallow's many voices drowning out mine with their dissent.

I reach down the back of my jeans and hand Tanvi the Glock.

Then I dive into the trees, running for both our lives.

21

I'm not fast the way Tanvi says I am. Not anymore. Wracked with pain, my body fights me with each step. It wants to double back and lie down in the snow with Tanvi, just like I do.

The voices serenade me with their hate as I weave through the trees. One of them screeches, "And the smoke of their torment ascendeth up for ever and ever: and they have no rest day nor night."

Another voice I can barely make out slips in under it. I can't be sure, but I think it's my dad's and that he's saying something good. Letting me know he hasn't deserted me. The thought alone makes me feel a little better, and I pick up speed.

Icicles form in my hair. Frostbite can't be far behind. My feet keep sliding out from under me in the snow, making me work triply hard to keep my balance.

I don't know how to pray like Tanvi does, but as I run my mind singsongs my grandmother's old chant:

> Moon and stars, forever shine,
> Moon and stars, friends of mine …

I've spent so long under various shades of black that when the quality of the darkness shifts, I don't trust it. The murkiest, most somber blue is virtually indistinguishable from black unless you have something to compare it to. Every time I glance up at the patches of sky between treetops my eyes doubt themselves. After everything I've seen tonight, how can I be sure of anything?

My stares run longer with each crane of my neck, striving to detect the truth. With my eyes scrutinizing the atmosphere, my feet are left to themselves. My lower body crashes into something solid, waist-high. I bounce off it and tumble backwards into the snow. There's so much of it now that it softens my landing. Hoisting myself up with my arms, my eyes steer to the object that I smashed into — *that smashed into me*. An antique wheelchair, its seat bottom hanging crookedly down through the metal frame, iced with layers of snow.

My hypothalamus and nervous system go wild. My heart tilts. My muscles tighten.

Something grabs my neck, crushes at my windpipe. Something else whips up my shirt and slashes talon-like down my back, slicing deep.

I stumble forward, around the wheelchair. *No oxygen.*

The voices rise as one, the snow-filled air suddenly suffused with loathing. How can anyone hate someone they don't know so much? My feet shuffle on, my left leg kicking out from beneath me as an unseen force belts into my calf.

No air. No strength. No way forward.

I crawl on my hands and knees, gasping for breath, my brain scrambling for a way out. *Tanvi, I'm sorry, I don't know what to do.*

In my memory I hear her call out from behind me on the steps of the movie theater: "Hold up." Offering me a ride home. Offering me, in the end, everything.

Then my mind hops swiftly backwards, pages flipping. My dad after he was released from prison, watching me show off on my two-wheeled bike. Proud of me in the summer sun.

He must regret most of the things that came after that. He must be here, somewhere in the woods, watching me, and if this is the end maybe I should be thinking something else — my entire life flashing before my eyes like people say it does — but what I land on, the thought that stays, as I'm inching forward on all fours, is that I've been living in my father's shadow all my life.

"He's not that person anymore," Tanvi said just before I left her, and then my brain takes another leap — vaulting over the rest of my life and landing here earlier tonight. "Don't listen to them," she told us. *The voices.*

For the second time tonight I close my eyes against them, fasten my palms firmly over my ears. I creep forward on my elbows and injured kneecaps, imagining I can feel my father watching, willing me not to stop. Through it all, the same thoughts circle. An understanding I should have reached long before now.

My problems are mine. My father's left this life. I'm still here, and the longer I hide from the things inside me, the harder they'll cling. I have to wear them on the outside, like everyone else.

I'm damaged, but not beyond help. That's the real truth, isn't it?

Anyone living can change. The dead too, although usually we don't know it.

I never actually hit Tanvi. But I might have someday. I don't want to be that person; I don't have to be. But I have to deal with the demons inside me.

The fingers around my neck loosen. Is that what happens when you die? Everything lets go?

I keep my eyelids shut tight. If the white light is out there, waiting for me, I'm not ready for it. I want another chance.

> Vigor and wholeness hold me high,
> Turn my eyes to the endless sky.

They're the only words my brain has left. My grandmother's chant with the white candle. Her migraine cure.

I can't remember the rest, that's fallen away too. My mind loops over the same thirteen words until I lose sense of their meaning and hear only their cadence — the way your brain registers the sounds of a foreign language it has no practical knowledge of.

There's no feeling left in my hands. The numbness spreads quickly to my kneecaps. My elbows, my face, my toes. I'm disappearing inch by inch, swallowed by a cold blackness I can't see, scared out of my skull. Not of death, not exactly. But that I never fully took a shot at living.

Seventeen years, and I never got it right. Seventeen short years for Tanvi too, when she should easily have had seventy more.

The light in the tunnel must be bright, just like they say. Because suddenly there's warmth on the back of my head and the bridge of my nose. The ice that's formed on my neck pops, my own personal fault lines breaking. If this truly has to be the end, I don't want to miss it. There are worse things than death. I've seen them here tonight, and I don't want to remain in Shantallow with them.

My eyelids open into the light. My hands slide away from my ears.

There's no tunnel. No malicious voices. Only the sound of birds chirping to greet the day.

Yellow morning sun beams down on me through the thinning trees. In the distance, another clearing stretches out ahead of me. If this is a trick or a dream, the cars and uniformed men and women in the road will fade. Night will return with a vengeance.

Not a dozen feet away, fallen brush crackles. My neck pivots, my eyes whisking to the left. A coyote stares pensively back at me, its muscular frame nearly large enough to suggest a wolf but the sheen of its silvery-red coat unmistakable. It yawns dispassionately as it turns away, returning its gaze to the street.

The mess of emergency service vehicles and personnel seems

closer now. I stand on trembling legs that retain only the most basic comprehension about their function. My will marches them through the remaining trees onto a country road where thick tire tracks have compacted snow into multiple grooves.

Lurching past two police cars, I fall into step with a trio of paramedics wheeling a gurney in the direction of an ambulance. The patient's strapped down, an IV running from his arm, his clothes dusty black. Greg's face comes into view on the gurney, still breathing. The paramedic next to me — a woman in her thirties — surveys me with eyes that understand everything in three seconds flat. "Hey," she says calmly. "It's going to be okay. Let's get you some help."

Two other paramedics, flanked by a pair of police officers, instantly surround me. "A girl," I mouth, my voice only a trickle. "Back there in the woods. You have to go get her."

Another gurney slips behind me. Someone tells me to lie down.

"Back in the woods," I insist, volume rising sharply. *The woods, the woods, the woods.*

A cop with stony blue eyes and a stern jaw pins me in his crosshairs. "Son, they're okay," he promises with improbable gentleness. "We got your friends. You're the last one out."

"They're okay?" I echo, as I lie back, heart throttling.

"Some frostbite. Other minor injuries. But they're going to be fine." He nods firmly. "You'll see them at the hospital. Don't worry. Just sit back and enjoy the ride now."

Both cops disappear into the crowd as the paramedics begin strapping me in. "What about the others?" I mumble.

"Three of the kidnappers are dead," one of the paramedics responds. "They just loaded the fourth — with multiple gunshot wounds — into an ambulance."

Glancing up at the sole snowflake left in the sky, I momentarily fumble my words. "Why is it — why, the snow?"

"What's today's date?" the same paramedic asks, his head suddenly leaning over me so that I can see the nick on the underside of his chin where he must have cut himself shaving earlier.

The date? My brain's temporarily lost that too. "Early September," I mumble. "Thursday, the … I don't know. Can't remember."

"December nineteenth," the paramedic declares, peering at me worriedly. Head injury, he must be thinking. He's probably right, too. But what neither he nor any of us five survivors will ever comprehend is how Shantallow held us within its grasp for three and a half months of darkness.

And what I alone will understand, down all the days and years ahead — after graduation; after future girlfriends; after becoming an uncle to twin girls; after counseling with a guy who only seems to own four shirts but who makes me talk and think and take myself apart and then put the pieces back in a different way; after becoming not an engineer but the kind of teacher who tries to go the extra mile, even for the students they don't like; after falling in love and then having a girl and boy of my own who never have reason to be afraid of me and who are as smart, brave, and compassionate as I'd ever hoped they'd be — is how in some bizarre twist of fate one of the most evil places on earth saved the rest of my life.

Acknowledgements

Special thanks to the Ontario Arts Council for helping make this book possible through their Recommender Grants for Writers. Your support is much appreciated. I can't stress that enough!

Barry Jowett, thanks for your invaluable help in sculpting *Shantallow* into a made-of-steel book with your editor-vision super powers. Thank you, also, to the entire Cormorant team for their outstanding work: copyeditor extraordinaire Andrea Waters, book designer Tannice Goddard (for always making my books look terrific), editorial assistant Sarah Jensen for her keen eye, cover designer Emma Dolan (your fantastically eerie cover sends shivers up my spine!), publisher Marc Côté for his continuing support, and Renee Newton, Matthew Doyle, Jessica MacDonald, and Jessica Carter.

Thanks to Greg Coleman for his horror acumen, for being an earlier reader of Shantallow and for lending a character his name.

Deborah Kerbel deserves a standing order of gratitude for making each of my DCB books possible when she offered an introduction to Barry years ago.

Most of all, thanks to Paddy, who is the best thing that ever happened to me and who makes everything else possible.

Cara Martin is the author of several acclaimed novels for young people published under the name C.K. Kelly Martin. Her most recent novel, Stricken, was released in 2017. A graduate of the Film Studies program at York University, Cara has lived in the Greater Toronto Area and Dublin, Ireland. Within the space of 3500 miles she's worked a collection of quirky jobs at multiple pubs and video stores, an electricity company, a division of the Irish post office, a London toyshop, and an advertising analytics company. She's also been an image editor for a dot-com startup that didn't survive the 90s, and a credit note clerk for Canada's largest national distributor of General Merchandise. Cara currently resides in Ottawa, Ontario with her husband and is still afraid of the Child Catcher from the film adaptation of *Chitty Chitty Bang Bang*.

We acknowledge the sacred land on which Cormorant Books operates. It has been a site of human activity for 15,000 years. This land is the territory of the Huron-Wendat and Petun First Nations, the Seneca, and most recently, the Mississaugas of the Credit River. The territory was the subject of the Dish With One Spoon Wampum Belt Covenant, an agreement between the Iroquois Confederacy and Confederacy of the Ojibway and allied nations to peaceably share and steward the resources around the Great Lakes. Today, the meeting place of Toronto is still home to many Indigenous people from across Turtle Island. We are grateful to have the opportunity to work in the community, on this territory.

We are also mindful of broken covenants and the need to strive to make right with all our relations.